I0594205

ABUSED

A CASEY CORT LEGAL THRILLER

AIME AUSTIN

AIME AUSTIN
www.AimeAustin.com

LOS ANGELES, CALIFORNIA

ALSO BY AIME AUSTIN

Judged

Ransomed

Caged

Disgraced

Unarmed

Kidnapped

Reunited

Contained

Poisoned

ABUSED

A CASEY CORT LEGAL THRILLER

AIME AUSTIN

Abused

This edition published by
Moore Digital Media Inc.
1125 N Fairfax Avenue
Unit 46071
West Hollywood, CA 90046
www.aimeaustin.com

Copyright © 2021 by Aime Austin
ISBN 13: 978-1-64414-070-3
eISBN 13: 978-1-64414-069-7

This is a work of fiction. Names, characters, corporations, institutions, organizations, events, or locales in this novel are either the product of the author's imagination or, if real, used fictitiously. The resemblance of any character to actual persons (living or dead) is entirely coincidental.

The author acknowledges the trademarked status and trademark owners of various products referenced in this work of fiction, which have been used without permission. The publication/use of these trademarks is not authorized, associated with, or sponsored by the trademark owners.

Cover Designer: Wicked Good Book Covers
Cover images © Depositphotos, Shutterstock

Abused/Aime Austin. — 1st ed.

To tell a story is inescapably to take a moral stance.

— JEROME BRUNER

There, but for the grace of God, go I.

— JOHN BRADFORD

1

Nicole Long
September 11, 2007

I thumbed at the edges of the cheap manila folder on my desk. Inside, there were sure to be gruesome crime scene photos. Maybe bruising, maybe blood, possibly worse. I hated this part of my job because looking at those pictures almost assured there were going to be nightmares in my future.

There had always been.

There always would be.

On the one hand, I hated the missed sleep and waking up in the middle of the night, my body gripped by sheer terror.

On the other hand, that terror drove me to put the bad men who did the bad things in jail where they belonged. Ninety-eight percent of the time, at least.

That other two percent who escaped justice kept me up at night for an entirely different reason.

My mouth watered. A taste of Maker's Mark would make this whole thing a lot easier. The one coping mechanism that I used to get me over the hump and back to sleep was the one thing that could end my career. The terms of my probation required that I refrain from alcohol. I'd been mostly good.

Pushing that thought aside, I took a swig of Diet Coke. That bitter aftertaste was the closest I was going to get to whiskey. It was a poor substitute.

With a sigh, I turned the file over so the back cover of the folder was facing me. Police detectives loved to tell the story of a murder investigation in chronological order. The crime scene photos would be in the front. Their investigative conclusion along with copies of the search warrant for the suspect's house and finally that doer's arrest warrant would be in the back.

Mind you, I didn't read the end of a hardcover mystery before I knew who the victim was. But I always read the end of a detective's murder book first.

The cops kept the order.

They'd come to me for the law.

I rolled my chair back so anyone casually passing wouldn't be able to see me. It was a move I'd perfected for adjusting my hose or fixing my bra strap. Our office culture equated a closed door with corruption. Mine was always three-quarters of the way open.

Sure I was out of sight, I slipped a key from my pencil tray to the lock of the bottom right-hand drawer where I stored my purse. The lock turned smoothly. Some WD-40 had made the glides soundless as I pulled. Tucked in a dark corner was a small bottle. On the outside, the tan and brown label read Madagascar Vanilla. I twisted off the tiny metal cap and lifted the bottle, poured the contents into my soda can. That next sip of Diet Coke was far better than the first. I was sure I could handle the pictures now.

Despite the fortification, hesitation kept me frozen for countless seconds before I was ready. Carefully, so as not to disturb the glossy photos sure to slide out with their shiny surfaces offering little purchase, I lifted the back cover, laid it on my desk blotter. Took in the information I'd need first and foremost when I drafted the indictment for consideration by the grand jury.

A tiny jolt of surprise shook me in my office chair. The bad man I was going to have to put in prison was in fact a woman. Digital mug shots were so very sharp compared to their decades-old film counterparts I'd seen in older files.

My soon-to-be defendant was an unassuming woman who, with her light brown hair and clear blue eyes, could have been the woman who raised me, albeit a decade and a half younger. This middle-aged person was an anomaly among Cleveland's usual defendants.

She was white.

She was a woman.

She was a mother.

I would have to push all that aside because she was still a murderer.

The victim? Her estranged husband, Kendrick Walker.

I looked at the slim watch I only took off to shower. It was three in the afternoon. For once I was grateful that it wasn't near quitting time. Though cases lingered in my thoughts, I tried not to take actual paperwork home with me. Even if the tiny hands staring back at me from my vintage diamond-and-gold watch, the red crocodile band the only color I ever wore, had read five o'clock in the afternoon, I'd have stashed this folder in my briefcase and carried it home.

Because there was a story here. Not the usual one-dimensional tales that filled courts and jails: a drunken one-punch homicide or drug dealer revenge scenario. Something told me it was going to be an interesting one.

I hunched forward and peered closer at the paper. The defendant was forty-three, from Cleveland Heights or Shaker Square—there were two different addresses listed. Her name was Juliana Rose Clarke. Her profession?

Painter.

I flicked my eyes toward the defendant's mug shot.

Obviously not a house painter, but the kind with a light-filled studio in the Heights and canvases and oils and drop cloths.

So much didn't add up that I closed the folder and carefully turned it again so that the front was facing me. I was ready now for the pictures that would surely transport me to the scene of the crime.

The first photo was of a kitchen. Half of my not-small condo could have fit in this room of stark white cabinets, stainless-steel built-in appliances, and pickled wood flooring.

In the center of the photo, there he was, Kendrick Walker, splayed out on the floor, a pool of blood surrounding his head. I had to wonder if the wood was permanently ruined by the stain. I'd left a similar blemish on my family's precious floors years ago. It had never come out.

Refocusing, I leaned over the glossy picture. There was no dignity in death. What human animals could do to one another had stopped astounding me right after college.

In this instance, his wife had bludgeoned him. Where the front of his head would have been, a high forehead meeting a short curly afro, was instead a crater of blood, skin, and gray stuff I knew had to be brain matter. I flipped to the second picture. In that one, the forensic photographer had zoomed in on Walker's head.

I'd read the crime scene report and coroner's report to get the full picture, but right now, I wanted to absorb the details I'd live with, wake up, and go to sleep with for the next few months. Next to Walker, there was something white. Probably the murder weapon. I had to squint and turn the picture this way and that before I could put it in context.

The weapon was a cheese board. The marble kind that came with decorative handles and probably a set of matching stone-handled knives and slicers.

A cheese board?

I tried to picture how the whole thing could have unfolded. Juliana Clarke had probably come to her family home, the one she no longer occupied but had lovingly bought and furnished and renovated and tended for a decade or more.

Clarke and Walker had probably argued or even physically tangled. She'd picked up the board from the granite counter, then what?

Thrown it?

Beaned him in the head?

From what I could see, he was a big guy, but hitting even the strongest person upside the head with solid stone would take them down. No matter a person's size, their head weighed about eleven pounds, their skull...a quarter of an inch thick.

I pushed the pictures to the side and skimmed to the end of the autopsy.

Five wallops.

That's what it had taken to end his life. One whack, then another, then another, then another, then one last on the back of his head.

Clarke had pounded the cheese board against his skull not once, not twice, but four separate times until the blood and life had left him. One dent came from his fall against the stone counter. I looked at the pictures of Walker's body and the mug shot of Clarke. Flipped between the two a few times.

I tried to reconcile two conflicting ideas in my head.

Marriage.

Murder.

Their marriage had to have started out like anyone's. Her in a white dress. Him in a tuxedo. Smiling and joyful family and friends surrounding them. I'd never been at a wedding where I imagined the marriage ending in murder.

Divorce, maybe.

Death from illness or accident, possibly.

But murder?

Never.

That was a completely different interpretation of "until death us do part" that the sixteenth-century authors of the Book of Common Prayer didn't see coming.

Proof of motive wasn't a legal requirement for a jury to decide the defendant did it. Before twelve of Juliana Clarke's peers would return a guilty verdict, they'd surely want to know why though. By law, the jury couldn't ask. But I'd have to give them an answer anyway.

Adrenaline and anger were a combustible mix that spared few who experienced its wrath. I took a deep breath and sat back in my rolling chair.

I could feel the shift in my bones. I was about to step into my first, possibly headline-making, murder trial. This case could be the one that cemented my shaky career. Juliana Clarke was about to change my life at the same time I was about to change hers.

2

"If you hear nothing else I say today, Casey, hear this. Your life is going to fundamentally change. I know that you like to chase newspaper headlines, but a baby will be your main story. Got it?"

When I didn't move or respond, Dr. Fowler closed her eyes as if gathering strength, opened them, then asked, "Do you have any questions?"

Somehow I'd blinked and my life had become an episode of Maury Povich. If I hadn't been pregnant, I'd have gotten off the exam table and thrown a chair.

Questions?

I had so many damned questions. The most important of which the good doctor wouldn't be able to answer. I hesitated a moment longer. Maybe she could?

I wondered if it was possible to spare myself an appearance on the confessional stage. What did I know about the state of modern scientific progress?

"How..."

How? How could I push past my shame to ask how to find out what I wanted to know? I came to a realization that answered my own question.

Alexis Fowler was my primary care physician. Our conversation was covered by the same kind of privilege I had with my clients. The sacrosanct kind that meant she had to keep all my secrets. Despite that rationalization, my stomach still went slightly queasy at the idea of admitting the mistake I'd made—sleeping with two different men back-to-back without any contraceptive barrier between any of us. I didn't fear the telling as much as I feared the humiliation the question would bring.

Awash with mortification that was heating my face, I sucked in air and tried to slow the beating of my heart. No good Catholic woman past thirty should be in my predicament. At least that's what my parents would have said if I had the guts to tell them. That revelatory conversation was a can I was kicking all the way down the road to the next county.

"I've heard it all, Casey," she soothed. "We share the same duty of confidentiality," she said as if reading my mind. "You understand that more than most."

Though she was ten years older, Fowler's face was unlined. It held such compassion that I relaxed my vigilance. I was done protecting my shame like it was a small animal in need of shelter. I plowed ahead before I lost my nerve.

"Is there any way I can find out who my baby's father is before he or she is born?"

I waited a beat, ready to be scolded for successively having unprotected sex with not one but two men. It didn't come. Her tone, when she spoke, was matter-of-fact. Gasping and pearl clutching weren't hallmarks of a good bedside manner.

"Depends. When you check out with reception, you'll get my list of OB-GYN referrals. In about two or three weeks..." Fowler's wiggling hand indicated the vagaries of human fetal development. "...maybe four, you can schedule your first ultrasound. When they get in there, the radiologist will be able to measure the fetus. From there, the date of conception and the due date will be a lot clearer. Does that help?"

I wondered if my face was more tomato red or beet red. Either way, I imagined this is how my mother felt when a sudden hot flash came upon her. Humiliation wasn't menopause. I took another deep breath and spoke the truth while shaking my head.

"It was two days apart. Friday and Sunday."

To Dr. Fowler's credit, she didn't even blink. Instead she shifted my paper file from the crook of one arm to the other.

"That narrows things, of course. The other option to get an answer before birth is far more invasive, unfortunately. The OB can insert a needle to either extract amniotic fluid or blood from the placenta, then compare that to the fathers' DNA."

"The fathers?"

"It's just a cheek swab, so not invasive for them."

"But I'd have to tell them."

Dr. Fowler rewarded me with a tiny smirk.

"Yes, I'm sure you're aware that medical exams without consent are illegal."

I wanted to tell her to preach that one to arresting officers in emergency rooms or to jail doctors, but decided a criminal defense attorney soapbox rant wasn't appropriate right about now. Instead I tucked that little conundrum—of how to get Justin's or Ron's cheek cells—away for later consideration. I'd only need it from one of them, which in a way made the idea of asking easier.

"My due date again?" It was a question that Dr. Alexis Fowler could answer. One that I'd have to factor into not only my court calendar, but...my life.

"Probably April. But that will be confirmed at your first ultrasound appointment. You don't need a referral. We'll call in some prenatal vitamins as well. Do you have a preferred pharmacy?"

Obstetrician? Gynecologist? Pharmacy? The first time I'd been here, it had taken me three tries to even find my doctor's office on a block of quintuplet medical office buildings, none of which seemed to have any visible address numbers.

"Can I just have a paper prescription? I'll figure that part out later."

"Casey, I know that you're a busy lawyer, but babies are not like moles. You can't just wait until later to figure all this out. You have to do it now. Maybe the father part you can put off...maybe even indefinitely, but the baby-growing-inside-you part? No."

I wondered if I'd been too honest earlier. It had been two and a half weeks between the pee-on-a-stick test and finally coming in to have a doctor confirm it with…another pee-on-a-stick test. Dr. Fowler had been quick to tell me that blood draws were a thing of the past.

"I…uh…"

"Oh gosh, I'm…I need to backtrack." That came out in an embarrassed rush from Dr. Fowler. "I just assumed you'd keep the baby. But you have down on your forms that you're single, and earlier you said… Do you need a different kind of referral? One for termination?"

My heart sped up again, but for an entirely different reason.

"No, no. I'm going to keep the baby," rushed from my mouth. Not for a single moment in the last seventeen days had I thought of an abortion, not that I had a religious or moral objection. But first I'd had to mourn the idea that anything in my life was going to happen the traditional way. "I've always wanted a family. Not in this order, but I'm going to take it as a blessing, nevertheless."

Dr. Fowler's shoulders came down from around her ears.

"Well then, my first recommendation stands. You'll need to get in to see an obstetrician sooner rather than later."

My phone rang, giving me a jolt of adrenaline I didn't need. I hadn't realized I'd been holding it in my hand the entire time. I'd hated that habit in Miles, my ex-fiancé. I made a mental note after months with him to not become "that" person who needs a doctor's scalpel to surgically extract their phone.

I silenced it with a single button push. From my glance up at Dr. Fowler, it didn't seem like a good time to joke about surgical removal. Kept that to myself. But I could feel myself relax into the humor with a smile.

"I'll do it today. Thanks," I promised, already distracted by the real world crowding in on me.

My doctor was out the door before I could get out a proper goodbye. I was about to stand up when my forgotten phone chirped again. This time I didn't silence it but looked to see who could be calling me. The number was local, but wholly unfamiliar. That was my life though. Strange people calling me—soon to become clients—a person whose secrets I would know and keep.

"Casey Cort," I answered after I accepted the call.

"Peyton Bennett."

The name sounded both familiar and not. In case it was a client who was going to soon put cold hard cash in my hands, I made my voice as helpful and solicitous as possible.

"How can I help you, Mr. Bennett?"

"I'm a partner at Bennett Friehof and Baker. You may have heard of us?"

May have heard of them? That's like asking if I'd heard of the Cleveland Browns. Of course, I'd heard of Bennett Friehof and Baker. It was one of the firms that had turned me down for a job when I was desperate for gainful employment. I put a hand to my chest. The usual constriction wasn't there. Ten years and I was just beginning to shake the bitterness.

Bennett...I wanted to ask him if he was a founding partner. He couldn't be, of course, he'd have to be like a hundred years old. I patted the paper gown down around my legs, as if he could see me through the little gadget, then, realizing I'd been quiet far too long, spoke.

"Yes, of course," I acknowledged. "Again, how can I help?"

"I have a proposition for you."

That was a phrase that could go either way. I'd either get a referral for some kind of pedophile serial killer I would be loath to represent. Or maybe it was an opportunity to get on another million-dollar case. I held on tight to the phone. People did win the lottery twice. I'd read about one such person in a magazine right here in this selfsame doctor's waiting room years ago.

"A proposition?" I mimicked.

"Can you meet me in my office in an hour?"

I looked around the room I was in. Thought about getting dressed, retrieving my car, sticking something bland down my throat so I didn't throw up what was still in my belly from this morning.

"I'm just ending a meeting on the east side. Maybe two hours. Would..." I glanced at my trusty Timex. The watch had seen me through everything and it kept on ticking. I laughed at my own joke. Justin would have liked that one. At the twinge in my belly at that thought of that man, I shook my head. "Would one o'clock work?"

"I'll have a visitor pass ready for you. I'm on the twenty-third floor. Reception will show you in." Like any important person, he ended the call when he was done. Not a lot of pleasantries with those kinds of people, law firm partners that was.

My mind whirred while I disposed of the paper gown, put on my clothes, and got down to my car. What could Bennett want? Was it another job offer? For someone who'd been a pariah for so long, I was suddenly very, very popular. A formal written, open-ended offer had come from Morrell Gates in the spirit of "if you can't beat them, join them." Miriam Shively hadn't been blowing smoke up my ass after all.

One tuna hoagie, a quick trip home to drop off my car and pick up some seltzer, and two hours later on the dot, I was in reception at Bennett. I had to wonder if there was some giant cloning machine that stamped out law firms. The wood, and brass, and glass were cookie-cutter.

I could have been at Morrell accepting that job offer or at Lulu's reception at Dalton Lacey which was in this same building, albeit five floors up. It was only the polished brass law firm name affixed to the wall that distinguished this one from the others.

"I'm here to meet Peyton Bennett." That was for the two women in reception, neither of whom made eye contact when I'd gotten off the elevator.

A very dapper man with gray hair, but young eyes, came toward me. He took my two hands in his in a very paternalistic handshake.

"I'm Peyton Bennett. You must be Casey Cort. So good to meet you. I've heard some great things about you."

From whom? I wanted to ask. For a very long decade, my name had been mud in Cleveland legal circles.

"Yes, I'm Casey," I said while extracting my hands and swinging my messenger bag around to my front. In one practiced motion, I pushed at the tuck lock clasp, lifted the thick leather, and felt around until I'd found my business cards. I gave one to Bennett. "Nice to meet you."

He took the card into his smooth palm.

"Come on back to my office so we can talk." He only moved once I started down the hall in the direction he'd pointed. In front of a large corner office, the size of my living room and dining room combined, he paused. "You want coffee? Tea?"

"Can I actually have seltzer? I…my stomach…"

"Coming right up," he said, while nodding at a curly-haired woman in a little cubicle in front of a large office that the smaller brass name plate affixed to the dark wood door told me was his. "Have a seat. Bonnie will be right in with that drink. In the meantime, tell me a little bit about yourself. What kinds of cases do you handle when you're not in the Plain Dealer?"

"I don't quite know how to answer that."

I thanked Bonnie when a glass, coaster, and small square napkin appeared in front of me. I took a long sip, held in the burp that was threatening to escape, and spoke again to Bennett. "Not to be rude or anything, but this whole thing"—I waved my hand about indicating me, him, his office, the water service—"feels a little odd." It was a weird fishing expedition and—second winning lottery ticket or not—I was not taking the bait.

"You're right. I'm sorry." He held his hands wide. His blue eyes were full of warmth. I didn't get a single antagonistic vibe from him. I wondered if that was his litigation superpower.

Some attorneys yelled.

Others were great storytellers.

Maybe Bennett's was extreme empathetic disarmament.

"This is awkward," he admitted. "I don't know exactly where to start."

However his superpower could be described, it worked. I wanted to lean in and try to help him solve whatever puzzle was perplexing him.

"How about at the beginning?" I offered.

Bennett's nod was stiff, formal, acquiescing.

"Have you ever heard of Fernsby?"

I shook my head. Law firms, I knew. Random names, not so much.

"It's one of the world's leading architecture firms. They're headquartered in New York and London. They opened a Cleveland outpost when all the construction sprang up with the new hall of fame, stadium builds, and Gateway renovations. Now they're handling a number of these historical downtown, near east, and west side conversions."

I nodded and sipped at the carbonated water. Cleveland had been a hot bed of construction despite its shrinking population. The first domino was the Rock and Roll Hall of Fame, then it was a completely modern update to Jacob's Field, making it into a camera-ready baseball field. Gateway for the Cavs came next, and the Browns stadium right after.

Now buildings just outside downtown to the east and west across the river were being converted into mixed-use type housing that had long graced New York, Philadelphia, and Chicago. I didn't know who was going to live in them or who could afford to live in them. But maybe it was like Field of Dreams, "Build it and they will come." I waited for Bennett to continue. Silence was my superpower.

"Our firm has represented them as a corporate and occasional litigation client since they came to town. It's run by a man by the name of Kendrick Walker, he's a Fernsby partner and chief architect. Is any of that familiar?"

I shook my head again and drained the glass. My stomach had settled down since my bout of late-morning nausea. But now I had to pee like a racehorse. I wanted to motion for him to move it along, but I could tell he was savoring the telling. Juries loved a good storyteller. I shifted so there was less pressure on my bladder and waited.

"Walker was murdered two Sundays ago in his home in Shaker Heights."

"Murdered?" My mind spun. And I thought that first conversation with my doctor was going to be the oddest of the day. This was quickly kicking my little paternity problem to the curb. After I let out a long breath, I said, "I think I saw something in the Plain Dealer."

Murders of the poor didn't merit much soy ink, but anyone with money, political influence, or social status got top billing in the city's largest paper.

"The Cuyahoga County prosecutor's office has already indicted a suspect for the crime."

I let that sink in. Justice was rarely swift, so there must be more to this than a garden variety murder. Not that homicide was ever ordinary. Or maybe it was too ordinary. I was going to unknot that philosophical conundrum on a day when I wasn't vaguely nauseous, didn't have to pee, and wasn't trying to listen to a law firm partner pontificate. His kind were never fast speaking nor got to the point right away.

"Who?" I asked although I had no idea why I was suddenly front and center to some random murder in our fair city.

"His wife, Juliana Clarke."

"Oh. Okay." I shifted in my seat again, half because I was truly interested in getting to the punch line—the reason I'd been summoned—and half because I really did have to pee.

"She called me, yesterday. Mrs. Clarke has asked me to represent her."

"In a murder case? Where she's facing a possible life sentence?" I didn't mean my tone to sound as incredulous as it had come out. But there were two types of lawyers. Those who sat up in these brass-fronted ivory towers not getting their hands dirty.

Then there were criminal defense lawyers. The kind who kept the popular lawyer bar, the Tipsy Jurist, in business. Unless my people skills had taken a powder, Peyton Bennett—from the bespoke wool suit that sat on his frame like royal robes, to his manicured nails—was not, and probably never had been, from the second group.

"For the last ten years, I've been heading up the firm's pro bono practice," Bennett said. I flashed on Ron for a second. He'd headed up Dalton Lacey's pro bono group for a few years before he'd made junior partner. Maybe that's where I'd heard Bennett's name.

My head tilt silently broadcast my next question.

"It's my way of giving back," Bennett answered. "I know that many law firms aren't the most egalitarian. Since I can't really lose my job here, I've spearheaded both our diversity committee and have taken on some of the more challenging criminal cases judges assign."

"You're on the assignment list?" I'd once been on that list myself. But the pay-to-play aspect—having to make donations to the judges assigning cases—had been unworkable on my shoestring budget. Now that my fortunes were about to change, that was yet another thing I'd have to revisit. The fact that it took money to make money wasn't only true in finance.

Bennett nodded. "We have greater resources than many solo practitioners can offer." His blue eyes widened for a moment at his faux pas. "No offense."

"None taken," I responded almost automatically. I was evolved enough that I no longer took offense at the truth. "But if this woman was the wife of a—by the sound of it— successful architect and lived in the Heights, I'm not reading destitute."

The whole idea of pro bono was that attorneys should represent the poorest for free. A kind of Robin Hood type scheme for the legal profession and its poverty-stricken beneficiaries.

"She's not, exactly. She and the victim were in the middle or maybe even at the end of their divorce process. She's an acquaintance and doesn't have the cash on hand to bankroll a murder defense."

"While all of this is kind of interesting, I have to ask. Why am I here?"

"I want you to be my co-counsel."

He could have knocked me over with either a feather or an anvil—the cartoon variety of course. My biggest worry this morning had been whether I was really, really, really pregnant and what that meant for my life. For my complicated relationship with Justin. For my budding relationship with Ron. For my life eight...make that seven months from now. A murder trial had not been on my radar. For there would absolutely be a trial. Only fools and poor people took a plea.

"Me? I've never tried a murder case in my life. Ever. I mean, this Juliana Clarke has a big problem in her life. I'm not sure she'd be happy to add my inexperience to it."

"She trusts me. My judgment. Don't undersell yourself. I want you on the case."

"Why? I mean, look. I think I'm a pretty good lawyer. It's taken me ten years to come to terms with that. I know my way around a courtroom. I'm even mostly good at client management which turns out to be no more than managing expectations—managing down expectations. But murder?" I plumbed the depths of my memory from studying criminal law for the bar exam. "The possible sentence is fifteen to life, right? That's a long time."

"She's not guilty."

"Aren't they all." I tried not to roll my eyes. I could count on exactly zero fingers the number of clients who'd come into my office proclaiming guilt.

"Seriously." His face and voice were equally sober. He was on board the innocence train. I wanted to tell him that train almost always derailed. "She's not, and even if she were, there are extenuating circumstances."

I had two pressing questions. I chose one.

"Why me?"

"I've been following your career since your representation of Sheila Harrison Grant."

Even with my newfound confidence, I could feel my face warm. That case had been an exercise in snatching defeat from the jaws of victory. I'd nearly won on appeal, only to have the panel of judges dismiss my winning case because my client, a judge, mind you, hadn't had any trust in the justice system and had fled the jurisdiction before her daughter's case could successfully wind its way through the courts.

"That was a long time ago," I said.

"You were on that Baldwin case. The Container case. You got that guy off not once, but twice. And now the papers are reporting that you took on Strohmeyer and reached a class action settlement worth millions. All of that says that you're a force to be reckoned with."

Despite my full bladder, I had to agree that it all sounded really good coming out that way. His retelling left out meals of ramen noodles, paying my secretary when I didn't have the funds to pay myself, and the many months when lint was all I had in my wallet.

I stood abruptly. "I need to use the restroom." If I was all that and a bag of chips, he could very well give me five minutes.

When I was back, I drank the refilled glass of water that had left condensation rings on the coaster, wiped my lips with the little cocktail napkin. Which of course wasn't what that was for. Somewhere Miss Manners was rolling over in her grave.

This time when I adjusted myself, it wasn't to relieve pressure on my bladder, but to make myself more comfortable because I thought the second big question was going to require a much longer answer.

"The extenuating circumstances?"

"She was the victim of domestic violence." I'm not sure why the term gave me a jolt, but it did. I was glad I'd emptied my bladder.

"In her marriage? Didn't you say that she was divorcing? Were they still in the marital home together?"

"No, she'd moved out. Bought a condo in Shaker Square."

I shivered for a second. She lived in my neighborhood. Probably less than a quarter mile from my own front door.

In many ways, the world of many of my clients—criminal defendants—seemed so far from my own. Already this was feeling a little close for comfort.

"Where was the husband murdered?"

"In their former marital home. The one in Cleveland Heights."

"Why was she there?"

"Do all these questions mean that you'll consider my offer?"

Probably not, I thought. My curiosity had gotten the better of me. Back to reality.

"While you're the son or grandson or whatever of the name partner—"

"Son. My dad retired years ago, so I'm the only Bennett here now."

"As I was saying...son of the name partner and can work for free and still pay your mortgage in your house in Bay Village or Orange—"

"Moreland Hills. You were close." His smile was unrepentant. "I like how you can read people."

"Moreland Hills, then. I can't afford to work for free. My two landlords as well as the folks to whom I owe thousands for student loans aren't interested in anyone's egalitarianism. They deal in cold, hard, cash. So while I appreciate the offer—"

My feet hit the floor, I was ready to push myself back from my side of his desk, pack up to go and work for clients who paid.

"I didn't say you'd work for free."

By their own volition, my heels dug into the carpet beneath my feet. Maybe I wasn't ready to go quite yet.

"You want to hire me for a case you're taking pro bo-no?"

"I said that Juliana Clarke couldn't pay. I didn't say she was broke. If you co-counsel on this case with me, the firm will pay you a flat fee of twenty-five thousand dollars as an independent contractor."

Ten years ago, a twenty-five-hundred-dollar retainer from the aforementioned Sheila Harrison Grant had been cause for me to do a happy dance. A decade later, ten times more and I was as cool as a cucumber.

Silence took over the office.

The only sound was that of a mantle clock ticking on Bennett's mahogany-stained credenza. I couldn't have said if it was the money or the mystery, but he'd hooked me. The new me. The Casey that was no longer living small wanted to grab at any great opportunity with both hands. It had already worked once this year. If I wanted the streak to continue, I couldn't shy away from a challenge now.

"I'm intrigued," I admitted. "I daresay I'm interested."

"Good. Good." Bennett steepled his fingers, ready for my conditions. I may have been good, but he was probably better.

"Before I commit, there are two things. First, I need to know what the missing element is. And there's something I'd need to disclose, because it may change your mind."

"As I said, Juliana is claiming complete innocence. If, however, that doesn't turn out to be quite true, then I want to put forward an affirmative defense."

Bennett was likely suggesting self-defense. It was some-thing that Juliana Clarke would have to prove, a legal anomaly because in ninety-nine percent of criminal cases, the prosecuting attorney was on the hook for proving the defendant had committed the crime beyond a reasonable doubt.

"Which is?"

"Battered women's syndrome."

He may as well have said that we'd have to prove the existence of God. For the briefest moment my best friend Lulu Mueller's face flashed in my mind.

As quick as it was there, it was gone. Lulu and her married live-in lover, Sinclair, had a lot of issues, but I'd probably blown them all out of proportion in my mind because my friend had indicated nothing of the type.

I took a deep breath, ran a finger through the tiny puddle that had spilled from coaster to desk, which should have been soaked up by the misused cocktail napkin.

"I'm in," I said for the second time that year. The first had been one of the best professional decisions of my life. I hoped this would be another. "But I do have to tell you something about myself. Something that I'm not sharing outside this office, for now."

Peyton Bennett squinted. His blue eyes scrutinized my face and for a long moment I felt like all my secrets were laid bare. I blinked and pushed that thought away. He couldn't read minds any better than the rest of us, which was to say that he couldn't.

"I'm pregnant. I'm due in April. If that's a disqualifier, tell me now," I rushed out. It was only the second or third time I'd said it out loud. The first two people to hear it could keep a secret. Telling Peyton Bennett felt a little bit dangerous.

Bennett nodded his head as if I'd just handed him the best Christmas present ever.

"Speedy trial should have us in court long before that. I'd like, after conferring with you, of course, to push for a trial in December—between Thanksgiving and the holidays. I don't want Juliana, our client, to miss any time with her family."

Bennett pushed back his chair, stood, and sifted through stacks of papers on his credenza. He located a file, pulled out a stapled stack, handed it to me.

"Representation agreement. Let's do this. I'll set up a meeting with Juliana, and after she tells you her story—if you'll take the case—sign this and return it to me. The firm will cut you a check, then we'll start mounting her two-pronged defense."

I pushed the clasp of my messenger bag, fished inside for another one of my business cards, laid it on Bennett's desk. When he thought I wasn't looking, he'd palmed my first card, then laid it on the ledge of his assistant's cubicle. There were so many ways that could get lost. For twenty-five thousand dollars and the most interesting criminal case to come down the pike in a minute, I did not want him to lose my contact information.

"My schedule is pretty clear right now. Call me with a time and place and I'll be there."

He stood. Shook my hand stoically.

"It's good to finally meet you in person after all these years. I think this will be the start of a great working relationship."

It wasn't until I got outside that I realized I was dressed all wrong. The midday eighty-degree weather had turned cold. It wasn't more than sixty now, and with the sun setting, the temperature was dropping rapidly. Once I was on the crowded Rapid, what I was beginning to recognize as a hormonal pregnancy fog cleared just a little.

After all these years, Bennett had said. What did that mean, more than the "following my career" excuse he'd given?

The tram jolted to a stop at Shaker Square and I was happy to get out and get home because I was exhausted. A late afternoon nap sounded divine. I'd think about Peyton Bennett, how close I was to paying off my loans, finally having financial freedom, and meeting Juliana Clarke tomorrow.

3

Tallulah Mueller
September 21, 2007

My heart was going to beat right out of my chest. I was sure of it. The RAV4 jumped forward when my nerves had me pressing the gas prematurely. I slammed my foot hard on the brake to avoid a fender bender. Then I gave a half-hearted wave of apology to the car in front I'd been centimeters from plowing into. Then another to the one behind that had nearly rear-ended my Toyota. My leg had been nervously jiggling so much it had slipped off the brake on a stretch of Carnegie Avenue that had a downslope pitch.

Once I was on an even keel, I chanced a look at the instrument cluster. The car's clock read six thirty.

Only twenty-two minutes separated now from eight minutes before seven. Sinclair had asked me to come home by sunset which today was at precisely six fifty-two. If my mother or father had asked, I'd have known it was for an impromptu Shabbat dinner to impress one of my mother's donors. With Sinclair, I had no idea what the request represented, but I knew if I didn't comply, I wouldn't like his reaction.

My boyfriend, Richard Sinclair, was ten years older than me but sometimes acted more like a father than my actual father did. It was the downside of dating an older man. I was working double time to break him out of the habit. Maybe it was because that in addition to my lover, he was kind of my boss at work. And that had put him in a paternalistic place. I knew he didn't treat his wife this way for sure.

The honking in my ears let me know that my left turn onto Murray Hill had been a tad aggressive. Something about the thought of Doctor Deborah Bloom upset me, caused jealously to curdle in my stomach like spoiled milk. Maybe it was because my boyfriend was her husband.

I sped through the last of the drive ignoring the horns that blared in my direction.

"Hey!" I called out when I finally walked through my apartment's front door, but it appeared there was no one to receive my greeting. The lights were dimmed. The dining room table was set with unlit candles. What smelled like roasted chicken wafted from the kitchen.

Chicken?

Sinclair hated chicken.

"Sweetie!" Sinclair came down the hall from the back of the apartment. He was wearing the "hot guy" apron I'd given him as a joke for Christmas last year. The very tan and very buff guy screened on the cloth was only clad in a Speedo. "I miss you when you're gone," he said. I tried not to let the plaintive note in his voice get to me.

"We went to lunch together today," I pointed out. Breakfast too. It was what happened when you and your partner—who was also a partner at your law firm and de facto boss—lived and worked together.

"I can't get enough of you, sweetie. That's all. It's been nearly five hours since I've been able to look into your eyes or hold your hand. Let me take your jacket."

He hung my newly acquired subdued gray overcoat on a hook by the door. He took my oversized Proenza purse that sometimes served as a kind of briefcase/work bag/computer bag from my shoulder and set it down.

That was quickly followed by his hands rubbing along the sides of my neck. I tilted my head, first right, then left as I relaxed into his touch. This was all I wanted. These moments. The kinds my mom and dad had. Where a couple was in a bubble that no one else could break into. Where the rules and dynamics were our own.

"Why does it smell like chicken?" I asked. My voice was deliberately soft. Not an inquisition, just an inquiry.

"That's the surprise," he said as he stepped back a couple of inches. He pulled his brand-new iPhone from his pocket. He poked at it until the time flashed on the screen. He showed it to me. Nodded in confirmation of the facts. "You almost missed it."

My inability to show up on his time clock was a fight I wanted to avoid, so I steered the conversation back to food.

"But you hate chicken." His distaste for fowl made eating out and well, eating, hard as hell. Half of any supermarket butcher aisle was chicken. And restaurants? I never realized how much chicken was on every single restaurant menu until Sinclair and I got together. I'd learned to call first or Google whether there was beef or fish or even lamb on a menu. Sinclair was never ungracious, but I could see that paying top dollar for limited options pained him.

He guided me, hand firmly on the small of my back, from the vestibule to the dining room. All of my best stuff—stuff my mother hand handed over when she'd given up on saving it for my marriage to a nice Jewish boy from the temple—china, silverware, cloth napkins were set and on display on the table.

"Sit. I've taken care of everything. All you have to do is relax."

He disappeared into the kitchen then. I lifted a cloth towel only to find a perfectly braided challah underneath. The warm yeasty smell brought back memories of dozens of the sporadic Shabbat dinners my family had made and had insisted my siblings and I attend.

I dropped the towel. Quickly, I rearranged the folds just as they'd been. Sinclair came back with a small plastic package labeled "Shabbat Candles" in gold lettering. According to the foil-embossed box, they'd been handcrafted in Israel.

"These are beautiful," I gasped. And they were. The bottom half of the colorful five-inch candles were like a sand sculpture. Gradient color, white tree branches etched in the wax.

"They were made in the ancient clay of Safed."

"I'm going to pretend to know what that is." I laughed, but Sinclair's face was serious as he chose two fat candles, both on the blue side of the spectrum, fitted them into holders, then lit them with a lighter he extracted from his pocket.

He waved his hands over the tips of fire, and intoned, "Baruch Atah Adonai Eloheinu Melech Ha-Olam asher kid'shanu b'mitzvotav v'tzivanu l'hadlik neir shel Shabbat."

Blessed are you Lord our God, Ruler of the Universe, who has sanctified us by your commandments and commanded us to the light of the Shabbat candles.

"We're not supposed to blow them out," I said preemptively.

"I'm not an idiot." His brows had creased into the tiniest frown. "I researched this. Be quiet and let me finish."

I'd always wanted a real man. One who was comfortable being the alpha. I only had to sit back and let him do his thing. So I smoothed down my gray blouse, straightened the bow at the neck, took a deep breath, and let everything go as he shuffled to the kitchen.

He bustled back in a few moments later with a platter of roasted potatoes in one hand and some kind of slaw in another. He left and came back with a plump golden-brown chicken that looked and smelled delicious. I peered around wondering what protein he'd made for himself. Maybe there was a brisket coming.

Not meat but wine came next. I watched as he placed everything so very carefully, then blessed them in succession, his Hebrew to my Reform ears nearly perfect. I took the bread he'd sliced and salted and took a bite, then drank some wine. It was too sweet as always which was why I never drank it. But to avoid any unneeded friction between us, I tried not to grimace as I swallowed.

Finally, all the rituals done, he sat to my left.

"I can't believe you did all that," I said as he carved breast meat and laid it on my plate, then spooned sides for me. "I was okay not going to my parents' house. They just invited me...us because they rarely do the Friday night dinners. Maybe a few times a year. I try to accommodate them."

"But you don't like your family. How many times have you said that?" Sinclair lifted a chicken leg and thigh away from the bird, plopping the entire thing on his plate along with a healthy helping of everything else.

"It's not that I don't like my family," I rushed out quickly. Maybe I'd been too openly critical of them. "I dearly love my parents and my brother and sister."

"Then why do you push back so much about spending time with them?"

I took a big bite of chicken rather than answer because explaining all this to him over and over felt so complicated. I was so articulate at my job and with my friends, but it was like I lost my grasp of English in front of my boyfriend.

"I'm thirty-six years old. I don't want to have to explain myself or my life choices to them. I want tolerance." I took a sip of the wine. The sweetness was growing on me because the side effect of the alcohol was so calming. "Not tolerance. No one wants to be tolerated. I want acceptance. I don't think that's too much to ask."

"You're right. Until you get that acceptance, I don't think you have to continue to subject yourself to their criticism."

I didn't agree or disagree. Family dynamics in the face of always having been the odd child out was one thing. Something I'd actually come to grips with. The new dynamic of their disapproval of Sinclair was something else entirely. I didn't point out that he was the cause of our latest rift. I'd set the boundaries he'd asked and had stopped seeing them. That had to be enough—for now.

"What's up with the chicken?"

Sinclair had a short beard and moustache that covered a lot of his face. That said, I think I saw a blush coming up. It was charming.

"I have a confession," he said. "I didn't bake the chicken. Or any of it. I ordered it all from Heinen's. They gave me a cheat sheet on finishing off everything in the oven. That's why the timing was so crucial. I wanted you to get home before sundown, exactly the moment when everything was ready."

"I did," I soothed. "I made it."

"Barely. I was so worried about you. You didn't even answer my texts or calls in your car. I had that Bluetooth car kit installed so we could connect while you were on the road."

"I was driving pretty fast. I didn't want to take my eyes off the traffic while I was trying to get here."

"I worry. In the future—"

"Yes." I cut him off. I didn't need to say I'd never make the mistake of ignoring his calls or text messages again. That went without saying. "How do you like the chicken?"

As if someone at the upscale grocery could somehow change a lifetime of preference. I wanted to know about that because it was a superpower I wouldn't mind having. Maybe there was a clue to getting him to finally divorce his wife somewhere in there.

"The chicken is great." I watched, waited while he sliced the meat from bone, then took a huge bite. Chewed. Swallowed. "They do a great job, don't you think?"

"But you don't like chicken." My voice was tentative because what he'd said in the past wasn't lining up with what was right in front of me. That incongruence gave me pause.

"I never said that, Tallulah. Chicken is the staple of many American diets."

I lifted my wineglass and drained the contents.

"But you never eat chicken at restaurants," I started.

"Yes, you're right." He nodded. "It's often too dry. Sometimes overpriced. I don't want to pay upwards of twenty dollars for a few ounces of fowl. But otherwise, I love chicken. You know that I eat everything. I'm probably the most flexible person when it comes to preferences."

Before I could pay attention to what I was doing, I was lifting the wine bottle and refilling my glass. First, I sipped, then I drained that one as well.

"Stop that," he snapped. "You're going to be drunk before eight o'clock at that pace."

Sinclair paired his words with a swift grab at the glass in my hand. I didn't let go fast enough and before I knew it there was a purple stain spreading down the front of my gray blouse. Thanking God it was rayon and not silk, I popped up, ran to the kitchen for seltzer and tore off the blouse. Under the fizzy water, purple liquid ran to clear.

In my bra, my blouse balled into my fist, I stalked to the bedroom, not happy with myself. I don't know why I was upset. Obviously I'd made some kind of mistake.

Misunderstood?

After I hung up my skirt, grateful there was no splatter, I pulled my softest sweats from the drawer and slipped them on. Zipped the matching jacket to my neckbone so that my braless boobs weren't exactly hanging out.

Comfortable and relaxed from the wine, I padded barefoot back down the long hall to the dining room.

"Sweetie. I'm sorry that you misunderstood," Sinclair was saying.

I moved a little more quickly because I hadn't realized he'd been talking to me the whole time. Apologizing. Sinclair hated one-sided conversations.

"No, I'm sorry, babe. I didn't mean to—"

Sinclair was holding his new phone up to his ear with his right hand. The left was waving frantically at me. My stomach knotted.

He wasn't talking to me.

I'd have bet my entire Dalton Lacey salary that he was speaking to his wife, the one and only Doctor Deborah Bloom.

He turned away, paced from the dining room, through the vestibule and into the living room. I couldn't hear him then. Muffled words were all that filtered through the thick plaster walls. I mopped up the spill that had beaded on the highly polished wood. Instead of the wine on the table, I went and filled my glass from a bottle in the fridge, drank that down, then filled it again, halfway.

The food that had looked so appetizing a half hour earlier had lost its appeal. Sinclair took his chair again after he shoved the phone into his pants pocket.

"That was Deborah."

"Your other 'sweetie.'" It was one hundred percent passive aggressive. It was a crappy, jealous-girl kind of thing to say and for once I didn't give a shit.

"Don't be like that. It was a twenty-three-year marriage. I've loved her my entire adult life. I just can't turn that off like a switch."

Why can't I be the only woman in your life? Why can't I be the only woman you love? Why can't you leave her? Why can't you divorce her? Why can't you let her go?

My wheedling internal voice was screeching while my real voice was silenced. It was too hard all of a sudden. All the effort he'd made to host a Shabbat dinner free from my parents' judgment and criticism suddenly meant nothing.

"I can't do this, Sinclair. I can't keep doing this. I love you and want to be with you. But I'm not love triangle material."

"Don't be like that. If I had a single ounce of feeling left for that woman, I wouldn't be here with you. But I don't love her anymore. My marriage was over years ago. I stayed because our daughter, Sarah, needed us. Now that she's grown and in her junior year at Vanderbilt, you're the most important person in my life. I've put you above Deborah and Sarah. What do you think moving in here was all about?"

Sinclair stood, his arms snaking around my waist. For a long, long moment I was as stiff as a board. He whispered a single, "I love you," into my hair, and in a flash my body softened like a boiled noodle. He smelled so good. He felt so good. He made me feel so safe.

It would so be stupid of me to give up something and someone so good just because he hadn't legally and financially untangled himself from the good doctor.

His reasons were valid. As an attorney, I understood them better than most women would. He and Doctor Deborah had a house. He was part owner of her medical practice. She probably had an equal stake in his Dalton Lacey partnership equity. There was their big Tudor house not too far from here. Retirement accounts and all of that weren't as easy to split as a restaurant tab.

Sinclair's hand found my right hoodie pocket.

"What's this?" He pulled a pregnancy test stick from inside. My body went stiff again. Now it was cold as well. My tongue ping-ponged between a lie and the truth.

"It's a secret," I started. A flash of something came and went across Sinclair's face so quickly that I wasn't sure I saw it. But whatever it was had me spilling my guts like vivisected fish. Without a second thought, I threw my best friend under the proverbial bus. "Casey's pregnant."

He lifted the test stick to the light, scrutinized it. "But this only has a single line."

"I took a test with her out of solidarity," I said. That at least was a half-truth.

"Were you sad when she was pregnant and you weren't?"

"No, it was a relief, actually."

Sinclair pushed me back. Hard enough that my elbow hit the fireplace's mantle. Pain exploded from my funny bone. Tears smarted from the corners of my eyes.

Realizing he'd gone too far, he pulled me close. Kissed my elbow. Shushed me. His eyes locked with mine.

When he did that, stare at me with enough love to fill Bryce and Grand Canyons put together, I couldn't look away. I couldn't deny him anything. A frisson of love and desire and warmth filled my entire body. God, I loved this man from the top of his salt-and-pepper head to the bottom of the leather slippers he was wearing.

"Don't you want to have my baby?" He was whispering now, his blue eyes so intense. I leaned forward to make sure I heard him. "I want you to."

"I don't know. I at least think we should wait until you're divorced before we talk about this."

"You don't have much time left. Conditions don't have to be perfect, Tallulah. That's childish thinking. Kids are always a blessing even if they don't come at exactly the right time."

"I'm up for partner this year." It was another excuse. He heard it for what it was.

"I'm already a partner, my love. I can easily support all of us, whether we stay in your little apartment or buy a house somewhere. Let's not fight. Let me make love to you without anything between us."

"I don't think—"

"You do too much thinking and not enough feeling. I want you to feel how much I love you. Feel how much I care. Feel how much I want you to be my future."

"I want..."

"If I knew you'd say yes, I'd propose to you right now."

The bottom dropped out of my stomach. He really did want it all with me.

Marriage.

Babies.

I let Sinclair kiss me and pull me toward the bedroom. Dreams, that I wasn't even aware I'd had all along, were about to come true.

4

When I'd been here at the Cuyahoga County jail in May to see my sex trafficking clients, Jarrod Carter and Dion Fortune, I'd thought the visit would be my last.

After that case, like others before it, the moral ambiguity of the law's efficacy in managing human behavior made me consider quitting criminal law for the hundredth time.

Here I was though, having arranged for a visit with a potential new client. A woman who could be my first murder client. I shook my head as I took in the cold institutional setting. There were twenty-five thousand reasons why I was back.

A guard who'd flirted with me in the past lifted two fingers of his right hand.

"Good to go, Casey," he said dipping his head. His smile was unusually big.

"That's our cue," I said to Peyton Bennett. He'd been mostly silent as he let me take the lead in my domain. That my home turf was the county jail said more about me than I wanted it to.

"Popular here?" the older attorney asked. I didn't know him well enough to know if his lips had quirked up a slight smile or if that was just the normal set of his mouth.

"If he knew I was pregnant, I think my stock would drop," I deadpanned. "It's in between counts, so let's hustle."

Though there hadn't been a county jail breakout in recent recorded history, the deputies counted the prisoners at least five or six times a day, if not more. Everything stopped until the number of prisoners equaled the number on the updated daily roster. If the count was off, even by one, they started again until they got it right. Counting nearly two thousand people one at a time could take an hour or more.

Bennett followed behind me as the guard led us to the attorney interview rooms. The deputy came inside as I counted to make sure there were at least three chairs.

"Lawyer visit," I said as I pointed to the camera in the corner where walls and ceiling met.

"Gotcha," the guard replied. "I'll get her now from the holding area."

"What's that about?" Peyton asked when we were alone, his chin jutting toward the all-seeing spheric eye of the black camera.

"They sometimes record meetings. They say it's for public safety. I'm not sure I've ever believed that. Either way, I don't want them recording us by mistake. My request not to record is on camera. If they don't stop it now, we have a constitutional violation and grounds for a mistrial if it came to that."

Bennett's cufflinks glinted in the flickering pink-hued fluorescent lights as he moved his hand in a circular motion.

"You think they'd actually record?"

"Phone calls certainly are recorded. Call me skeptical, but I don't trust the system." Saliva pooled in my mouth with the swiftness of a Pavlovian dog. "If you'll excuse me a second."

I pulled a sleeve of saltines from my bag and a small green glass bottle. Chomped through three, then twisted off the gold metal cap and took a swig of the seltzer. Tried to let out the world's tiniest burp behind the hand in front of my mouth.

"Sorry—"

"I have...three...kids, Casey." Bennett shook his head. "No need to apologize. From what I've witnessed, morning sickness usually ends about a third of the way through."

I nodded my thanks and took a surreptitious look at him when I bent to put my snack away. There was something about the way he'd counted his kids that reminded me of an old client. One of the first women I'd represented. I'd asked her how many children she'd had and months later I learned there was one extra she hadn't mentioned.

I shook my head to rid it of the old images of my early years of practice. These hormones were making my mind go to weird places. Of course law firm partners could count their kids. He'd had the same nineteen years of schooling I'd had.

The door opened and a forty-something woman was led into the room, stopping at the doorjamb. The deputy removed her handcuffs. He held them up and looked at me questioningly.

I shook my head in response to the sheriff as I studied Juliana Clarke. No need to cuff her in the room. I wasn't scared of this one. She had that Sara Jane Olson look about her. I wondered if she shared a background similar to the former Symbionese Liberation Army member. Upstanding community member with a little bit of a felonious side.

I tried my best to swallow my judgment. Clarke shuffled in, then made herself as comfortable as was possible in the awkward metal chair. The deputy gave one last salute. His shoes squeaked on the pristine linoleum as he turned and exited, closing the door behind him. It locked with no way to open it from our side.

"Juliana, this is Casey Cort." Clarke lifted her hand across the table. I shook it. It was very fine boned, and cold as ice. I let go of it slowly, wondering if she'd taken a life with the hand I'd just held. "I've asked her to co-counsel with me on this case. She's been practicing in the criminal courts for years. You may have heard of her, she worked on the Container case."

I swallowed again, but it wasn't nausea that caused the bile to rise in my throat this time. I wasn't sure how I felt about my twice successful representation of a child sex trafficker serving as my claim to...infamy and apparently my ticket to a first-degree murder case.

Clarke let out a humorless laugh that mirrored my own ambivalence.

"I read about that. Sex trafficking in our own east side backyard. Never thought I'd have anything in common with that guy."

I didn't say anything about glass houses and stones. It was so adult a move on my part that I felt instantly ready to graduate from the young bar association despite the fact that I had a few years until I officially aged out at forty.

"All who are accused are entitled to a vigorous defense," I said. Though after my little constitutional speech, I wasn't sure who exactly I was trying to convince.

Backing up my chair, I laid my bag on my lap and unclasped the leather flap that had started to curl back on itself. Today's pad—pink—plunked on the table in front of me. I'd decided a few weeks back that I deserved to have fun colors for a job that wasn't always fun. With pen in hand, I got as close as possible to the table, to Juliana Clarke.

"What's the story?" I asked.

"Story?" Her face said she'd expected an entirely different approach from a twenty-five-thousand-dollar criminal defense attorney.

"I've just met you this moment. I'm meeting you as a woman who is indicted for murder. Even as a lawyer who staunchly believes in innocence until proven guilty, I have to assume that where there's smoke, there's fire. So I'm asking what is it you want me to know."

"Just an open-ended question? You're not going to give me a bunch of warnings about what I can and can't say?"

Clarke's wild-eyed stare landed on Bennett. Second-guess was written all over her face. I was grateful when he did nothing more than nod at me. He wasn't playing at patriarchy today.

"This isn't TV." I put my pen down. "All that smoke and mirrors conversation is not how I do it."

I saw Juliana's eyes go wide with fear as they ping-ponged between me and Bennett.

Her response was interesting. I decided to give her a break, then get back to her story.

"Where were you born? You don't have a Midwestern accent."

"You sound like everyone here." She rolled her eyes, huffed a bit at us provincial Clevelanders. "We, Ken and I, that is, moved here twenty years ago. My daughter was born here and yet people treat us like we just plopped down from outer space."

"If you're not from Cleveland, then where?"

"New York City. Mount Sinai to be exact. Upper West Side or near enough to it. I grew up in The Osborne."

"Translation?" I asked. Even though I'd seen all the episodes of Sex and the City, I didn't understand what she was saying.

"First luxury apartment building in Manhattan. Pre-war as in World War I not II. Central Park views and all that."

I paused for a moment. If there was one thing I'd learned in my last years of going up against the Strohmeyers and Brodys, it was that there was a single thing rich people never talked about—being rich. Clarke had violated about a dozen rules all in a single sentence. Leaning a little on the table, partially as an intimidation tactic, and partially to ease my roiling stomach, I probed.

"Where'd you go to school?"

"Chapin all the way through. Cooper Union. Penn."

I had no idea what Chapin was. Though I suspected it was the New York equivalent of Hathaway Brown, the tony, all-girls private school in Shaker Heights.

Though her speech was still clipped, I chalked that up to the Big Apple. Clarke's shoulders had come down from around her ears.

"Where did you meet Kendrick Walker?"

"Penn. We were in the architecture program together."

"You were divorcing, though?"

"I filed last year."

I scratched down a note to search the basement records room of the Lakeside courthouse for the active domestic relations file. Probably nothing but a bunch of pleadings and financial disclosures, but I didn't want to leave any stone unturned.

"Not final?"

"According to Madeline Montgomery, we're probably going to trial."

Noted the present tense. Kept my head down, made another note to talk to one of the busiest if not most successful family law attorneys in the city. I didn't point out to Clarke that the matter of the divorce was moot. Death had ended her marriage to Kendrick Walker. If she weren't in jail for said death, I'd probably have made her day with that announcement.

"Why did you file for divorce?"

"Irreconcilable differences. The same story I'm sure every middle-aged woman gives. We grew apart. He gave all his days and nights to Fernsby. I quit my job when Sienna was born and pursued my art around raising a daughter. Woke up during her junior year at Hathaway Brown and realized I didn't have much of a marriage anymore."

One hundred points to me, I thought. I'd been right on the money on the school. Like mother, like daughter, no doubt. Justin would find it hilarious. Until I realized that we weren't working together anymore, so this meeting was full of secrets I couldn't share with him. That and I hadn't seen Justin in weeks, because until I decided what to do, we were pretty much over.

I put a cap on my pen. Laid it on the pad. Leaned back in my chair. I looked between Bennett and Clarke. Took a breath. Huffed it out. Got to the meat of it.

"Why do the Cleveland Heights police and the county prosecutor's office believe that you murdered your estranged husband?"

"Because my husband's new girlfriend found me lying over his body with a marble cheese board in my hand."

5

"Detective?"

It took everything I had to keep my jaw up off the floor. None other than Darlene Webb was standing on my threshold. The last time I remember talking to this particular police officer, she'd been in the grand jury witness chair. We'd been discussing Marc Baldwin and the death of an unarmed Black man, Troy Duncan. It hadn't been anyone's finest moment.

Webb had been a rookie beat cop back then. Now she stood before me in a navy-blue suit hanging from her thin frame as if her shoulders were no more than a wire hanger. A single thread dangled from the hem of her jacket. The rayon-blend fabric was as limp as her hair. She reminded me of one of my nieces playing dress-up. I wanted to lean forward and snip that string off for her. That and hand her a bottle of conditioner. Dismissing her appearance for now, I decided to tackle that when the time came for her to testify and I needed her to at least try to look authoritative.

"I didn't expect to see you here," I continued when she didn't reply to my greeting.

"Switched departments. Took the civil service exams. Got promoted. I'm out in Cleveland Heights now." Her response was clipped.

So that had been how they'd bought her out—"they" being a moving target. Maybe it was Cleveland chief of police, Kelley McCormick, or the Cuyahoga County prosecutor and my boss, Lori Pope. Or maybe even the Brody family. Who knew? Everything in Cuyahoga County was a transaction.

Fortify the blue wall. Make detective, albeit in a smaller department. I'm sure the pension and seniority transferred over.

I believed what Webb said was true on the surface. She'd taken the right tests, no doubt. Her passing scores helped to hold up the thin veneer of propriety.

I certainly could cast no stones. My own job here was transactional. I'd taken the fall for Tom Brody and now I was heading up the Major Crimes unit. We were both standing on hollow pedestals.

"They let you on this case?" I was kicking at hers but couldn't help myself. I hadn't had a murder case in a good long time. This would only be my second, actually, not that I'd admit it aloud. That was a lot of inexperience between us.

I couldn't ask for help, though. Showing weakness would get me pulled from this job faster than I could say,

"I'll have a sidecar." Nothing less than perfection would do. I almost let out a bitter laugh at how that was a mirror of the demanding family I'd left back in Louisiana.

"I may be young." Webb paused, crossed her arms so tightly the bulge of her shoulder holster and gun became prominent. "I may have been stupid once upon a time. You know what, Ms. Long? Lesson learned. I take my job seriously and am working hard to get seriously good at it."

"Touché. I'm in the same boat, I guess," I admitted.

"I'm not sure about that, Ms. Long. They let you on this case?"

"I'm sorry," I backpedaled. Webb and I had been in this quasi-confessional space too long. If I was going to prove that I deserved to stay in this job, I needed to win this case with Webb or in spite of her. I scooted my chair closer to my desk, clicked my pen, and looked at Webb expectantly.

"Tell me about Mister Walker."

Webb helped herself to one of the chairs in the office. Tom had been in here alone for as long as I could remember. He was special like that; his uncle, Liam Brody and the predecessor to Lori Pope, had presided over the prosecutor's office before he became attorney general.

For me, I expected this two-attorney space to be filled before the end of the month. That gave me only a few more days alone. I stood and closed the door behind Webb making the best of the privacy while I still had it.

Webb flipped open a black binder that I hadn't seen her carrying.

"Kendrick James Walker. DOB June twenty-third, 1960. He was forty-seven. African American. Architect. Lived in Cleveland Heights, but born and raised in D.C. Works...worked downtown here."

I wanted more. A bigger story. She wasn't there yet, as a detective. Didn't know if she realized that jurors were bored by facts.

With first-person shooter video games and TV like it was nowadays, blood splatter and badly harmed corpses barely caught their attention or shocked them into demanding justice. They were moved by the same thing that moved humans time immemorial—story.

The big questions of who, what, where, when, and most of all, the one the law didn't require us to prove, why needed to be answered before they'd return a unanimous verdict.

It was the why, in my opinion, financial crimes were often so hard to prosecute. When the answer to "why" was a Gordon Gecko-style "greed is good" response, juries were hardly swayed.

Throw in betrayal or jealousy, though, and I'd have them hooked from the first words of my opening statement. Architect and ex-wife feuding over money would not keep anyone up at night nor keep my potential jurors from nodding off.

"Why did his wife kill him?" I wanted to get to the heart of it. The meat of it. The core story I could build my case around.

"They were in the middle of a divorce."

I sighed. She was disappointing me.

"And what, she wanted the washer and dryer and he said no?"

"Probably the usual domestic issues. Money. Million-dollar divorce case, looks like. Her lawyer was Madeline Montgomery. His was Gerald Popovic."

I held up my hand for a moment of silence.

"So contentious, then? No one hires Gerald Popovic for a run-of-the-mill case. This was a dog fight. He's a bulldog. Montgomery's a pit bull. This does not read as exactly amicable."

Webb shrugged, then continued, "He was gonna owe support—marital, not child. Their girl is a college freshman. Didn't want to pay her to sit on her 'bony ass.'" The last was in air quotes. "Said that to too many people."

"He said what exactly?"

"That he was..." Webb looked at her notes. "Quote, 'done supporting a starving artist. That a bony-ass white woman could figure out how to support herself, but was done being the Black man who supported her. That she could easily find another sucker to take up the cause.'" Done reading, Webb looked me in the eye.

"So, on September second, the wife comes to pick up something. They fight," I started, trying to fit the pieces together. "From what you're telling me, there was no love lost between them. She hits him on the head with a marble cheese board. Either that, or the subsequent hit his head took on the counter killed him."

I was quiet for a second thinking how that would play to a jury. Except for the potential jurors listed as "homemaker" on the venire list, starving artist wouldn't play in working-class, blue-collar Ohio.

I scratched a note to toss stay-at-home moms from my jury if I could. Every one of them with a side hustle could be sympathetic to Clarke. It still wasn't a lot to work with. I dropped my own pen and met Webb's bold stare.

"If every ex-spouse drive-by and pickup yielded a death, half the city wouldn't be alive." If people could just stay away from each other. Domestic issues, bar fights, and drug deals were about ninety-nine percent of the cause of misery that I came across. Social animals with homicidal tendencies is all humans were.

"True," was Webb's response.

I'd get the story later, I guessed. And if there wasn't much meat there, I'd work with her to craft the best tale we could, given the facts we had. Made a note to see what our investigators could dig up. Since Webb was now a woman of very few words, I cut to the chase with my next questions.

"Witnesses?"

"No, but the crime techs and forensics are ninety-nine percent sure how it went down."

"Who found him? Not the daughter. Please tell me not her," I said out loud, though my mind cast a short film of what it would be like if indeed the daughter had found him.

One girl crying, especially if she was biracial and pretty, could get a guilty verdict from a jury of twelve faster than I could say, "convict."

"It's early to have that kind of trauma," is the socially acceptable thing I said out loud and what I personally believed.

"Maybe she'd take a dead body over her mother in prison for killing her father," Webb said with a dead-eye stare.

"There is that." I shifted in my seat.

"It was the girlfriend who found him."

"His girlfriend? How long has she been around? Clarke filed for divorce only eighteen months ago."

They always had a girlfriend. They could never wait until the divorce was final. Sometimes I think I'd have been better off living in a time where immorality was more strongly condemned.

Thinner. Younger. Blonder. A trifecta that wouldn't make my victim as sympathetic as I'd like. Social animals be damned.

"How long had he been separated before he got the girlfriend?" Now the fictional jury in my mind was coming back, the word "acquit" on the foreperson's lips. A crying, orphaned daughter weighed on one side of the scales of justice. An unsympathetic victim who'd "moved on" with a younger, blonder model weighed on the other. A balanced scale did not equal a verdict in my favor. I needed a thumb on my side.

"A year or a little less."

"Is she younger, blonder?"

"Monica Mae Ellis. She's twenty-eight. Hair color's about the same, though."

I tried to remember if Webb used to have anything that resembled a sense of humor. I'd have even settled for the ever popular among law enforcement gallows type. Nothing about that Troy Duncan, Marc Baldwin situation had warranted a smile. Nothing. Neither did this one, but still those of us on the right side of the law needed tension relief that didn't come in a cocktail glass.

"What's your theory?"

Webb finally relaxed the tiniest bit. She acted, though, like I could knife her at any second. She was warier than an inner-city teenage boy. And in my experience, those were the jumpiest motherfuckers ever.

"Got a couple of ideas." Webb shifted in her chair, leaned forward a bit. "Maybe Clarke went over there to pick up a canvas or her favorite running shorts. She and

Walker got into a fight about money. She got mad and lifted the cheese board, and when he said something else,
implying she could wait for hell to freeze over to get what
she thought was due her, she hit him. Or they got into a
fight about his new woman moving into a house that she's
still part owner in."

"That's enough motivation?" I asked. Cops, prosecutors,
we all spun out theories. It was the only way to make
sense of something—killing or harming another human
being—that didn't really make much sense at all. But the
story still needed to hold together.

My one and only goal was to get a conviction. In ninety-five percent of the cases, it was as easy as bullying the
defendant into a plea deal. In the other five percent, it was
about swaying a jury. After the Container case, after Tom's
perfidy, I couldn't afford to lose. Especially a high-profile
murder.

"He was starving her out," Webb replied.

"How do you mean?" For all Juliana Clarke's problems,
I didn't imagine that she was standing in line behind the
homeless at the local food bank.

"He refused to pay child and spousal support."

I almost shrugged. That was typical in divorce, I imagined, par for the course. Expected. Not a motive for murder.

"You said that Madeline Montgomery was repping her."

"Yeah. Well, the court finally ordered support after a
lot of delays. Surprise, surprise. He's not paying it. He's
technically self-employed, so garnishment is more work."

When I'd been in the dog house, I'd been busted down
to prosecuting deadbeats for the county's Child Support
Enforcement Agency. Ohio had been revolutionary in be-

ing one of the first states to universally garnish wages of payors rather than relying on their goodwill. For the unemployed and self-employed, though, it was often like getting blood from a turnip.

"Got it. Does she have other resources?" What I meant was well-off parents or siblings or a trust fund, but I didn't exactly say that out loud.

"Her parents cut her off twenty years ago." Webb hadn't pretended to misunderstand.

"Cut her off? This isn't the nineteen fifties. Why?"

"For marrying a…bl…an African American man."

Right.

I should have guessed that. I was from Jefferson Parish. I knew that playbook backwards and forwards and upside down. Men never got disowned, but women always did.

"She's not going to bond out," I said. "The judge set it for one million." Even if Clarke couldn't put up the full amount, she could put up ten percent through a bondsman. "That's still a cool hundred thousand." Even if I had that in my savings account, I imagine most people didn't. And even if Clarke was that kind of woman, her husband's refusal to pay out support meant that she'd probably burned through whatever savings she had.

I tried to communicate the gravity of the situation with my next words.

"You know what that means."

"I know." Webb nodded. "Speedy trial. Will she waive?"

"She's got a private attorney. I put the chances at twenty percent."

"They never waive with private attorneys," Webb said. "Why twenty?"

"Her lawyer is Peyton Bennett of Bennett Friehof and Baker," I informed her.

"What does that mean?" Cops were familiar with the top criminal defense attorneys, but unless they'd had a hard cross-examination from one of them, I think most of the rest of the bar was forgettable.

"It means that he's a civil attorney. I hear he's been slumming here in the criminal courts for a minute. Probably out of some sense of civic duty or guilt or a well-meaning pro bono initiative, but he's not from here."

Self-aware white-shoe lawyers would deny it, but absolute truth of the matter was that they were the gazelles on the plains and we were the cows. Everyone knew that cows and gazelles didn't munch the grass on the other's field.

"So, are we moving ahead as if this Peyton Bennett is taking this to trial in ninety days?"

"Yes. Always. There are no shortcuts in the law." I bent to do a quick calculation on my desk calendar. "We have to empanel a jury by December thirteenth. That's seventy-seven days to prepare. Sounds like a lot, but it's not for murder. We have a lot of ducks to get in a row. Forensics, witnesses..."

A knock on the door took my attention away from Webb. It was the file clerk on the first of his twice-daily rounds.

"I don't have anything for you today, Tony," I said. Many of the documents in any case had to get stamped by the county clerk and were added to the official court file for the judge.

"Got something for you. Just came in. You said to expedite anything tied to the Clarke case."

He held out a slim fold of papers in his hand.

"Okay. Give it to me."

He did, then took his cart and rolled it down the hall to visit the other offices with looming court deadlines, which was most of them. I glanced down at the pleadings. "Notice of Counsel," it read.

I skimmed for the punch line and there it was. Casey Cort was going to be added as co-counsel, probably second chair, maybe first. Peyton Bennett, gazelle extraordinaire had gotten himself a cow. I knew my comparison was unkind, but didn't care. He was starting things off by tipping the scale his way.

"Clarke isn't going to waive for sure," I said to Webb. I thrust the notice toward her.

"Casey...Casey Cort." Webb's face screwed up in recognition. "Is she the same one who represented Marc Baldwin?" The newly minted detective wasn't yet an expert at hiding her feelings. After Marc Baldwin had shot an unarmed Black man, Webb had become collateral damage. Baldwin had hired Casey and covered all of his bases. He'd stayed out of jail. Had gotten a job elsewhere. Had kept his pension. Casey had made the cop Teflon.

Webb had been on her own, twisting in the proverbial wind until she made whatever deal had landed her the plum homicide assignment in Cleveland Heights.

"One in the same." The woman was like a bad penny in my life. This would be my third trial against her. I'd lost the first two. I needed to change the outcome this third time. The stakes were much higher for me. My job and reputation were on the line.

"I don't know how I feel about that," Webb admitted.

"Neither do I. But one thing's for sure, we've got a fight on our hands." I pulled the Walker file closer, made sure my pen was working. "So let's get to work. Tell me again how it all happened. Start as far back as you need to."

6

In the end it was just Justin and me.

We stood alone on the steps of the new federal court-house. The Lake Erie wind tossed detritus down the quiet street. I know I was shell shocked. Justin was less so, but he was not unaffected. I couldn't think of a person who wouldn't be by what had happened moments ago.

"Thank you," I said. It was the understatement of the year. Turning to face him head-on, I gave him Buddhist prayer hands and a slight bow of my head.

"For what?" He looked genuinely perplexed. That altru-ism was one of the things I really loved about him. He was unselfish with everything. Well...nearly everything.

His affection, the kind I could really take solace in, that he kept for himself or for someone else he found more worthy. I blinked away my armchair psychological analysis.

All those questions and thoughts and decisions were for another day. This was a moment to take stock of the huge win we'd scored.

"Brighthill." I shook my head, disbelief dissipating in fits and starts. "Magistrate Judge Carol Wheeler approved it. The whole settlement. The attorney's fees. There's no more to do. We got everything that you said we'd get at the outset. Justice for our clients. A big win for ourselves."

Saying all of that out loud made my head fizz. My brain was still trying to get aboard the fact train. I met his eyes. Felt that zing of connection. Did my best to not look away because we were colleagues first and foremost. "You're going to get a check for three million dollars from Strohmeyer."

Which meant that after expenses were paid, we'd each get a little bit less than one and a half million dollars.

"I'll cut you a check or, probably better still, wire you the money to your business account," Justin said. And as if he'd snapped his fingers, about half of my decade-long lingering problems would be solved in the blink of an eye.

Despite what people often said, money problems could be solved with money.

The baby I was carrying in my belly. The one whose father was as yet unknown. Money was going to do nothing about that. I didn't open that can of worms with one of the potential fathers. Instead I took a step forward on the courthouse stairs. A step toward my future.

"I did the math," I whispered as I started down. He followed me to a sidewalk flanked by post-9/11 concrete barricades.

"Me too," Justin admitted in an unusual show of openness.

"So we're not quite millionaires," I said. After substantial federal, state, and city taxes, we'll each net about eight hundred fifty thousand. "At least not me. I'll solidly be at eight hundred fifteen thousand at the end of the year," I qualified. "This settlement and my Subaru are my only assets in the world."

Justin squinted. Whether it was the sunlight or me, I couldn't tell. I tilted my head in question.

"Why only eight fifteen?"

"Student loans."

"You graduated in ninety-six, though. You're not paid off? Hudson?"

Ron had referred me to the Hudson adoption agency. I'd become their main referral counsel for finalizing international adoptions. What I'd thought was going to be a morally clean and—more importantly—lucrative practice had been sullied by Hudson's dodgy behavior.

Justin had pushed me to quit, and I'd taken his advice because as a solo practitioner, I couldn't get on the wrong side of the state bar. It was too easy to lose my livelihood.

But quitting had meant the flow of attorney's fees from eager-to-be parents had ended just as abruptly, leaving me as broke as when I'd started, with nothing more to show for it than a moderately expensive couch, coffee table, and other decorative doodads.

"Hudson paid off my credit cards and for furniture I couldn't really afford from Arhaus," I admitted. "The student loans? I refinanced those at eight and a quarter percent for twenty-five years. I'm only eight years in. Amortization favors the lender."

"But pretty close to millionaires," he said. "This has to make up for Hudson." It was the first time he'd taken responsibility for pulling that rug out from under me. Problems solved, his face brightened. "We should celebrate."

I looked toward Huron Road, mostly empty of civilian cars leaving the street littered with lots of different agencies' law enforcement SUVs. I'd suspected Justin was going to say as much. I'd done a great job of avoiding him the last few weeks. Though I knew I was going to keep the baby, I had zero idea what I was going to say to him, and arguably more importantly to Ron—a man who actually wanted to commit to me.

When I hadn't seen Justin, I hadn't had to think of what I was going to eventually have to say. There had been no avoiding this hearing, though. Actually, I hadn't wanted to miss it for the exact reason I was glad I'd attended. Without blinking, Judge Wheeler had given us everything we'd agreed to in the Morrell Gates conference room in August. That was a feeling I needed to absorb in person. Otherwise I might not have believed it in the retelling.

For the first time in weeks, I really looked at Justin. From the top of his brown hair, to his stocky frame that I knew all too well, to his court shoes—tasseled loafers suitable for a man twenty years his senior—I marveled at how much he'd changed my life, from steering me toward juvenile court a decade ago, away from Hudson a year and a half ago, then back toward Brighthill six months ago. Not to mention the fifty percent chance he was the father of my growing baby.

More than I wanted to, I'd missed our Sunday night romps.

When I'd seen myself naked in the last couple of weeks, I didn't exactly look pregnant, but I didn't look the same either. Men were very visual when it came to sex, and I suspected that he'd have a few too many questions I was unwilling to answer.

I easily demurred any time he did his low-key ask of whether I was free. His no-strings attitude meant he didn't push too hard against my flimsy excuses.

"Casey?" he prompted.

"Sorry. My mind wandered," I said. Who in the heck knew what I missed while my thoughts had spun out on pregnancy and Justin and Ron, then sex. In between bouts of nausea, I thought of sex a lot these days. I craved the very thing that had gotten me into this predicament. That had to be the definition of irony Alanis Morrissette had been looking for.

"Want to get drinks, maybe dinner?" he asked, his near insistence out of character. I had to wonder if he'd missed me. "The Indians are in New York," Justin continued, "playing the Yankees, so it shouldn't be too busy down here tonight."

"I...uh...planned dinner already."

"Oh. With Ron?" Justin's blink was long and slow. "I get it. Maybe we can celebrate on our own on Sunday."

We had no hold on each other. That had been the defining parameter of our relationship—casual. Well, that and co-counsel and colleagues on this Brighthill toxic tort matter. All of a sudden, a gaping pit of guilt and obligation opened up in my stomach.

"No, not Ron," rushed from my mouth before I could think to stop talking. "Lulu and Sinclair. I didn't think you'd want to hang out with them."

"I love Lulu," he said.

There was a tiny bit of an inward wince at his easy declaration of love for my best friend when I was sure there would never be a similar one for me.

"Then I'm sure there's room for one more." My tone was fake jovial. He didn't notice. "Can you drive? It's on the east side, though."

"If I can stay at your place for the night, then for sure."

I mentally walked through my apartment. The prenatal vitamins were in a kitchen cabinet. There were bags of maternity clothes stuffed in the back of the closet because even I wasn't one hundred percent ready to deal with what was coming. I hadn't even told my parents.

I was giving myself that "first trimester" cone of silence many women did. I didn't want to get everyone riled up when maybe nothing would come of this. That gave me three more weeks to figure everything out. The first of November, the first day of my second trimester, was not tonight.

Tonight was for celebrating. Suddenly being a single mom who was not going to be broke made for a much different future than the one I'd first imagined when I'd seen those two lines on the positive pregnancy test.

"Of course you can stay over." I checked my watch. "If you're coming, let's meet on Public Square at six. That will give us time to drive across town and get to dinner at seven. That work?"

Justin nodded. His smile was infectious. I was happier just seeing it.

"I'll run home," he said, "take care of Morro, and be back in front of your building at the appointed hour."

For a long moment I felt bad. Staying at his place had been helpful for me; it kept needed distance between us, but it had been convenient for him because of course dogs couldn't really stay alone for more than a few hours.

"What will you do with your dog?"

"I have a neighbor who loves him," he said. "Just have to do the handoff."

"See you in a bit, then." Before I could turn away, he pulled me into an embrace. A hug was what I expected. The kiss on the mouth, shouldn't have been—but was—a surprise.

There was nothing I could think to say or do after that display of affection, so I walked away. Shaking off the effect he had on me while I took myself down Superior Avenue.

"This is it," I said three hours later when Justin and I pulled up to Blake's Seafood Kitchen in his gray Ford Explorer.

I kept up a constant stream of chatter to cover the awkwardness I felt with us being in a car together for forty long minutes. Chagrin Falls was the name of the town where we were about to eat. It was also the view we'd have from our dinner table.

For years I'd skimmed *Cleveland Magazine* and read Elaine Cicora's restaurant reviews in the *Scene*. I'd never been able to afford any but the most modest recommendations. Tonight Lulu had offered to pick up the check. But I liked knowing that for once in our decade-plus relationship I could pick up the tab if I had to.

There were three men in red vests waiting at a stand under a giant umbrella adorned with fish.

"A vest of valets?" I tried.

Justin laughed even though it didn't quite work.

"How about I let them park the car. That's how we roll, now, right?"

While he handed over his Explorer's keys, I waved at Lulu through the plate glass windows fronting the eatery. She and Sinclair were already there, seated next to each other.

I tried not to chafe at the idea of sitting next to Justin for the next few hours. Just because we were "casual" didn't mean I wasn't very attracted to him. Something I made a strong effort to keep in check as he'd told me in no uncertain terms that he was not interested in anything more than casual with me. He was in search of the perfect girl and I was so far from flawless it wasn't even funny.

I had to smile at the whole thing: the expensive restaurant, the valet, my companion. My life never went as I'd planned.

"That's how we roll," I parroted. I let one of the vested men help me down from the SUV. Justin's hand was at the small of my back as we made our way into the restaurant and as the host directed us to the table.

"Congratulations, lady!" Lulu crowed the minute we got close to the table. She jumped up and I hugged my best friend, close to feeling like equals for the first time since law school. "You too, Justin," Lulu added.

"Thanks," I said, selecting the seat closest to the window. I wanted to take in the beauty of the water flowing over rocks and through tree roots. The view in front of me, of Sinclair, was not exactly what I'd bargained for, but I didn't think I could ask him to switch with Lulu without seeming rude.

"Sinclair, nice to see you again." It was my best Catholic schoolgirl voice. The nuns would have been proud of my manners. "This is my friend, Justin McPhee."

"Have we met before?" Sinclair half stood from his chair extending his right hand over the table to shake Justin's. "Your name sounds familiar."

Justin flicked his eyes toward me for a second, then shook his head.

While we were sitting and scooting, I could have sworn I saw Lulu's leg move as if she'd kicked her boyfriend under the table.

I flicked my own eyes toward hers. The shake of her head was subtle and almost completely unnoticeable. I saw it, though. Looked at Justin and had to return the broad smile of a man who'd pulled a metaphorical legal rabbit out of a hat. It was infectious. I let a server unfurl the napkin and place it on my pantsuit bottoms.

"It's pretty here," Justin whispered in my ear as he leaned toward me to take in more of the view. I shivered.

"You cold?" he asked.

"No...I'm okay," I demurred.

There was no space to admit that he was the one who made me shiver. Our relationship had no place for that kind of vulnerability.

Sudden longing for Ron pierced through me. He didn't make me shiver, but he made me feel safe. I knew that one day I could be vulnerable with him. There'd been no repeat of our single night, though. Passion isn't a word that came up when I thought of Ron—not in the way it did with Justin.

"I've always wanted to come here. Now I can finally afford it," I whispered back.

"It's on me," Lulu said.

Justin looked at me, eyebrows raised slightly. Apparently we weren't as quiet as we thought.

"Can we get you something to drink?" a server asked, delivering me from the awkward moment.

"I was thinking the Veuve Cliquot," Lulu said.

I swallowed my knee-jerk reaction to refuse alcohol. I'd have a sip to play it as normal as a non-pregnant person would.

"Very good." Our server nodded. "Are we celebrating?"

"They won a big case," Lulu said with a point and small clap in our direction.

The server turned toward Justin and me.

"Congratulations to you two, then. It'll be a moment, the champagne. The sommelier will have to go to the wine cellar." She made as if to walk away and put in the order. Before she could take more than a few steps, Sinclair cleared his throat loudly.

"You know what? Let's change that," Sinclair said. He snapped the wine menu closed with authority.

Lulu looked like she was going to say something, but a single glance from Sinclair seemed to make her think better of her impulse.

"The Ruinart Rosé is a better choice," Sinclair continued. "Probably more along the lines of Casey's taste." To me, he said, "This one has notes of watermelon. Sounds like it's up your alley. If you're drinking."

The last caused a tiny jolt. I brushed it off as a case of pregnancy hormones making me too sensitive. By this time of day, I'd usually evened out. Of course, Sinclair hadn't been making a pointed remark to me. Something odd was happening between Lulu and Sinclair which was none of my business. I'd politely ignore it.

"I'm game for anything," I said. It was the best I could do to smooth over the tension between the couple across the table.

"The rosé it will be, sir." The server promptly left before any of us could change our minds. A few minutes later, she was back with water and requests for appetizers.

"We'll share fried calamari and shrimp," I said. Justin smiled. It had been the appetizer during our first real dinner. I'd have said first date, but that would have been overselling it.

When Sinclair dropped his menu on the table, he used his now free hand to smooth Lulu's hair. My best friend's smile toward him was warm. I hoped I didn't look like that. Her face said in love. I wanted my face to read serious lawyer who'd just taken down her decade-long nemesis and was celebrating life as an almost millionaire.

"Cast iron chicken meatballs," she chose. "We'll share too." The server disappeared again.

"Chicken?" Sinclair's face had morphed from kind into a sneer so quickly that it was as if the previous expression had never existed. "What am I supposed to eat?"

I chanced a look at Justin. His eyebrows lifted in a reflection of my own surprise.

"What do you mean?" Lulu countered. "That diablo sauce and house-made ricotta sound divine."

"I don't eat chicken," Sinclair said. His voice brooked no argument.

"Since when?" Lulu's voice was laced with a certain helplessness.

"Since always." His blue eyes cut hers like a diamond on glass.

"But what about the Shabbat dinner? It was one of those rotisserie chickens from Heinen's. That's what you said."

"That was for you. It's the kind of thing I do for you. Maybe one day, you'll do something for me. Sacrifice can't only go one way in a relationship."

I was more than happy when the sommelier came to the table with an ice bucket, the champagne, and a pristine white towel in hand. Someone followed behind him and made sure each of us had a sparkling clean flute.

"The Ruinart Rosé," the sommelier announced. Sinclair with his salt-and-pepper hair was clearly the elder in the group, so he got the label display. My ex-law school professor nodded as if the world owed him.

Carefully, the sommelier peeled the peach foil until the cork and cage were exposed. I shifted in my seat to make sure I wasn't bopped in the head. He was good, the sommelier. The cork stayed in the towel. The pop was so quiet that I only knew it happened when mist rose from the dark green bottle.

Pink liquid graced the bottom of Sinclair's flute. He sipped, then nodded. My glass was filled next, then the rest of them.

When it was just the four of us again, Lulu went to raise her glass, but stopped when Sinclair put a heavy hand on her arm.

"Let's raise our glasses for the happy couple. Congrats on your win. Indeed it was a coup for the two of you."

"To life," Lulu interjected.

"To life," we all parroted.

"Thanks," I gushed. Couldn't help it. I could not remember the last time I toasted to career success that was mine and not Ron's or Lulu's or anyone else's.

At the waiter's prompting for our entrée choices, I chose the shrimp platter. Justin ordered Lake Erie walleye fish and chips. I kept my mouth shut about my disgust at the idea of eating anything that came out of Lake Erie.

After reading the expert reports on Brighthill's contaminated water table, I hoped the fish was coming from the Canadian side. Lulu got Alaskan salmon. Sinclair huffed and puffed so long, I thought he was going to blow down a house of twigs.

Eventually, he barked out a request for a sixteen-ounce rib-eye. It was the most expensive item on the menu. A week ago, I'd have panicked in case I had to pick up a check that was clearly going to exceed four hundred before tip.

"Good choice," I said with my newfound calm. "If you don't finish it all, we should get a doggy bag for Morro. That's Justin's dog. He's a mutt, right? Always hungry..."

I trailed off when I was the only person who laughed at my canine humor. I tried not to be mad at Lulu for bringing Sinclair Buzzkill along.

I drained my glass because I was well deserving of a nice buzz and I did not have to drive home. When I looked at the empty flute, my pregnancy came back in full force. Well, that would be my last, I decided.

The appetizers arrived. At Sinclair's pout, Justin pushed the deep-fried seafood across the table and pulled the chicken meatballs toward us.

Glad that my early pregnancy aversion to poultry had waned, I took a toothpick and speared one of them, dipped it in the bright red diablo sauce. Popped it in my mouth. The mmmm that escaped my mouth was inevitable.

"You should try one." I nudged Justin with my elbow.

"What are you going to do with your money?" Sinclair asked. I pretended I didn't hear the impolite question.

"Lulu, when are they making partnership decisions for your class?" Justin asked. I was eternally grateful that at least my companion could read a room.

Sinclair snapped his fingers as if he'd just remembered something.

"You used to work at Dalton Lacey, I heard."

I tossed a glare at Lulu. Had she violated the girl code? The unwritten rule where we kept each other's secrets. She was glaring at Sinclair, though, and didn't catch my non-verbal reprimand.

I took another long drink of the champagne Sinclair had refilled unprompted. Just because I hadn't known about Justin's work past and Lulu hadn't either didn't mean that his crimes and misdemeanors weren't infamous among the Dalton Lacey partners. I could see how sleeping with a partner's wife could have become a story to be passed down.

"Short lived," Justin cut the inquiry short. Probably had some practice at answering that question. "I'm a lone wolf. That said, I do remember that they used to make decisions by the end of the year. Only a few weeks before everyone disappears for the holidays."

"I hope so," Lulu said. Her fingers were lifted above the table, and crossed. She waved them for good luck. "I've been trying to get cases of increasing responsibility. I've been having more client contact as well, so that's good. I don't know though." She threw a thumb toward Sinclair. "He won't tell me anything. Mum's the word and all that."

"Some secrets are meant to be kept," Sinclair said, but he was looking at me. "Speaking of which, you must not be pregnant anymore. When did you decide to terminate?"

I swallowed very deliberately so that the meatball that had been in my mouth did not end up all over the white tablecloth and ruin everyone else's meal.

Silence stretched for long seconds. I could hear the murmur of the other diners' conversation, the clinking of ice in glasses, the sound of forks on ceramic plates. Cars cruised by. Water rushed over the falls.

"Casey?" Sinclair pushed.

"Terminate?" It was the only word I could get my brain to formulate and tongue to speak.

"You had some champagne. Most pregnant women don't drink."

"Who had the shrimp platter?" A woman had flipped open one of those webbed things that look like a hotel's suitcase stand, laid down a huge brown tray. At my nod, a plate of buttery shrimp was placed in front of me. Fish and chips slid in front of Justin.

"Be careful, hon," the server said. "The plate is hot."

Sinclair and Lulu got theirs. The server practically curtsied when she asked if we needed anything else before she left.

I wanted to ask for a thousand condiments and three different kinds of water. Anything to prolong her departure. Shock glued my mouth shut. So she nodded and backed away taking her apparatus with her.

"You were pregnant?" Justin's brows knit together as he turned toward me.

"I am pregnant," I said to Sinclair. "It was just a little bit of champagne, by the way. I just wanted to celebrate." What I wanted was to kick myself for making excuses.

"Were you...am I..." Justin stuttered.

What the hell? is what I wanted to ask Lulu. But there was no time to address her betrayal.

Justin would want answers.

Deserved them.

I didn't have any.

"I'm not feeling that good." My chair was so loud scraping back from the table that half the conversations in the restaurant came to a grinding halt. "I'm just going to step outside for a minute."

I didn't wait for anyone to say anything else. Instead I stood, tossed my napkin on my chair and wove my way through the tables. When I could have turned toward the bathroom, I turned instead toward the exit. I stepped out into the rapidly cooling evening, angry at having forgotten my blazer. I rubbed my hands at the goose bumps under my blouse's thin sleeves, then crossed the street and took a path to the water that gave Chagrin Falls its name.

When nausea threatened to overtake me, I doubled over the bridge's railing and gulped air into my starved lungs. It took a minute to gain my equilibrium.

"Am I the father?"

I didn't need to turn to know that Justin had followed me from the restaurant. If I could have disappeared, I would have, but there was no place to go except into the falls.

That wasn't an option. If it had only been me, I don't know what I would have done. But I was suddenly very protective of the life growing inside of me.

Slowly, I turned toward him. He kept moving until he was mere inches from me.

"When were you going to tell me? Are you going to keep it? You didn't answer the first question. Is this why you've been avoiding me?"

"That's three questions, Justin."

"Then just answer the one, Casey. Am I the father?"

"I...I..." My hands flew to my face, shielding my eyes from his. I couldn't take the searing look he was giving me.

Even though I couldn't see, the hands that enveloped my fingers were warm. They gently pried mine from my face. Held them against his body. Justin's heart was beating so rapidly, it felt like it would jump out of his chest and into my hands.

"Casey? Am I your baby's father?"

I gave him the exact same answer I'd given Lulu one month earlier.

"I have zero idea."

7

Casey

October 4, 2007

"Casey Cort. Good to see you," the deputy sheriff said. "Are you here for Juliana Clarke again? Or taking on some new clients?"

For the first time I really took in the black rectangular name tag affixed to his left breast. "P. Nowak" was embossed in white.

"What's the 'P' stand for?" My voice was friendlier than usual, attempting casual.

"Paul," he answered, the single syllable ending on a squeak.

"Nice to finally know that," I said. For a second, I put out my hand to shake, but I drew it back. Flirting had never been one of my superpowers. Instead of offering my hand, I tried batting a lash or two at Nowak. "Have you heard anything about Juliana Clarke while she's been holed up in here?"

"Keeps to herself mostly, I think." Nowak's answer was accompanied by a shrug. "Not a lot of her kind of people here."

"What's her kind of people?"

"Rich? Got all her teeth. Isn't in withdrawal."

I didn't have a comeback for that. He wasn't wrong. Most people were in county jail because they were poor, couldn't afford to post bond or pay their fines or child support or whatever was necessary to leave. No one who could get out, stayed in.

"That's true for her." I backed away from this go-nowhere line of questioning. Not sure what I'd expected anyway. "How long before I can see her today?"

"Fifteen minutes, tops. Someone's gone missing or the computer roster isn't up-to-date. It'll be squared away in a few once everyone is accounted for."

"Thanks." I made to walk to a bench at the far corner of the lobby, but Nowak reached out as if to grab my hand. Like mine had earlier, his faltered before making contact.

"Can you stay a second? There's something I'd like to ask you."

"Sure. Do you know someone who needs an attorney?"

Nowak took a quick glance over his shoulder, then exited from behind the large reception desk. The other deputy glanced up and nodded, indicating that the area was covered. I followed Nowak to one of the benches I was planning to occupy earlier.

"How do you like your job?" he asked after we'd both sat. I paused for a beat wondering what Nowak was fishing for. I decided that a modified bit of honesty might be called for.

"It's great most of the time, but like most jobs, there are downsides."

"Like what?"

"Not being able to get what the client wants. Sometimes the long hours get to me."

"Do you have time for stuff outside of work?" Nowak was fishing. What for, I didn't know. I threw out the most neutral I could come up with.

"Like hobbies?" I offered.

"Or dating." Before I could put the kibosh on what was coming next, Nowak jumped in. "I know that I'm probably younger than you. But I think you're really pretty and I like talking to you. I was wondering if you're free to go out on Saturday night?"

Nowak rushing in headlong with the enthusiasm of a puppy made me nostalgic for a time when things were simpler. When I wasn't kind of in love with one guy and possibly pregnant by another. Though none of the guys loved me the way I wanted. That wasn't the deputy's fault. If I hadn't been pregnant, I might have said yes.

"I can't—"

"The murder thing. Right. I'm sorry. That was stupid of me. You're here to see your client, and if she's in jail, that means her trial is right around the corner."

"It's not that," I demurred. "I'm already dating someone." Like my earlier answer that was mostly true. "Actually, I'm pregnant," I revealed. Rejection was hard for men to take sometimes, so I put a fine point on it, just so he wouldn't take it as a rejection of him and make client visits harder than they had to be. I'd seen asshole attorneys get on the wrong side of county deputies. It wasn't pretty when you had a hell of a time seeing the people paying you for representation.

"Oh. I had no idea." He glanced at my left hand. "You didn't have a ring. Congratulations."

"Thanks. You're cute. You'll find someone."

"Ouch! You sound like my mom."

"Moms are often right. Just because she gave birth to you, doesn't mean she doesn't have two eyes in her head."

Nowak laughed. It was good natured and it gave me the tiniest flutter. It wasn't that I was attracted to him. It was that he was nice and not hard on the eyes and easygoing. I needed more easy in my life.

"Anyone who lands you will be lucky," I said patting his arm with my ringless hand.

He actually blushed above his stiff collar and brass studs. He tilted his head toward the big desk that sat like an island in the lobby. "I'll check to see if your client is down."

When I went to rise, he put a hand on my arm. "Stay put. I'll give you the heads-up when they're ready."

I wanted to protest, but I took the offer in the spirit given. He was a kind guy underneath all the stiff polyester and nine-millimeter gun.

Normally I was annoyed at the time I spent waiting at the jail. Criminal cases were always flat fee, so hours wasted were just that—wasted. Today though, I spent the time working out an approach that would get more from Juliana Clarke. After the visit with Peyton that hadn't yielded much, he'd tried again solo with even less to report.

When Nowak flagged me, I got up and followed him down the familiar corridor to one of the attorney rooms. I went in and got set up with my pen and pad and the file.

Less than five minutes later, he led my client into the room.

If she was surprised to see me alone, she didn't let on. Money also seemed to go hand in hand with impeccable manners. Prisoner calls only went one way—from the jail—so there was no way to let a client know you were going to show up. They were mostly grateful, I found, because at least I broke up the monotony of people warehousing.

"I'm Casey Cort," I said.

"I remember."

My clients were usually chatty, so her reticence was a huge departure from the norm. We weren't friends, so I got right down to it.

"Ms. Clarke. I'm not sure what Peyton Bennett discussed with you last week, but I'm assuming you're okay with hiring me as I haven't heard different."

"He said it was a good idea."

"Speaking of good ideas, I should get right down to what I need from you."

Her response was barely a tilt of the head downward.

"Building a criminal defense is like putting together a wedding cake. There's the cake itself. The filling between the layers. The frosting. The icing. The decoration. A topper. They're not easy to build, but not impossible either.

"If I drove over to Corbo's and ordered a cake, they'd have some basic questions like what flavor or color or how many I'm serving. Bakers would do the rest, but at least they'd have a template to start."

When I got nothing, I moved on.

"I'm working on two pillars here. Meaning, I'm going to divide my time between the presentation of two possible defenses to the jury."

"What are they?" she asked. Her first show of interest in saving her own life. I took it as a positive sign.

"They're both different flavors of the same ingredient, like cocoa and Belgian chocolate. I think the best argument, given the circumstances and more importantly the evidence, is self-defense. As I see it, either you were in fear of your life right at the moment you hit your husband—that would be him coming after you right at that moment—or you had a generalized fear based upon his conduct toward you over the years of your marriage. Do you understand?"

I searched her eyes for a flinch of recognition, for a glimmer of understanding. Clarke closed them against my scrutiny. When she opened them again, she took a breath, then looked everywhere but at me.

"Yes, I understand."

"I can do a lot of things in my job, but suborning perjury is one thing I can't do without risking my license or my freedom. I'm interested in neither."

I took a pause. Waited. Met her unblinking eyes.

"You didn't ask a question, Ms. Cort."

"Right. Of course. What time were you at the house on Shelbourne Road?"

Clarke, who'd been so dead on in her stare, looked away from me right at that moment.

"What time do the reports say he died?" she countered.

I looked at her wrist for a watch, then remembered she was in county jail where such things wouldn't be allowed.

"Do you remember what time you got there? Or at least what time you left the condo? Does your car have a clock?"

The headshake was mutinous. Her lips were closed as tight as a willful two-year-old's being fed a mush of green peas.

"How did you get to be at the house? Can you answer that one?"

"Sienna texted me. She'd gone out with a friend to a movie or something. I don't know that part. She's eighteen. But she left her car in the garage because they drove wherever together. Her plan had been to pick up some clothes or shoes for college. I thought her friend was going to wait outside and drive her back to Shaker Square."

"But that didn't happen?"

Clarke shook her head. I scribbled down notes as fast as I could. Those were the most words I'd ever heard her speak and I didn't think she'd repeat them if I missed anything.

"What's your daughter's friend's name?"

"Bryan Sheffield."

"Is he a friend or a boyfriend?"

"He's a year younger. At University School. A friend."

I wondered what age and school pedigree had to do with romance, but didn't ask. Maybe that's what it meant to have money. You didn't fall in love with a person, but instead merged resumes.

"How did you know that Sienna needed a ride?"

The use of her daughter's name was foreign on my lips. I wonder if that's what made Clarke's face snap up, her eyes meeting mine.

"She texted me."

"Where's your phone? Did the police confiscate it?"

"No. I didn't take it into the house."

That was the first admission that she'd been in the house on the night of the murder. Even though hundreds if not thousands of questions remained unanswered, I finally felt like I was getting somewhere.

"Where is your car?"

Clarke shrugged.

"You didn't drive it back." I flipped through the file. "There's no receipt for impound. What kind of car is it?"

"Volvo. One of the SUVs. I'm not good with the model numbers." I raised my eyebrows, trying Clarke's method of repartee. "Sienna drove it home...to my condo. The car is probably in the garage."

I took a long moment to look at the file while I gathered my thoughts. Something wasn't adding up.

"Let me get this straight. You were home on September second. It was a Sunday. You get a call from your daughter that she needs a ride, but from your old house, not the movies or this Bryan's house, so you go to Shelbourne. Is that right?"

"Yes, that's correct."

"Can you see my dilemma? Your sole purpose in going to the house was to retrieve your daughter. So how is it you two didn't come home together? Why did you go in the house in the first place? Why were you in, but she was out?"

I watched Juliana Clarke's face in the same way a juror might. Looking for the truth, a lie, a tell.

"That's more than one question."

"Then let me start with an easy one. Did you go to Kendrick Walker's residence with the intent to kill him?"

Her headshake was swift, almost involuntary.

"Okay. Good."

Relief flooded through me. For a split second there, I got a feeling that there was something huge I was missing. I could see it now. Maybe Sienna was tired of her parents arguing. A child frustrated with years of fights driving off in a huff, leaving the adults to it wasn't beyond reason.

Before I could ask Clarke just that question about why the girl had left, there was a knock at the door. After I indicated it was safe to come in, keys jingled against the door, the knob twisted, and Nowak poked his head in.

"Sorry to cut you short today, but she has to go back for dinner and the count."

"It's okay. We're done for now."

It wasn't perfect, but it was enough to get me started. I had a narrow path to walk. Now I needed to start by putting one foot in front of the other..

8

I knew it was coming, the reckoning with the higher-ups, but not the exact day or time. Turns out that time was now.

"Lori Pope is expecting me," I announced to the county prosecutor's assistant as I marched into the top honcho's office.

"Have a seat," the assistant said. "She'll let me know when she's ready."

I hated the power move. Pope and her predecessor before her, Liam Brody, were famous for the hurry up and wait. They required your immediate presence but kept you from the inner sanctum. I had to wonder if it was part of the asshole-boss training manual. Not that Lori Pope was an ass, per se. She was only the second female prosecutor in the county's history to break into the boys' club.

A nearly silent buzzer vibrated somewhere.

"She can see you now."

I stood, smoothed my black pencil skirt. Tugged at the collar of my ice-blue blouse. Hoped I looked presentable. Even if I didn't, there wasn't anything I could do just now, so I put one high-heeled shoe in front of the other until I was through the large double door entry.

"Ms. Long. It's been a while," Pope said in greeting. Carefully, quietly she closed the doors behind me until the lock caught. Somehow the slow and deliberate movement made me nervous.

Since Pope didn't extend her right hand, I kept mine firmly at my side. There was no indication as to what I should do next, so I stood, waited.

"Please have a seat," Pope finally said before taking her own high-backed chair. I sat in the guest chair on the right. The one farthest from her felt safest.

"How are you liking Major Crimes?" Pope's voice was so mild-mannered, I was immediately on alert. That question was its own minefield. I wasn't interested in getting blown up.

"It's been interesting so far. I'm enjoying coming back to felony work." My answer was as noncommittal as I could make it.

"A little birdie told me that you got a murder case," Pope said. The Clarke case had come to me when Pope's number two had been out of the office. I had a sense that I'd never have been assigned otherwise, but it was impolitic to take a case away without good reason. It especially stood out when it happened to women. There were only two women on a similar level to me and they handled sex crimes and children—areas where go-getting male prosecutors had very little interest.

"Yes, that's true." I worked to make my voice firm, authoritative. Pope didn't know I was shaking in my metaphorical boots. "It'll probably go to trial. The defendant has private attorneys."

"The defendant is Juliana Clarke?" Pope peered at a spreadsheet on her desk.

"Yes. I didn't bring the file," I said. She was probably looking at the list of prosecutors and case assignments. "Your assistant didn't mention what the meeting was about."

"That's okay. Since my name goes on every single pleading, I keep myself abreast of goings-on here."

"Anything in particular you'd like to know?" I asked, ready to get up and get the file if necessary. Without Tom to oversee my work, maybe she didn't trust my skills.

"Can you win?" Pope held me in a dead-eye stare.

"I think so…yes," I stuttered. "Clarke was caught red-handed with the murder weapon in hand. It doesn't get any more slam dunk than that."

"I don't think I have to tell you how important this case is to your…longevity here."

"Yes, ma'am."

It was common knowledge among everyone here that I was nearly permanently on probation. I was that cautionary tale everyone in the office shared with baby attorney trainees. Whenever I thought I was an anonymous face, one of the new ones would catch my eye, shake their head, move away like I was contagious.

"Oh, I sometimes forget you're from the South. The reason I called you in here was to speak to you about your posting as acting director of Major Crimes."

"Yes, I've been wanting to speak with you about that. I still haven't received notifications about any of the management meetings. It was my understanding from Tom Brody that in addition to trying my own cases, part of the job was assisting in managing the other attorneys in the unit, distributing the caseload, acting as an ad-hoc mentor for those in the department who need it. I called your assistant about getting on the email distribution list, but so far, I haven't received a calendar invite."

"That's what we need to discuss. You're not on the list because I'm not ready to commit to making this appointment permanent."

Though Pope's words were expected, it was a hard blow to my ego. Of course I wished she'd see how brilliantly I was handling the job and anoint me without further vetting. That, obviously, was some very wishful thinking.

Mentally, I pulled up my big-girl panties.

"What would have to be in place for me to make it permanent?"

Lori spun around, putting the back of her leather chair toward me. The windows from her office gave anyone looking an expansive view of Cleveland. It was a rare sunny day and the view across the Cuyahoga River westward went on forever.

I don't know how long it was before Pope stood, but I remained silent the entire time. Pope walked to her credenza, fiddled with a stack of paper, then turned to me, resting her elbows on the back of the high chair.

"Nicole, you've gotten yourself into a hole. It's a long climb out and I'm not sure you have what it takes."

I did not live in the world of the nebulous.

"Give me the concrete steps needed. I'll let you know right now if I can't handle them, and then you can look for someone else to take the job," I said. I was calling her bluff. The mess Tom Brody had made of the office and the call for one ethics investigation after another had made the post radioactive. I was here because no one else was stupid enough to take the job.

"You'll need to stay sober. I checked with HR and there are no legalities barring routine screening."

"Screening?" My voice went up an octave. I hadn't been one hundred percent sober. I just made damned sure to stop drinking before midnight so I was good the next morning.

"I'm ordering random screening by breathalyzer."

"Oh, that will be absolutely fine," I lied. "What else?"

"I'll need to see your win numbers up. And not just on easy-to-convict felonies, but the bigger cases too. Like this murder of Kendrick Walker. No one likes to see the murderer of an upstanding citizen go free."

"Like I said, it's a slam-dunk case."

"So was that sex trafficking ring."

That last from Pope was a low blow. She had to know that Tom had thrown the case. At least I was sure that he'd lost on purpose, dragging me along in his unspoken decision to protect himself from prosecution above all else. Pope's knowledge and complicity was all conjecture on my part. Neither Brody nor Pope was ever going to substantiate my claims.

"Nicole. I'm going to be completely honest here," she began. No good ever came from that phrase. I braced myself. "Ever since you started here, I haven't had the best feeling about you. Unfortunately your behavior has borne that out."

I hoped my face wasn't turning red. I rarely blushed, but the incident she was alluding to was a humiliation I'd like to forget. During my orientation to the prosecutor's office exactly one decade ago, I'd gotten too drunk and had maybe been dancing on a bar when she'd walked into the establishment with her then boss and Tom Brody's uncle, Liam. That maybe was because shame made the memory a hazy one.

"I think I've paid my dues. I did five years in child support enforcement and three on the grand jury." Both were non-challenging assignments for newbies and fuckups.

"You showed up to a rape trial drunk, Nicole."

"I'll admit that was a huge mistake. I was under great pressure and not using the best coping mechanisms."

"The best. You were drinking in the middle of the day."

"With all due respect, that was five years ago. I took the demotions. I was always a good lawyer. I'm still a good lawyer. I just need..." I trailed off. I didn't want to say what I was thinking which is that I needed this opportunity at redemption.

"Here's your last chance. If your breathalyzer ever comes up positive, you're out. Not demoted. Not child support. Not juvenile court. But out."

"Okay." I tried not to panic. I was running out of road, but I wasn't ready to give up alcohol. I needed something to smooth away the sharp edges that evening brought. There could be no breathalyzer at night, though. She wasn't going to knock on my door. I'd simply need to figure out the latest I could have a nightcap and vow to stop then. It seemed so unfair. Half my colleagues were at the Sidebar nightly and I was the one being singled out. I made as if I was ready to lift my butt from the chair, but Pope held up a hand.

"I'm not done. If you make any mistakes, withhold exculpatory evidence from the defense and I find out about it or you lose this case, you're also out."

I was starting to think she was making any excuse to get rid of me. Maybe this wasn't a true second chance.

"Juries," I replied, looking for an out from her ultimatum. "I can't control the jury."

"You know all those eloquent arguments you used to do with the Bible verses and all that? I suggest you pull whatever rabbit you need out of whatever hat you have in your closet to make sure you do just that."

"Of course. I understand. And those management meetings? When can I get on the invite?"

"If all goes well, January."

"Can I at least get a commitment of extra investigative support if it's necessary?"

"You said the defendant was found over the vic with the murder weapon. Doesn't sound like much to investigate. Have you spoken with the detective on the case?"

I almost mentioned Webb by name, then decided against it. "Yes, I'm working closely with the detective on the matter."

"Sounds like you have everything you need, then. Your caseload otherwise appears light. Assaults. Drug charges. Most, if not all of those, will plead out. You have one real case on your plate. Win it.".

9

I took a deep breath, trying to slow down the heart pounding in my chest. My life plan did not include a heart attack at thirty-six. I had no idea how Casey had gotten used to all these damned stairs. I think I'd counted forty-eight between the tiny mailbox-filled vestibule and the top-floor landing between her apartment and her neighbors'. My own second-floor apartment was a breeze in comparison.

"I'm surprised to see you here," a voice behind me said when I got to the final step.

Speaking of the devil, I thought.

Turning around, I saw Greg Salazar slipping into bike shoes and tweaking something on what looked like a racing bike Lance Armstrong would have ridden. Along with one of those tight cycling jerseys and even tighter bike shorts, I had to wonder where he was racing to. Shaker wasn't France.

"Is Casey not home?" I asked. This time it was panic speeding up my heart. It had taken all of my courage and three long days of beating myself up to get in my car and come—goodies in hand—to beseech forgiveness from my best friend.

Salazar twisted himself into a pretzel shape, tucking an Allen wrench into the bulging zip pocket above his butt, then stood.

"No, she's very much home."

I stood, silent under his withering scrutiny.

"After the stunt you and your boyfriend pulled at dinner, I'm astonished to see you is all."

I hefted the large wicker picnic basket that had made the climb to the fourth floor even more difficult than usual.

"I come bearing gifts." The high pitch of my voice signaled my uncertainty.

"Is it a bottle with a genie put back in?" His question was laced with laser-accurate sarcasm.

It would have been kind of funny if the tragedy part hadn't loomed so large, but tears leaked out instead of laughs.

"I'm really sorry, you know." I put the basket down in the wide hall. Swiped at my tears under my favorite cat-eye glasses. I'd put on the rhinestone-studded spectacles in straight defiance of the tame tortoiseshells Sinclair had bought for me and insisted I wear.

"I guess you're going to have to try that one on her. If you were my friend, this would have been a deal breaker."

I stepped back, but stopped when I almost felt my right foot slip on the carpeted stairs. Ten minutes ago, I'd have considered him and his longtime partner among my friends. Guess everything was not quite what I'd thought.

If Sinclair had been standing here, he'd have given me an "I told you so" look. Maybe he was right in that I didn't have nearly as many friends as I'd thought. Maybe what he'd said more than once was true, that what he called my fake "urban" persona had alienated everyone, but that those same people hadn't had the guts to say anything.

Until now.

"Gotcha. Have a good ride." I watched Salazar heft the bike on his right shoulder and heard the clips of his shoes make muffled thumps on the forty-eight stairs down to North Moreland Boulevard.

I took the world's deepest breath, then knocked on the door of a woman who I hoped was still my best friend. Greg Salazar was an acceptable casualty. I wasn't ready to lose everyone in a single day.

"Lulu." Casey breathed my name through the wide-open door. I examined the expanse of white painted wood rather than look at my friend.

"You still don't have a peephole." I shrugged.

Casey didn't respond. She just looked at me. She wore a purple T-shirt over gray sweats. The color looked good on her. Made her eyes greener than hazel. I didn't say any of that though. She probably wasn't the least bit interested in my observations of her personal style. I was certainly learning I wasn't a fan of that kind of thing when Sinclair harped on mine constantly.

"If I did have a peephole, I might not have opened the door."

"Ouch. That hurts." And it did. It was like a physical punch in the throat.

"That hurts you?" Casey sucked in air. "I don't even have the words for this." She turned and walked back into her apartment. But…but didn't slam the door in my face. I took that as an invitation.

"I'm…Sinclair…" I stood at the threshold trying to articulate the inexcusable.

At the sound of his name, Casey whirled around. Her face was like thunder.

"What the ever-loving fuck, Lulu? What. The. Fuck. It was the most important secret I've ever shared with you. All I expected was common courtesy. Which, I'll inform you, would be to keep the secret to yourself. Instead you spread my business to Professor Sinclair, then he spouts it all over the dinner table like he was spitting red wine on a white tablecloth."

I took two steps into the apartment. Lifted the brown basket up high.

"I came bearing gifts?" My voice may have squeaked again.

Casey hadn't turned, but glanced over her shoulder. Then she walked a few more steps to the living room. She sat on the couch, curling in on herself, then lifted the remote and flicked a button so the sound of a Law & Order episode resumed. Chris Noth and Jerry Orbach were standing outside of a New York City building.

I came around so I was standing in front of the fireplace opposite Casey on the other side of the coffee table. I did not block the TV, though, because one boundary violation was enough for a lifetime.

"My mom has a friend who lives in Pasadena." I had to raise my voice above the sound of a woman crying in a dark and dingy corner of a tiny Manhattan apartment. "That's in California. A suburb of Los Angeles. Anyway, she sent a bunch of goodies from a store they have out there called Trader Joe's." I lifted a flap on the basket, then hefted out a heavy dark bottle that looked like beer, but Casey cut me off before I could launch into an explanation of its non-alcoholic nature. She pressed mute, then hit me with a glare.

"Is that another bottle of pink champagne?" she groused. "Maybe I can drink that, give my baby fetal alcohol syndrome, and pile on more reasons for Justin to hate me."

"It's just sparkling cider." I took two plastic goblets from the basket. "Does he...hate you?"

"No, Lulu, he doesn't hate me. That award goes to Richard Sinclair. You know, I'm starting to think he really wanted to hurt me. For the life of me, though, I can't figure out why. I've never done a single thing to him—ever. Nor to you, for that matter. How could you tell him? I mean I get that he's your boyfriend"—she air quoted—"and that 'couples share things.' But this is a man who's lying to his wife or to you or maybe to both of you. I can't believe you thought you could trust him any farther than you could throw him."

I shuddered at the implication of her air quotes and the truth of her words.

"That's not fair." My retort was as weak as my evidence of unfairness.

"In this circumstance I think it's entirely fair."

Ignoring that last, I pulled cracker boxes and cellophane bags from the basket.

"Have you seen these? Chips made from vegetables other than potatoes. Olive and fig crackers. My mom's friend says at this store they have an out-of-this-world cheese selection. Sounds like this place would beat Heinen's any day. Don't know why we can't have anything cool here."

"Because maybe people in Cleveland don't deserve nice things. Especially when things like expensive seafood dinners are so easily ruined."

"What do you want me to say, Casey? I can't go back. It's just that Sinclair—"

"If I never hear that fucking name again, it won't be too soon. What in the hell is going on with you? This guy says jump and you say how high. One of the things I used to love about you is that—"

Casey shot up from the couch and ran through the still-open living room door. I heard a feline sound of protest as my friend came back through the door into the living room, her cat in hand. Simba spilled from her arms like water from a glass. This time, Casey shut the door firmly behind her.

"What you used to love about me?" I whined.

"Was that you were never one who didn't speak her mind. I never had to worry that you didn't say what you meant. Now it's like this guy has some kind of Svengali-like control over you."

"Svengali?"

"Everything you're doing is out of character. Spilling secrets, arguing about chicken, bringing me make-up gifts. I don't even know who you are right now."

"What else can I do to say I'm sorry?"

"Turn back time. Do you know how complicated you've made things? I had no plans to completely hide my pregnancy or even the paternity question from Justin or Ron, but I needed time. I needed time to get past this first trimester. I needed time to not focus on these guys, for once, but instead on my first murder case."

Birth and death in the same breath was a shock.

Murder?

"Murder case?" I asked. I'd stopped fiddling with food and drink. "You have a murder case? Oh my gosh! Who got killed? Who's on trial? Why didn't you tell me?"

I was so proud of Casey. She'd said that she was going to stop being so meek and go balls to the wall with her career. And she was doing just that. Challenging herself in all these different ways without a man second-guessing her. Pride gave way to a wave of envy.

"Why did you tell Sinclair I was pregnant?"

Murder and snacks weren't going to make her let that one go.

"Casey. I'm sorry." I sunk to my knees next to the coffee table. "What else can I say or do?"

"Answer me that one question. Our whole relationship was built on the idea that we were each other's secret keepers. I thought that's what had been going on here for the last twelve years. Now I don't even know that anymore."

"Where's the question?"

"Don't effing lawyer me. Why did you tell Sinclair I was pregnant?"

"Of course," I backpedaled. "Of course I've kept all your secrets. I'd never share anything you told me, ever. The pregnancy thing. It's...I don't know how to even begin to explain it. Sinclair had prepared Shabbat dinner. I barely made it on time and he was mad. Then his wife called and I got mad and took off the clothes he made me wear and put on my Juicy sweats."

"While this recitation is interesting, can you circle around to the point where you put my business out on the street?"

"That's funny. You sounded like me for a second there." My attempt at levity fell flat.

"The old you. I thought maybe if I spoke your language, I could get an adequate explanation."

"Anyway, I came out of the bedroom in my sweats and Sinclair put his hands in my pocket to pull me closer, to hug me. The negative pregnancy test was still there."

"What did any of that have to do with me?"

"I don't know. I just blurted out the truth. I didn't tell him to keep it a secret. I didn't think it was necessary."

"That's because any normal person wouldn't be stirring up shit during a dinner celebrating something entirely different."

I couldn't change the past. Not one single bit of it no matter how much I wanted to.

"So what are you going to do? What did Justin say? He just came in and got the food boxed, then left. Except for requests of the waitress, he even didn't speak."

That had been one of the most awkward moments of my life. Even more awkward than when I'd forgotten the Chatzi Kaddish in front of our temple's entire congregation when I was bat mitzvah and my mother had cried for a solid minute while I fumbled around until the rabbi saved me.

"I think I'm going to keep the conversation between Justin and me to myself for right now." Casey mimed turning a key at her lips.

"Oof. Oh, okay. You want some of this sparkling cider?" She shook her head. I fished around for a different bottle. "Lavender lemonade?"

"I'll try that. I have a hankering for tart stuff right now."

"So how are you feeling? Morning sickness?"

"Lulu. That's off-limits right now as well. I haven't even told my parents."

"The murder case, then?" I asked, desperate for some kind of common ground.

"I'll tell you what was in the Plain Dealer. Kendrick Walker, head architect at Fernsby, was killed. My client, his wife, Juliana Clarke, was indicted for murder."

"Wow, this is huge. Congrats. This is just the biggest coup for you, criminal law-wise at least. How did you end up on the case?"

"You know Bennett Friehof and Baker?"

"The bigger law firm a few floors down from us? Who doesn't?"

"Peyton Bennett called me in to co-counsel. I said yes."

When someone pounded at the door, I nearly poured the lemonade all over Casey's new furniture. A sticky spill would have been icing on the shit cake I'd built. Luckily, I rescued the bottle in time.

"Who is that?" I asked. I may have had my moments, but pounding was not polite.

"Probably Greg." Casey's head turn toward the moving door was slow. "Did you see him out there with his bike earlier?"

"Yeah. He adjusted something, then went down the stairs with it on his shoulder."

"He forgot his keys, then. Happens all the time. Jason is on call and stayed at the hospital."

She slowly unwound herself and got off the couch. She headed down the hall away from the door that opened into her living room.

"You have their keys too?" I asked, stupidly jealous. All of a sudden, I wanted my best friend back and all to myself. For a brief moment, I had a glimpse of how Sinclair must feel. I just wanted to block out the whole world until I could convince her that I loved her. That I was loyal.

That I was sorry. That she could trust me again and didn't need a whole slew of other friends.

"I'm the keeper of many keys, Lulu. Not just yours. Jason and Greg's, my parents', Justin's office. Probably have some old ones from Tom or Miles rattling around," she said as she jingled keys in a wooden box that she'd probably retrieved from the drawer below the telephone nook.

The pounding started up again while Casey swirled her hand through a lot of steel and brass.

"Get that, will you? Tell him it'll be a minute." She squinted and held up keys attached to an ancient friendship bracelet that looked vaguely familiar. "I think these are yours."

I set the bottle down carefully, then went to the door that was going to jump off the hinges. Why in the hell was Greg so damned impatient? I opened it.

"Ron?" OH shit, went my brain. Then all the swear words crowded in. "What are you doing here?"

Casey came back into the room, holding a different set of keys.

"Casey, thank goodness, you're here." Ron rushed into the room bringing the distinct smell of expensive cologne with him. To Casey, he said, "You didn't answer your phone."

"It's on the charger—" She gestured behind her. The keys in her hand jingled.

"Is it true?" Ron implored.

Casey's brain had clearly chosen freeze from the four panic responses: fight, flight, freeze, and fawn. I'd never actually seen a deer in the headlights in our suburban part of the world, but I imagined Casey's face was a carbon copy.

"Is what true?" Her words were slow, careful, cautious.

"I was checking some document review downtown, when Richard Sinclair came into my office—"

My best friend—make that permanently former best friend if this was going where I feared—turned her whole body toward mine. If Casey's eyes had been lasers, I'd have burned to a crisp standing right where I was, leaving only a pile of ashes and maybe my glasses melted into a blue and purple glob of multicolored plastic and rhinestones.

"He came into my office," Ron started the story. "Sinclair said, oh, I heard congratulations were in order. I was like, for what? I thought maybe it was about partnership, but that would have been a bit delayed, since we're already considering the next crop."

Ron seemed to notice me then. "Oh, I—"

Casey pinned Ron with a look. "Close the door. I'm tired of chasing the cat."

Ron did as directed. He came over to Casey then, took her hands in his.

"Sinclair said that you were pregnant. When were you going to tell me? I know this isn't to plan, but we both want a family. Let's just get married now, at the courthouse. Our son or daughter won't be born out of wedlock. Then we can plan a bigger affair with our family, Lulu, and your friends. I already knew I was falling for you. Let's do this."

With a glare at me, Casey slipped her hands from Ron's.

"There's something I have to say…"

I braced myself for a second time. Ron was going to have to hear all about Justin. Somehow I didn't think their nascent relationship could withstand Casey's admission to having a guy on the side. Not like Sinclair's and his wife's

Teflon one which was somehow surviving my own existence.

"I know it's all quick. It's the right thing to do, though."
Ron's voice was a plea. "I want you to understand this is
not because of the baby. This is not spur-of-the-moment. I
wanted to do this at The Baricelli Inn. I was planning res-
ervations for the weekend before your birthday in a couple
of weeks if I could talk to your dad. If not, then probably
Christmas or New Year's Eve like our first date. Either
way," he babbled on, "I already had this…"

I watched in both admiration and horror as Ron came
down on a single knee, after he'd pulled a small square
blue velvet box from his pocket. He tilted it open on its
tiny hinges. The diamonds sparkled in the white gold or
maybe even platinum setting, catching the light from Casey's new floor lamp.

"All the bling," slipped out of my mouth. Fortunately, I
think they were too busy absorbed in each other to have
heard me.

"Will you marry me, Casey? Whether it's this month or
after the baby makes no difference to me. Either way, I
just want us to be together for this journey."

I looked between Ron and Casey, waiting for her to fess
up, to admit that he wasn't the father for certain. That she
had a connection with someone else. She may have denied
it up and down, but I could tell that she felt something for
Justin, especially that night in the restaurant, and from the
window as I'd watched them talk. They were so clearly in
love even though neither of them would admit it.

None of that happened, though. I watched Ron slip one
hell of a ring—the big stone had to be two carats, plus lots
of tiny diamonds besides, sparkling on the three bands that
crisscrossed artfully—onto her ring finger.

What I didn't hear from Casey was "yes." Maybe I'd missed it when the ring had nearly blinded me. She looked happy enough. He looked thrilled. I must have missed her big acceptance.

I watched my best friend kiss her third fiancé on the lips. Then I saw them hug. Over Ron's shoulder, Casey's glare said it all. She was going to hold me personally responsible if Sinclair fucked up her life any more.

"Congratulations," I tried to enthuse, both uneasy and jealous at the same time. I hefted a bottle in each hand. "Good thing I brought the non-alcoholic drinks!"

10

"Congratulations are in order, I see," Peyton Bennett said after he'd confidently strode into the conference room and plopped a thick stack of files on the highly polished cherry table. It was easily eight feet of burnished wood. The gleam had nearly blinded me when Bennett's assistant had showed me in.

Bennett pulled out one of the leather rolling chairs and made himself comfortable. He took off, then laid his folded sport coat on the seat next to him. Unbuttoned his cuffs and rolled them effortlessly into something that looked Kennedy-like, both fashionable and comfortable. Then his eyes met mine.

I had to envy that, his ease and comfort at walking through the world. I'd have stood in front of a mirror for hours fiddling with my sleeve fabric and would have never gotten it right. I'd have self-consciously messed with my shirt, frustrated the entire day.

For me, this was the true mark of wealth. It made you comfortable with yourself. It made it such that you didn't crave anyone's approval. I pulled my mind out of a pit of self-recrimination and looked at Bennett, not just his sleeves. I focused on the pad he had in front of him and the pen he had in his left hand. His hand was sure as he put what was probably Juliana's name and today's date at the top of the blue-lined page.

"Congratulations? For?" I asked, then looked around. We hadn't stepped foot in a courtroom yet. All I'd done was draft a whole slew of preliminary trial motions. I assumed that's what was in at least one of the many folders that lay between us.

There was a crinkle at the corner of his eyes. They were warm, fatherly. Reminded me that I'd been avoiding my own father whose eyes were also warm, albeit hazel like mine instead of blue.

Bennett's gaze zeroed in on my left hand. I followed his line of sight and tried not to be surprised.

The ring.

I'd get used to it eventually...the many diamonds large and small that encircled the third finger of my left hand. One day this sparkly ring would melt into the background of my life.

"That's a lot of sparkle that you didn't have just last week." Bennett tapped his pen on the table.

The one I'd silently accepted because it had seemed easier than offering yet another complicated explanation. The one I hadn't told my parents about because I knew they'd have a lot of questions—warranted questions—this third time around. Questions I didn't want to answer.

"Right." My finger wiggled, involuntarily throwing rainbow facets of light around the ceiling and walls. "Yes. Thanks." I could hear the lack of enthusiasm in my voice. Couldn't do a damned thing about it.

"Who's the lucky guy?"

The chair almost scooted right out from under my butt when I jumped at the question. But it was a normal question. I had to remind myself of that so I didn't get startled the next time someone asked. With a ring this size, there were going to be a lot of someones.

"Ron Pinheiro," I answered after I stopped moving and the casters quieted. "He's a partner at—"

Bennett's face lit in recognition.

"Dalton Lacey. Met him at a Cleveland Bar fundraiser. He's head of pro bono over there. We talked a bit about how we can get our firms to do more for the community."

I had to fiddle with my bag and pretend to consider my pen choice for today's meeting to conceal my face. No doubt they were at a ten-thousand-dollar-a-table event, in tuxedoes they owned, talking about how to help the less fortunate. I'd never met a big firm lawyer who appreciated when I pointed out the irony of that situation.

"So, when's the big day?"

"Nothing's decided yet," I said. I arranged, then rearranged all my own stuff on the table in front of me. Then I gestured toward my middle. "Going to have to plan around this."

"I get it. If you want one of the judges to officiate though, you should book them early and plan around that."

"Thanks for that bit of advice." I hoped my small smile deflected any further questions about due dates and wedding dates and my nonexistent arrangements for all of the above.

A buzzer sounded in the room. Bennett stood and strode to the sideboard where bagels, water, soda, coffee, and tea service obscured a slick black phone. He pressed a button and a disembodied voice filled the space.

"Jacob Lambert's at reception," came over the speaker.

Ah, he was finally here—our investigator. The reason for this meeting.

"Show him in. We're in the—"

"Huron conference room," she replied. "I'll go get him and bring him to you."

I'd already done the pen maneuver, but I wished I had something else to fiddle with. My stomach was churning and not because of morning sickness. This time I was panicking because suddenly I felt out of my depths.

How did I think taking on a murder case with co-counsel who also hadn't ever represented anyone facing this long a stint in prison was a good idea? I felt like we should abandon our planned meeting and instead start working on the ineffective assistance of counsel brief Clarke's appellate attorney would surely file upon appeal of her almost certain conviction.

"Have you seen her since our jailhouse meeting?" I asked Bennett instead of tearing out my own hair. I'd shared what Clarke had said to me during my solo visit. Bennett and I had decided there were even more questions than answers. Fortunately trial motions and prep were fairly standard no matter the case.

I'd done my part in preparation so at least there was some forward movement on the case. In a criminal trial, time was always the defendant's enemy. The prosecutor and cops had done a world of investigation before filing charges. When clients didn't waive their right to speedy trial, the ninety-day clock ticked loudly. Half the job of criminal defense was playing catch-up.

"No. I didn't think there was anything new I'd get from her," Bennett answered. "I thought we could do another visit after this meeting."

"Today?" I asked with a deliberate glance at my watch.

"Maybe. Maybe not."

Before I could delve into the delicate dance of the con-stitutional right of unlimited lawyer visits versus the prac-ticalities of running the county jail, the sound of footsteps got loud, then the door opened. Bennett and I stood at the same time.

"Casey Cort. Long time no see," Jacob Lambert said as he came through the door, Bennett's assistant behind him. Bonnie Medina came through and picked up the bagel platter and moved it to the table. Tubs of various cream cheese flavors followed.

"Anyone want tea or coffee?" she asked.

I wanted tea, but I was super sensitive to my position as the only other woman in a room asking a woman to serve us. So I shook my head emphatically.

"We'll serve ourselves," Bennett replied. Bonnie took that as a cue and left the room, pulling the door closed behind her softly. I had to wonder if there was ever a loud sound in this place of plush carpet and muted colors.

Lambert pulled me into a hug. I did my best to extract myself and extended my hand instead. He ignored it, so instead I gestured to my co-counsel.

"Jacob. This is Peyton Bennett."

"The man who's signing the checks." That earned Ben-nett a hearty handshake from Lambert. "Great to meet you." To me, he said, "Casey, it's been a long time. I always hoped that we'd get to work together more after I left the prosecutor's office."

"My clients have to be able afford you," I retorted.

"Good people cost money." It was something he'd said whenever I'd broached him about a discount. It was a lesson I needed myself.

"From your lips," I said.

"Have a seat," Bennett offered. Lambert took a chair at the head of the table after he'd snagged half a bagel and a bottle of water. "What have you got for us?"

The investigator smeared chive cream cheese, then took a big bite of bagel, then held up his hand while he chewed. Once he swallowed, he hefted his own messenger bag to the table. He took out a manila folder, flipped it open. He handed me one of the thick stapled stacks. The other went to Bennett.

Like the good Catholic school student I'd been, I moved the papers in front of me, but didn't open the packet or thumb through the pages. The nuns had always said it was rude to read when someone was speaking to you.

"What did you find?" Bennett asked. He didn't beat around the bush or hesitate.

"Your lady, Julian Clarke, was probably abused. You may not have enough for a defense. That battered woman thing, I don't know about that."

Lawyering was best left to lawyers, I thought as I shook off the urge to respond. I stole a brief glance at Bennett. From the millimeter rise of one of his eyebrows, I knew that he agreed with me.

"What makes you say so?" I probed. I...Bennett and I could weigh the arguments later. For now, I wanted to be persuaded. To think of how I'd persuade a jury.

"I talked to her parents and friends in New York City."

"New York?" I asked, as if New Yorkers were somehow devoid of phones or email or other forms of communication. I tried to imagine what it could have been like for Juliana Clarke growing up in New York City. Only images from two television shows Law & Order or Felicity flashed through my mind.

While Cleveland was technically a city, it had barely four hundred fifty thousand people in this brain drain era. On any given weekday, downtown streets could be completely empty. The lights and vibrancy that made a city a city were rarely found here. New York was in a different league altogether.

"Her family may not speak with her, but they haven't moved from where she grew up."

"They haven't exactly disowned her, I think," Bennett interjected. "But I know they've distanced themselves from her for marrying a Black man."

"That's just it," Lambert said. "That her interracial marriage had caused the rift, had been my assumption as well. It's common enough in this country. Although in my experience, in many cases the white families come around when the couple has kids. The urge to grandparent trumps racism sometimes."

"But that didn't happen here," I pointed out. Not only did I want the backstory, but I wanted to know who could be a character witness for her. Families may be estranged for one reason or another, but I imagined murder would unite people like nothing else, even grandchildren.

"That's just it. It didn't happen here. Clarke was still in contact with her family during the first year or so of her relationship with Walker. She seemed to be sending out feelers to see what was normal."

"Feelers?" I sat forward, suddenly very curious. "What was she saying? And to who was she saying it?"

"She asked her younger sister, Calandra, why it was that Walker was always accusing her of lying and cheating, when she'd been doing nothing of the sort."

"Is she, or has she been a cheater?" I asked.

I could sell a lot to a jury, but for a group of Clarke's so-called peers, cheating seemed to be up there with pedophilia as something not tolerated in polite society. I'd read that nearly seventy percent of marriages have cheating, and may have made the mistake of spouting off those statistics one time.

Turns out, juries didn't like those kinds of odds. Some things were like cooties where the fear of being infected or the memory of having been infected was greater than the thing itself. I schooled my mind away from that topic as I thought of my deception of Ron. That was for another day. Now it was time for digging deeper into the Clarke-Walker marriage.

"No evidence of cheating," Lambert said.

"What caused the family rift?" I snuck a glance at Bennett. He'd been mostly quiet. It was unusual for a man of his gender, age, and stature. Most law firm partners wouldn't have been able to help themselves from taking over the meeting. But Bennett was giving me more than equal time. It was an interesting fact to file away for later.

"The first time he hit her. She ran home to her family. Stayed with them. Begged for help leaving him."

When I saw from Lambert's posture that he was going to tell it like a story, I closed my eyes, bowed my head, and listened.

"They rented her an apartment on Water Street," he continued, "in one of the then new buildings. Paid a huge broker fee, put down a hefty deposit. Furnished it straight from Pottery Barn."

I wanted to move in. Sounded like a dream come true. A perfect place to heal and figure all things out. I'd often thought if I'd had a year off all expenses paid, I'd have cracked the puzzle of life. Maybe that's what was coming in my future, just with a tiny person in the mix.

I'm not sure how long Lambert had been quiet. My eyes flicked open, collided with his.

"Then..." I prompted.

"She got back together with Ken. Her mom and sister called her almost daily in the beginning to check in on her. To let her know that the Water Street apartment was waiting for her. Even when the calls ended—"

"Wait. Why did they stop calling? Was it out of the blue or did something trigger it?"

"They moved. Clarke and Walker. Changed their phone number."

"Moved? From where to where?"

"From Coventry to the first house they had. That one was in Shaker."

"Sorry to stop you. I want to hear it all. But where in Shaker?"

"Chadbourne."

That was in the Onaway neighborhood. Pretty brick houses. Big green lawns. I sometimes walked there from my apartment when I needed to clear my head.

"Sorry. Go on."

Lambert spread his hands wide.

"They kept the apartment for her for a full year. The minute they gave up the lease, Juliana called again. This time they didn't make the same mistake, but offered her refuge in her childhood bedroom. She came this time—"

"For how long?" I asked.

"About two or three days. The minute Ken showed up with a dozen red roses and jewelry straight from Tiffany's and a mouth full of apologies, she went back. That's when they closed the door. It was a move straight out of the tough love playbook, if you ask me."

I refrained from mentioning that not once had we asked him to editorialize.

"What did she tell them? About abuse specifically?" I asked.

"Juliana told her sister that she and Ken were playing pool one time. She was winning. I guess he was a sore loser. He got mad and hit her pretty hard with a pool cue. Enough that it broke the stick and fractured one of her ribs. That's when they got the apartment."

"Jesus. Broke a pool cue. Broke her ribs." I tried to picture it. Tried to imagine the level of anger it would take to hit another person hard enough to break wood and break bone. I'd been the angriest I'd ever been at Sinclair during that dinner. Had probably had many murderous thoughts after the fact. But I can't imagine having picked up something from the table or even a chair and doing violence against him.

"Did she go to the doctor? Are there records?" The story Lambert shared was a solid brick in the foundation of a self-defense claim. Evidence I could show a jury was better.

"Family friend came and told her the hospital wasn't necessary," the investigator answered.

"Was her family friend a doctor?"

"Yes. Clarke had graduated, hadn't started a job, was uninsured. So he taped her up."

I did mental gymnastics in my head trying to work out if a family friend who happened to be a doctor added up to doctor-patient privilege. And if it did, would his "patient" Juliana Clarke waive that privilege. I made a note on my pad to research that.

"What about that second time? When her family didn't pay a year of New York City rent and just invited her home?"

"That's a little more murky. This time Clarke was having a series of accidents. Had felt like she was becoming clumsy. The call to her family came after a trip to London. It was an early Fernsby work trip. A huge opportunity for Walker to design a new building there. They were in the Tube...the train there."

"I've heard of the Tube even here in Ohio." I tried not to roll my eyes. What I liked about Lambert was that he wasn't from Cleveland, so wasn't biased in the ways natives were. What I never liked about Lambert was that he assumed we'd never heard of or seen anything outside of the state's borders.

"He kept telling her to mind the gap because she was going to hurt herself. They got off at Kentish Town to visit the British Museum, but her foot got stuck in the gap. She thought he'd pushed her into it.

"He claimed that he hadn't and the accident was her fault. But she was sure he'd done it because she'd dragged him away from his work to visit the museum with her. They'd been in London for several weeks, and Walker had only gone from work to their rented apartment and back.

"This day, when they were in the Underground, was the single day he'd promised her they'd do something she wanted. But he'd grumbled over breakfast. Argued the entire way down into the train. Lost his ticket twice. She clapped back that he was sabotaging things. Then the stop had come up, and next thing she knew, her boot was caught. It was only some eagle-eyed people who saw what happened and pulled her to safety before the train left the platform again, taking her leg along with it."

"Wow." She'd gotten lucky. If it had gone any other way, it could have been gruesome.

My mind stuttered, stalled on how her New York City-based family came into play.

"But if she was in London…"

"They both decided he couldn't work with her there, so she flew home. But to New York City instead of Ohio. When her family heard what happened, they said it was part of the pattern of ongoing abuse."

"And Clarke. What did she say to them?"

"She said it was just a very unfortunate mistake."

"Any hospital visits after this train thing?"

"This time it was a broken toe. Like a rib, there's no special procedure. Same family friend taped one toe to another toe and she went home after six weeks when she could walk better. And when coincidentally Walker had come home as well."

"Where's…Sienna in all this?"

"She was born in eighty-nine. Both of these incidents occurred before that. They were married in Philadelphia on May thirteenth in eighty-eight. That was a Friday, incidentally."

"They got married on a Friday? Okay, that's interesting. So these incidents happened in between what?"

"Graduation from Penn and the date they got married."

"She married him anyway?" All this happened before she was legally bound to him. "Why?" I asked someone who couldn't answer.

"I can't speak on that." No editorializing this time.

"Where are her parents now?" Bennett asked.

"On the Upper West Side of Manhattan," Lambert answered.

"I didn't mean geographically," Bennett retorted. "Will they be willing to testify on her behalf if we decide to go with a battered women's defense?"

"I thought I'd leave asking that question to you."

That's what I loved about Lambert. He left the finesse work to us lawyers. He could ask the hard questions. We could do a much softer approach. One that would probably work better with Juliana Clarke's family.

"What did you say to them?" Bennett asked.

"That she was in jail for murder, had a trial coming up, and we were investigating for her legal defense."

I couldn't imagine the turmoil Lambert's visit had caused. How many unanswered questions they might have. A visit from Bennett and I would probably be welcome at this point. I had a strong feeling that Clarke wasn't making collect calls to New York from her cell in the Cuyahoga County jail.

Bennett looked at me. His open face was easy to read. We were on the same page.

"Up for a trip to the city?"

"Can we see Wicked?" I was doing my best teenage girl voice in jest. "I've never been to a Broadway show."

Bennett saw right through my attempt at humor. His answer was straightforward.

"I'll have Bonnie arrange for tickets."

11

I lay in my bed paralyzed with fear. A man lying down beside me in the queen-size bed had jarred me out of sleep. I was on the edge, facing the wall, so I couldn't see him, but I could feel him behind me. His breath made the hair on the back of my neck move and stand at attention.

I held my breath.

Pretended I was sleeping if not already dead.

His weight had shifted the mattress so it tilted. It was all I could do not to slide toward him. I had to resist the urge to grab at the edge on my side. Movement would only spur him on.

Desperately, I tried to gauge if I'd be able to get out of bed and run for the phone before he grabbed me.

Hurt me. Again.

I waited a long moment while my lungs burned. He wasn't going to hurt me.

Not today.

The bed dipped as his weight lessened. I felt him climb over me, walk out of the bedroom, down the hall, and into the front of my apartment.

Finally, finally I let out my breath. Took in a necessary lungful or air.

My eyes came open. I listened closely. The only sound I could hear was wind from the lake. Otherwise the apartment was as quiet as a church on a Monday.

I clawed up through the murky depths of sleep. There wasn't anyone in the apartment with me. Only the specter of another waking nightmare.

It had been months if not years since I'd had one. I tried not to think about how the bad dreams coincided with my periods of sobriety.

Usually, I didn't wake up between the time I put my head on a pillow and my alarm went off at six in the morning. A good stiff drink or prescription sleeping pills were to thank for that gift. Maybe I was building up a tolerance to the pills. I didn't want to think about the implications of that. I wasn't ready to extend my sobriety that far.

I blinked. Lifted my eyelid, turned my dry eye toward the glowing hands of my analog clock. It was eight thirty? I turned my head the other way. The sun was poking around the edges of the blackout blinds.

Lakewood, Ohio's so-called Gold Coast, had sounded like the best of the bad options when I'd moved to Cleveland after law school. Somehow a thirteenth-floor lakeview condo had struck me as being a great idea to push back against the superstition I'd grown up around in the bayou. Now the few sunny days Cleveland had, all of which seemed to be in the autumn, were the bane of my existence.

While I was contemplating whether such a thing as black duct tape existed, my intercom chimed. I searched my memory for forgotten arrangements. I was sure that I hadn't set up a meeting for Saturday. Friends weren't exactly coming out of the woodwork. Women in Cleveland, and men for that matter, weren't lining up looking for companionship. Not from me at least.

Wracking my brain wasn't helping as the intercom buzzed several more times.

I wasn't expecting a delivery that the concierge wouldn't handle himself. After waking me up once to deliver a king cake from my mother, Derrick Henderson never, ever bothered me again.

I informed Henderson in no uncertain terms that whether blood or water or ice cream were dripping from whatever package was labeled perishable, that he was never to bother me with the fact of its arrival.

The buzzer chimed a fourth time. It wasn't Henderson. He wouldn't risk it.

I hauled myself from the very comfortable bed and into the cool room. I'd have to check the weather forecast before turning on the heat. Autumn was variable in Cleveland. Eighty one day, fifty the next. Owing to the now insistent noise, I wrapped a fleece robe around me and shuffled to the spot near the breakfast bar where the intercom had been installed.

"Who is this?" I barked.

"Darlene Webb," an unsure voice answered.

Webb? The police detective? Unless Juliana Clarke had killed someone in jail, I had no idea why this couldn't have waited until I was in the office on Monday. I didn't say any of that through the rudimentary communication system.

Instead, I pressed the button that opened the inner lobby door. Based on all my years living here, I calculated at least seven minutes between the time I triggered the unlocking mechanism and the time she would be at my door.

Hastily, I pulled blue jeans up my legs. Wrestled my tits into a bra and tank. Sniffed my pits to make sure I wasn't going to scare her, then threw on my softest college hoodie. By the time I'd jammed my feet into my tennis shoes, Webb's footsteps had halted at my apartment door.

After a quick glance through the peephole, I pulled open the door before she could knock.

"I'm sorry," Webb blurted before I could do the polite thing and invite her in.

"I thought my address was a secret," I said. It was a courtesy extended to judges, prosecutors, and cops. There were too many bitter people in the system who could target us.

Webb shrugged. She didn't pretend that she hadn't misused a database only police had access to.

"Has Casey Cort or that co-counsel of hers said anything to you about Juliana Clarke?" Webb asked, forgoing all pleasantries.

I stepped back from the door and opened it wider in silent invitation. Webb stepped through it. I took a seat on my denim-covered sectional. I had a corner unit and catty-corner floor-to-ceiling windows flooded the space with light. Webb perched on the edge of a wingback upholstered in white with bright orange, yellow, and blue flowers.

"In criminal cases, the discovery usually goes one way," I snapped.

Damn, waking up with a nightmare had made me groggy, disoriented. Abruptly I stood and walked into the open-ended galley kitchen from the living room side. I pulled the old filter from the coffee maker, tossed the cold, damp dregs, and started all over again with a scoop of fresh grounds. Once I added water, I set it to brew. When the smell of coffee started to fill the area, I stepped back in front of the couch. That whiff of caffeine helped me remember my manners.

"Gimme a sec," I said and went back to the kitchen. I pushed the button that paused brewing and poured myself an extra-large mug. Got sweetened condensed milk from the fridge and added in a hefty slug. Took a few big gulps and did the two-step process again. Only when some of the cobwebs cleared did I sit back on the couch, though I didn't let the mug leave my hand.

"What's the story?" I asked.

"I've been talking to the Clarkes' neighbors." Webb leaned forward on the chair. "Trying to re-canvas and reinterview anyone who might come forward as a witness."

The police had come upon Clarke with a weapon and Walker with a matching gash in his head. Witnesses were superfluous as far as I could see. I almost blurted out my scorn when I remembered that we'd talked about nailing down the timeline. Seeing if anyone had seen Juliana coming to the house. Getting a read on her state of mind.

"What are they saying?"

"It's not what they're saying. It's what Jacob Lambert was asking."

"Our Lambert? You're aware that he used to work for the prosecutor's office." I didn't need to say the word traitor out loud. Took a sip of coffee instead.

"I learned that when I pulled info on his PI license. He had a new number, but was older. I checked around and found out he'd switched to the other side."

"More money over there." It was true of private defense attorneys for sure. Not public defenders. We made more than they did. But private attorneys could charge people who treasured their freedom tens of thousands of dollars. A good chunk of that went to investigators. Cort and Bennett had probably been paid the equivalent of my yearly salary for this single case. Being on the righteous side of justice—not money—was what let me sleep at night.

"Anyway, I know it's Saturday, but I wanted to warn you that Lambert may be poisoning the potential witnesses."

The word poison got my attention. Witness tampering was a first-degree misdemeanor.

"What's he asking?"

"Whether there were any incidences of domestic violence between Walker and Clarke."

"DV?" I leaned forward and put the coffee on the table that shared its name. Remembering my manners, I looked at Webb. "You want coffee or water or juice or something?"

"I'm good."

My mother would have pushed, called in our housekeeper, Aubrey, to serve cake and coffee. I took Webb at her word.

"I need to get my files. I'll be right back."

I didn't have files exactly, but I needed a second to regroup and a minute to get a yellow pad from my dusty home office. I pulled open the drawer on the side of my desk. A small bottle of bourbon was there like I'd expected. If Webb weren't here, I'd have poured a slug in the coffee. Improved the taste considerably. I twisted open the top. Stuck my tongue in the bottle's neck. Realized the smell would probably be too strong on my breath, then screwed the lid back on.

Later.

If Webb didn't have a breathalyzer on hand, I was probably free of a Pope spot check for the weekend.

I waved the paper and pen like I was flying a flag when I got back to the living room. Without a taste of the liquor, I could not stay still. I dropped the writing stuff on the coffee table next to my unadulterated beverage and paced in front of the windows. The lake was as smooth as glass.

"He was asking specifically about what?" I turned back to Webb. "Fights? Physical altercations? Police calls?"

"All of that."

"What's the family's history with the police? Did you call your fellow officers?"

Webb nodded.

"No reports filed that I can find," the detective added. "Some of the Clarke/Walker relationship predates computers though. I'll have to take a second deeper dive. I did put in a few calls. Still waiting to see if there were any off-the-record visits."

Lambert wasn't intimidating witnesses. He was bolstering a claim of abuse. I walked up to Webb. Stood too close to the chair. Forced her to look up at me.

"This means she's likely to lodge an affirmative defense."

"What's that?"

"Not guilty by reason of self-defense."

"She's going to say that he was trying to kill her?" Webb opened the murder book on her lap, flipped through a bunch of pages. "There's no evidence of that in the file."

Webb held up pictures of Clarke the police had taken. "She's got no bruises. No defensive wounds. I didn't catch the case until after all the forensic work was done, but that's not something anyone working for any department should have missed."

I threw back more coffee not even caring that something other than careful sipping was proper.

"It's not immediate self-defense. It's battered women's syndrome."

"Is that even recognized by law. Here? In Cuyahoga County. In Ohio?"

I was careful not to roll my eyes.

"Wasn't this covered at the police academy?" I asked. "The law passed in November 1990." It was one of those weird bar exam facts that I never forgot. But definitely something Webb should have remembered. "That's almost twenty years ago."

"I don't know." She shrugged. "Maybe? Training focused on diffusing domestic situations and if necessary removing the guy from the house. I didn't do a lot of those calls. But every single one of those women I did meet was unreliable. One minute they'd be screaming at the guy, like bloody murder, and then when we'd ask if they wanted to bring charges, they'd back off in a heartbeat. Or we'd go up to trial and the woman wouldn't show up or she'd recant. I'm not sure that's a thing the police or courts should handle for that matter."

"Point taken. But if what you turned up means anything, then the issue is going to be heard by the jury and the court. The justice system will have to decide whether she was abused, and if so, was she entitled to murder her husband. So we're going to have to figure out what the heck we're all going to do about it."

Webb's headshake was so swift I wouldn't have seen it if I hadn't been looking directly at her.

"After the fact." She slapped the file in her hand. "If she had called the police beforehand, neither of us would be here. We could be on more worthy homicides. Drug dealers killing innocent civilians. Child abuse—"

I sliced my hand through the air cutting off the detective. We were not going down this road.

Worthy cases my ass. She'd hit on one of my triggers. There had been a time long ago when I hadn't been considered a victim worthy of respect.

"We can't choose the victims or the defendants," I set her straight. "We have to play the cards we're dealt. So why are you here?"

"I didn't want to wait until Monday, and while the BMV database has your address, it doesn't have a phone. Do you want me to investigate this abuse angle? This kind of thing is best done on weekends when everyone is home, so I wanted to get a jump start if you were on board."

"Yes." While I didn't like her methods, I did appreciate her initiative. "Nail down if there were any complaints. In any jurisdiction. Cleveland proper. Shaker. Cleveland Heights. For every possible incident she brings up, if she testifies, I want to be able to point out that not once did she call in the police to help her."

"Got it. Can I have your number?"

I wrote it on a corner of the page in front of me. Tore it off.

"Use it sparingly," I said.

Meeting over, Webb stood and I escorted her out. The moment I closed the door behind the detective, I opened a cabinet above the fridge. Wrapped my hands around the large square bottle. Tipped a bit of the contents into my nearly empty mug. Usually I'd have added more coffee, more milk to dilute the mixture, but not this morning. Leaning my head back, I swallowed all that was in the mug in one fell swoop.

I'd attempt complete sobriety tomorrow. Give myself a dry twenty-four hours before Monday morning office hours. As the noise in my head quieted down, I pushed away any guilt. I needed this hit because my very simple case was about to get very complicated.

12

I thought I was prepared for the meeting with Juliana Clarke's family. I'd researched her divorce records. I'd read and reread Lambert's report.

On the plane, I'd even read much of the psychological research and current case law on Ohio's interpretation of battered women's syndrome. What I hadn't spent any time thinking about was what it was like to grow up with money.

Unlike the meetings with the client and with the private investigator, once we arrived in New York City, Peyton Bennett had taken the lead. He hired a black car service that had whisked us from the airport to the upscale hotel on East 57th Street.

He arranged for rooms that made my own apartment look modest in comparison. After the same black car had whizzed us across the city, Peyton schmoozed with the Clarkes' doorman who'd keyed the elevator and escorted us up here.

Here was the two-story penthouse of the Clarke family. The small and dingy New York apartments I'd seen in films were nothing like this place.

"Tea?" Helena Hanover Clarke had asked while a large silver platter was placed on the table. I thanked God my European immigrant parents had injected some kind of manners and grace into my upbringing.

"Thank you." I nodded while she poured. I added a single sugar cube, stirred, then took a sip. The tray of tiny Italian cookies looked so appetizing my mouth almost watered. I had to imagine though, that the miniature sweets were for show. I did the gracious thing and declined politely.

"I'm sorry for the circumstances that bring us here," Bennett started after Mrs. Clarke had taken a seat on a love seat opposite the couch we occupied. A small Scottie jumped in her lap. From the corner of my eye, I caught the wince of Juliana Clarke's father, James. Dog on couch disagreements were probably common.

Footsteps sounded from well across the large room. The woman who approached us looked like a younger version of Juliana Clarke.

"Calandra Clarke Young." She held out her hand for Bennett to shake. I took it after him. Did everyone here introduce themselves by three names? It's how I imagined a Daughters of the American Revolution meeting started.

"Have a seat, honey," James Clarke insisted, his eyes on his daughter. Once Calandra placed her bum on the armrest of her father's chair, James fiddled with the buttons on his tweed jacket. If he weren't real, I'd have thought that he and the rest of the family were messing with me. In my wildest dreams, I didn't think people like this existed outside of Woody Allen movies. But here they were.

"I just can't believe she's somehow wrapped up in all this mess." Mr. Clarke shook his head. "This Walker character has been bad news from day one."

"What makes you say that, Mr. Clarke?" I asked. This meeting had to be open-ended. It was a fact-finding mission as much as anything else. Even though I would have liked to mold the story of Juliana Clarke's life into a bulletproof defense that could withstand anything Nicole Long could launch our way, the truth was more important.

What her family said here could be substantial building blocks of Clarke's defense.

"He was just too much," he said. Mr. Clarke hung his head as if Walker were the cause of so much misery.

"Daddy, hindsight is twenty-twenty," Calandra soothed.

"You were young then. I'm sure your perception would be more mature now."

I looked between the family and put down my tea. Squabbling would derail any productive conversation. I'd seen it many times in custody cases.

We needed background that we could use. They could debate the best way to reconcile their own inaction on their own time.

"Here's where we are," I interjected. "Kenneth Walker was murdered the first weekend in September."

"That guy you sent—Lambert, was it?—told us all this."

I continued as if Mrs. Clarke hadn't spoken.

"Juliana was found with the body and the murder weapon in her hand. Since then, she hasn't spoken much."

"Why not?"

I wanted to shrug, but resisted. With my hands, I gestured toward Bennett, punting the question to his greater expertise in all things Juliana Clarke.

"My best guess?" Bennett said. "Trauma. Post-traumatic stress disorder? We'll have an expert evaluate her, but that's not ongoing treatment, so there's no telling when she'll talk or what she'll say. In the meantime, the gears of justice grind on and we'll need to mount a defense no matter how helpful she is or isn't."

Mr. Clarke nodded sagely. I imagined he used that posture in whatever classes he taught at the Ivy League uptown where he was a professor.

"So what was your first impression of Ken Walker?" I asked.

"He was sweet," Calandra said. "Up until him, Juliana had dated all these artists. But assholes, you know. They smoked Gauloises or Gitanes or even clove cigarettes and scarves and it was all about their capital 'A' art. He was like one hundred eighty degrees from that. Kind of a relief from all that pretentiousness."

"How so?"

"She showed me this letter he'd handwritten her asking her out on their first date. He'd listed every single thing he'd observed in her. That she was artistic and clever and funny and pretty. He came to her apartment in Philadelphia and brought a dozen red roses when he picked her up for the first time. It was like that almost daily for the first few months."

"That sounds positive." Or overwhelming, but I didn't interject my own thoughts.

"But it wasn't, I don't think," Calandra said.

"What did you think?" I directed this question to Mrs. Clarke. Except for stroking her little dog's black fur, she'd been quiet after getting the tea and cookies out.

"Have you heard of the brainwashing that cults do?" she asked.

"It's called love bombing," Mr. Clarke finished.

"Sounds violent." I regretted the words as soon as they left my mouth. It was as if I'd left my manners down on the street. I picked up a cookie, bit it. Tried to mold my face into something more sympathetic. "Sorry. Love bombing?"

"It's the go-to technique of emotional manipulators like cult leaders."

"How does it work?" This was a first for me. There was so much more I'd have to learn about abuse. Re-watching The Burning Bed wasn't going to cut it.

Mrs. Clarke looked over at her husband. He nodded their communication wordlessly.

"These cult leaders, they find vulnerable victims. Then they give them all this love and attention. The target can do no wrong. These manipulators...they'll say whatever the target needs to hear."

"What did Juliana need to hear?" Bennett asked. I'd have tried to phrase that more artfully. From the look that passed from one family member to another I had to assume that they'd chewed through this a time or twenty over the last couple of decades.

"That she was a great artist. That he was her biggest booster."

"Did you mind her pursuing art?" I asked. From looking around this apartment in this historic building, I couldn't imagine that being poor or starving was any kind of worry.

But maybe having a bohemian artist in this family was off-putting.

Even now in my newly fattened-wallet state, I couldn't really imagine my parents signing off on "painter" as a new career path for their daughter.

"No, we didn't mind. It was fine. My own sister is a painter," Mrs. Clarke said. "It's just that she had so many gifts. I thought she'd be happier doing something more practical. It was my fault she went to Penn. It's James's alma mater. Practical felt important back then. I didn't want her to be just another woman with nothing to fall back on. Nothing to fulfill her should hard times come."

I didn't know a lot about New York City, but something told me that this apartment wasn't paid for with a professor's salary, even an Ivy League one. This situation had trust fund written all over it. There was probably something more going on here than potential hard times. Dickensian wasn't how I saw Juliana Clarke's young adult prospects.

Something that had propelled Juliana Clarke from the safe bosom of this well-off family and into the arms of a man they'd all but agreed was an abuser.

"I think we stumbled a bit," Mr. Clarke started. He'd spoken without prompting from either me or Bennett. "It's not that we're racist, but when Juliana brought home an African American man, it was a bit of a sh...surprise." He cleared his throat, then went quiet.

"Daddy, you made some joke about that Will Smith movie," Calandra huffed.

"It wasn't the movie. That play got a Tony nomination," Mr. Clarke corrected.

"Six Degrees of Separation. Everyone was talking about it," Mrs. Clarke said.

"It was at the Vivian Beaumont. The only Broadway theater not in the theater district," Mr. Clarke mused.

"So what did you say that may have alienated her?" I probed. I needed them to focus. To get back to the matter at hand, their daughter and sister was facing a long stint as a guest of the Ohio Department of Rehabilitation and Corrections.

"Daddy asked if he were Sidney Poitier's son. Ken didn't get the joke. He'd been so nice and I don't know...jovial up until that point. I tried to explain that it was a bad attempt at humor. But Ken, he sort of bundled up Juliana as soon as he could and took her out of here. They were supposed to stay. But they got into his car and made the drive back to Penn." Calandra stopped abruptly. I'd seen the move before. She wanted to say something, but it wasn't nice or polite.

"Did you see something?"

"This apartment has a front door and a back door. A lot of them in this building do. Anyway, I went out through the butler's pantry to put something in the chute. There's a window in that hall, you can see down to Seventh Avenue. They were there arguing. Obviously from up here I couldn't hear what they said."

I didn't point out that from up here you couldn't hear a damned thing. All the buses and trains and honking and city noise was missing from this apartment.

Money bought you silence.

"Our parking is a few blocks down. I saw them walking. I knew it was her because she was wearing this new ruby-colored trench she wouldn't let me borrow, so she stood out against the background. Anyway, Juliana said something. She was making angry gestures toward Ken. He pushed her, hard. She didn't fall because there was some building scaffolding that broke it. He walked up to her and pushed a hand up against her throat."

"You never told us this," Mr. Clarke said, his eyes going wide.

"Why didn't you call the police?" Mrs. Clarke asked. The little dog yelped and jumped off her lap. I wondered if she'd squeezed it too hard in her dismay.

"Because just when I thought he was going to choke my sister, or something worse, he pushed that same hand even harder against her neck, then he kissed her. Just like that she looked like she'd melted. I was younger than her. I thought that I'd seen something different than what I was used to, but not bad per se. Just some kind of relationship that was...unconventional...but consensual. After a minute, they both stood up straight, fixed their coats and started walking again."

"Did you ask her...Juliana...double-check that what you saw was what you thought?" Mrs. Clarke had turned full-on toward her other daughter. I could see Mrs. Clarke's maternal instinct war with her pride.

"How do you ask that?" Calandra shot back. "I asked some different questions, like if she loved him. Was he as nice to her as Dad was to Mom? Stuff like that."

"Tell us about the time you got her the apartment," I prompted. I was glad that Bennett had suggested we come in person. Lambert's report was thorough, but it was only an outline. Seeing the family tell the story filled in the picture.

"The bastard laid hands on her," Mr. Clarke said. His tone was strident. He was more animated than he'd been at any time so far.

"She called, crying," Mrs. Clarke added. "We drove eight hours to Cleveland to pick her up.

"She looked pretty bad," Calandra added.

"How would you describe it?"

"It was only the left side of her face. There was a bruise on her cheekbone. The side of her lip was split. We didn't know about the ribs until later. When we got there she said she was scared. We jammed all of her stuff that we could see in a suitcase and a garbage bag. He'd gone out and she didn't know when he would be back," Mrs. Clarke said, her face pained.

"Did you call the Cleveland police?" I asked, hopeful.

"No. We didn't want to stand around and wait and see what would happen," Calandra said.

I got that. I was pretty sure it was well known that the police response to domestic violence was all over the map. If not, I'd surely have to find a way to educate the jury on that. I added that to my notes.

"She wasn't like these other unfortunate women. She had a place to go. Family to help her. There was no reason to involve some twenty-year-old cop with no training," Mrs. Clarke added.

Bad experience with the police no doubt. Nearly one hundred percent of my clients could relate.

"Then what happened?" I asked.

"Ken brought flowers and jewelry and took her back." Mr. Clarke said that with such finality that I imagined there was a lot of pain in between Juliana's phone call and her return to Walker.

"What about her ribs? Who was the doctor who taped her up?"

All three shot each other looks. I had no idea what it meant. Calandra finally answered.

"Eli...Elias Phillips."

"Would he talk to us?"

Another look passed between the three. I wanted to jump up and say something about keeping secrets not helping anyone, especially Juliana, but I resisted.

"We'll give you his contact information," Mrs. Clarke said. She stood and walked from the room. In a couple of minutes, she was back with an old-fashioned black leather address book. The kind my mother still used to keep track of fellow parishioners.

She scribbled something, tore off a piece of paper, and handed it to me. I tucked it safely in the crease of my yellow pad.

"Can I ask what your take was on the London trip?"

"I think…" Mr. Clarke cleared his throat. His eyes met mine, didn't waver. "That she was lost to us then. Whatever he had done, manipulated her, brainwashed her…she refused to believe he'd done her any harm no matter what happened."

"We told her that we were here whenever she needed us, but we couldn't, in good conscience, continue to support her."

That was the end of the meeting. I could sense that without anyone having to say a thing. I stood and thanked them, shaking each family member's hand in turn.

On my way out, I scanned the room again, a little more closely than when I'd come in and the whole two-story penthouse apartment had felt overwhelming. There were a lot of family pictures, framed on the wall, framed on the piano. The faces were all white.

No Ken Walker.

No Sienna.

Had they cut off contact for their daughter's safety or their own sanity? It was a question a jury would wonder, but it wasn't a bad one to leave in their minds.

Bennett secured their detailed contact information and their promise that they'd testify if need be, then we took our leave.

13

"What are you doing?"

After I spun around in surprise, I took the phone from my ear. Jammed it in my cardigan pocket. Sinclair and I were standing in the room at the farthest end of the apartment. A skinny one with a wall of windows that faced Overlook Road. It wasn't much of a useful space, but I used it as kind of a reading room. And when I wanted privacy, it was a good fifty feet away from the back of the apartment where the bedrooms were. Sinclair had been working in the spare bedroom that he'd turned from my home office into his own study.

"I was...uh...I was just calling Casey."

His brows came down over his eyes in what looked like the start of a frown.

"You said she was in New York City."

Suddenly exhausted despite the pre-dinner hour, I sat in my favorite single-armed chaise lounge. One of Casey's boyfriends, Miles, I think, had once referred to it as my fainting couch.

"They have phones there. I wanted to check in. See if she saw Wicked like she'd planned."

"You called her about a Broadway show?"

Maybe that was a flimsy excuse.

"You can't understand," I tried to explain. "I need to talk to her. To get her to forgive me."

"What does she have to forgive you for?" Sinclair asked. He sat on the end of the couch, lifted my legs, then put my legs on his lap so that my knees were a pyramid over his thighs. As much as I loved him, I didn't very much like Sinclair in this exact moment. He was very calm for someone who'd unintentionally lobbed a few grenades into my best friend's life.

"Are you kidding?"

"From where I'm standing, you've been one hell of a loyal friend," he said. That was true. I'd made a small and understandable mistake. I'd owned up to it right away. I didn't love Casey any less for the position she'd put me in.

All that said, though, I very much wanted us to go back to how we'd been before that night when the first ordnance had exploded.

"But what about...you know...me spilling to you that she was pregnant. The guys she was with finding out she was pregnant before she was ready to tell them." I wasn't comfortable exactly laying blame at his feet, but I did want him to take responsibility for his part in this little debacle.

"Maybe she shouldn't have had sex with different men." Sinclair shifted, lifted his arms, cupped his head between his interlaced fingers. "She's lucky that pregnancy was all she got out of it."

"What do you mean?"

"Disease? HIV? AIDS?"

"Seriously?" I shook my head. "No one I know has these kinds of problems."

"It's not just poor Black women and working women."

"Working women?" Was he saying that Casey deserved a disease because she had a job?

"Prostitutes," he spit out. "Women of the night. Girls of ill repute. Deborah tells stories that would curl your hair. More than it already is." Sinclair plucked at one of the corkscrews on the side of my head. He held the hank of hair in such a way that a small twinge of pain shot through me before he let go and the coil sprung back into place.

"Every week," he continued, "Deborah came across one patient or another who was surprised they had chlamydia or syphilis or even HIV. They all thought going bare was fine."

My mind was swirling. I didn't even know how to respond. He thought Casey was promiscuous? He thought STDs were a problem? We'd never been tested together. He'd never used a condom with me even when I'd asked.

It's why I'd thought I'd needed the damned pregnancy test in the first place. The entire reason Casey had discovered she was pregnant and I'd been relieved to find out I wasn't.

My stomach twisted into a big knot.

Deborah.

Could he ever go one day without talking about his wife? I was ready for him to divorce her already and for them to put their marriage behind them so that Sinclair and I could start something new and fresh without Deborah Bloom's specter forever hovering.

"Casey's in a vulnerable place," I said after I pushed all those other thoughts out of my head. "She may be mad at me right now, but however it turns out with Ron or Justin, she's going to need someone solid in her corner."

Casey wasn't at that point yet. I think there was a lot of denial in my best friend's life. From my outside perspective, I could see how inevitable her baby's entry into the world was. Cleveland winters may have been long, but the end of April was just around the proverbial corner. No matter how things shook out with Justin and/or Ron, I planned to be a single steady presence in her life and the best aunt I could be.

"She has her parents." Sinclair took his arms down. Patted my legs with them. "You said they're alive and well. Flush too, considering the car they bought for her."

I took the Blackberry from my cardigan and jammed it as far as I could into my very small jeans pocket.

"She hasn't told them yet," I said, nearly sure it was the truth. After Sinclair's little stunt with first Justin, then Ron, it wasn't as if my longtime friend was confiding in me much. I still believed that kind of confession would surely have broken Casey's silent treatment.

"You've talked to her?" Sinclair was well aware of the rift. I hadn't spoken with or seen her since I'd delivered my gift basket a few weeks back. I only knew she was in New York because she'd texted me to ask about some New York logistics since my family went at least a couple of times a year.

"No. Not exactly. I...I've been leaving messages. She hasn't returned a single one."

"And this is your best friend?" Sinclair said as if he'd never had a rift with anyone.

"I met her first-year law school. It's been fourteen years. I love her like a sister. Maybe it's hard to understand because you're a guy," I explained. "Women can get really close."

"You think I don't understand love, friendship, or relationships. Is that what you're saying?"

Sinclair looked unjustifiably angry. I tried to piece together what I'd said in the last few minutes that could possibly have made him mad. I thought we were talking about how my best friend was freezing me out because of something he did.

"I'm not saying that at all. Are you mad at me?"

"I'm not angry," he yelled. He pushed forward suddenly, my legs fell off his, and I nearly slipped from the lounge. Then his voice quieted. His mouth, if it was possible, pushed into a pout. Sinclair doubled over, leaning his elbows on his thighs. His face when it turned toward me looked genuinely confused.

"I don't understand why you hang on to Casey. I can't see what positive influence she has on your life. She's constantly involved in cases where the morality is questionable. Her money situation is all over the place. I would bet that over the last dozen years or so, you've covered all the meals, some of the shopping trips. Anything you'd let her mooch off of you, she took. Add to that, she's doing her best imitation of a low-class talk show guest with the baby daddy mystery of 2007."

If he'd been anyone else, I'd have let out a "tell me how you really feel."

"That's not fair. She's a smart girl who had some serious setbacks. You were there for the first big one. She's done the best with what she's had to work with. In fact, I think she's done pretty good considering."

"Considering what? That she went to a fourth-tier law school. If she's so smart, why didn't she go somewhere better after Ohio State."

As if I'd been slapped, I scooted as far away as I could get on the little couch.

"I went to the same school. You taught there."

"I went to an Ivy," he said, as if Princeton and Columbia didn't already come up in nearly every conversation. He'd recently bought two college sweatshirts that he alternated between on weekends. "I came here only because Deborah wanted to work in a world-class medical community. It's the only thing that's top-tier in this city. I did her a favor. I did everyone a favor by bringing a little bit of Ivy League to your school. They were lucky to have someone like me on board for as long as I stayed."

"Do you think I'm not smart?" I asked. I knew I wasn't a neurosurgeon like my brother, or really lived up to my family's intellectual giantess, but I hadn't really seen myself as a slouch either.

"I love you for you," Sinclair dodged. "You're a great girl. I want to marry you someday. Have babies with you."

His forever words were like a balm that eased the sting of all that had come before.

"I want that too," I whispered. No one had ever loved me like Sinclair did. No one had ever tried as hard as he did to make me happy.

He pulled me close. Kissed the top of my head. Ran his hands down my back in a way that made me shiver not with cold, but with anticipation.

"I don't want anyone in the way of that, sweetie."

"Neither do I," I replied. I melted into him as hope burgeoned in my chest. He was saying that he was finally ready to let go of his other sweetie. That soon it would just be me and him—not the three of us: me, him, and Dr. Deborah Bloom.

"So you promise not to call Casey."

I leaned back from his embrace.

"What does my best friend have to do with us being together?"

"I don't think Casey sanctions our relationship. I don't think anything like this between us, something this new and fragile can survive, much less thrive with that kind of negativity."

"No one is really in favor of me living with a married man," I admitted. I'd only hinted at my family's condemnation.

"That's because they don't know me. Won't even give me a chance. If they did, they'd know, like you do, that I'm not that guy. I'm not leaving my toddler kids at home alone with my harried wife while I do the horizontal mambo with some unsuspecting woman."

"You aren't that guy," I agreed. "That's exactly the reason I trust you."

"It's all out in the open, Tallulah. There are no secrets, no indiscretion, no betrayal. Deborah's struggling with the end of our marriage, our daughter in college, maintaining a practice. It's just a matter of untangling a long marriage with professional partnerships and brokerage accounts and retirement and pensions and real estate. That's not something anyone can dissolve overnight."

Sinclair dug into my jeans pocket. Extracted my Blackberry.

"What are you doing?" I asked as he typed in the password he'd chosen and started using the tiny button to scroll.

He didn't answer right away, but kept manipulating the tiny buttons. After a minute or so, he handed the phone back to me.

I squinched my face in question.

Sinclair's face was open, inviting, free of anger or any kind of negative emotion. He shifted his eyes so they were locked with mine. I wanted to freeze the moment because it was the face that I'd fallen in love with. I wanted to snap a picture and share it with everyone who doubted us.

When he looked at me with such obvious love and devotion and admiration, I was unable to look away. It wasn't any different in this moment.

"I love you too," I said, though he hadn't said it out loud. I could read his eyes, his face, his heart.

I lifted the phone to see what he'd done. The black-and-white contact list was open. It was sorted pornstar-style and not last name first like the paper address books my mother still used.

Cara Guzman was at the top of the virtual page and an attorney with the firm, Carl Buchanan was next. With my thumb, I scrolled down the list until I hit Claire Henshaw. Without meeting Sinclair's eyes I used my thumb to go up and down the list again. There was only a single name missing, one that had always been in my favorites for years: Casey Cort.

My brain scrambled.

"Wait, did you...?"

"Did you a favor," he echoed. The kiss that came after was extra gentle.

"Deleted Casey. Now we can focus on us. It's time for me to file. Deborah will just have to live without me. It'll be hard for her, I know. Eventually she will adjust."

14

"Did it live up to your expectations?"

I wanted to answer Peyton Bennett's question, but I had to take a minute or ten to take in the restaurant first. If this is what money bought you, I may be a convert.

It made me think much more seriously about the offer from Shively at Morrell Gates. If I got a job making good money, then I could bank all of my settlement dollars. Save that money for a rainy day, for my baby's future.

"Cocktail? Wine?" a server asked.

"I've had enough of that," I said. Then, realizing the server was not in on my overindulgence at that celebration dinner, or my pregnancy, I answered, "I'm not drinking tonight. Thanks." I lifted my hand indicating it was Bennett's turn.

"Sazerac."

"Very good, sir. I'll be back to take your order soon. I hope you enjoyed your show."

"We did very much, thank you." The men nodded at each other as if they had some kind of secret language I wasn't privy to.

"How did he know we were at a show?"

"He's not a psychic. Just someone who's very good at observation. You have a Playbill on the table."

"Oh gosh, of course," I sputtered. "Well, I really like the view."

"Then it's good the restaurant shares that name."

It was probably the kind of place only a tourist liked, but I didn't mind being a lookie-loo as the restaurant turned and gave me three-hundred-sixty-degree views of the glittering city.

"Was it your first Broadway show?" Peyton asked.

"I guess," I started. I hoped I wasn't blushing. I may have been the most educated person in my immediate family, but that law degree hadn't come with instant sophistication. "I've seen a few traveling shows at the Palace Theatre. But this was very different. Thanks for arranging all of this."

I held my hands facing up indicating first-class plane tickets, black car on call, the hotel suite, the show, and dinner. I didn't know if it was from Bennett's personal budget or the firm's, but either way I was grateful. This weekend had parted the curtain and given me a glimpse on how the other half lived.

"How's your engagement?"

"I'm taking Ron home to my parents next weekend." I wasn't looking forward to it. Especially how I'd be doing it without the buffer of Lulu.

"Are they thrilled for you? Excited to be grandparents? A wedding?" Bennett was at that age where an adult child's milestones were celebrated.

"I haven't shared any of that with them."

"Oh. I'm sorry. Frankly, I don't know what to say without putting my foot in it any more than I already have."

"To be frank," I started, mirroring his words, "I haven't told my parents about any of it. I've had…and broken two other engagements. This is a delicate situation that requires a deft touch. I need a few more days to figure out exactly how to deliver that information."

"What's next on the Clarke case?" Bennett's change of subject was abrupt. I didn't mind as it very much ended that awkward moment between us.

"I think we need to talk to the daughter," I said.

"Sienna Walker?"

"Do they have another?" The question wasn't as farfetched as it appeared. Bonus kids had turned up more than once in my years of practice.

"No. I don't think her mom is going to like this."

"I don't like the idea of it. After talking to the Clarke family though, I think there very well is something there. Something to this defense. If Juliana Clarke is not going to help herself, then we're going to have to marshal every resource at our disposal. Unfortunately, at the crux of that is Sienna. I know she's lost her father and that her mother is in jail. None of that can be easy. But she's had at least eighteen years in that household. If anyone had a front-row seat to what's happened, it's her."

Peyton Bennett nodded. Steepled his hands. Took a sip of his amber drink.

The first of our three-course prix fixe menu arrived. I was proud that I'd chosen my beet and fig salad over Bennett's cream-laden bisque, but got a little envious after he savored his first bite. I wouldn't have said I was afraid of gaining baby weight, exactly. I was afraid I'd come out on the other end looking a lot more like my mother and less like Heidi Klum.

Conversation was mostly superficial through that first course and the main. I took Bennett's suggestion of a cheese plate over the fruit or chocolate dessert offerings. He had the server bring him a glass of port. I had seltzer.

"I have a confession to make," Bennett started.

I tried not to wriggle in my seat. That was one of the world's scariest phrases. I said nothing. Waited.

"I've been in Cleveland my whole life," Bennett started. "Grew up in the Heights. My dad worked long hours at the firm he'd started with some law school friends."

I leaned back in my chair and took a bite of blue cheese doused in honey and sprinkled with walnuts. The combination was surprisingly good. I took a second bite while I waited.

I could tell he was gonna tell the whole story from beginning to end. This wasn't going to be a cut-to-the-chase kind of conversation.

Old guys were like that. The food had been good. The view was even better. The cheese was good. The atmosphere was pleasant, so I got more comfortable in my chair and with my silence.

"In the eighties things changed at the firm," he continued. "Suddenly there was this emphasis on widening the pool of people we hired."

"What does that mean?"

"We started considering women, bl—African Americans."

"Did they stay?" I asked, curiosity getting the better of me, though I knew my question might derail the story. Even in my short time at Morrell Gates, turnover among those who were not white and not male was nearly one hundred percent.

Whether it was a lack of cultural fit, or being subtly pushed out with few good assignments or mentors, the result was the same. Lip service that didn't go far. It was the one reason I could cut Shively slack in her treatment of me. Being at a firm was an "every woman for herself" kind of situation.

"Most didn't. Half moved to government, a couple moved in house, some had kids and didn't come back. The usual. But there was one associate that I mentored and got close to. She was really smart, probably a lot smarter than half the people we'd hired. Went to a good school and put in all the work necessary to succeed."

I looked down at my abdomen, still as flat as it was previously, which was to say not very, but also not pregnant looking either. I had to speculate if there was some backhanded job offer coming. Maybe this whole Clarke case was some elaborate test to see if I was white-shoe law firm material. I wondered if I'd passed.

"When she was about to make partner, she messed up," Bennett continued.

"What happened?"

"My dad and his cronies didn't have a lot of room for forgiveness. So they put her up for judge."

For a long second my brain went haywire. Bennett hadn't answered the question I'd asked and what he did say set my antennae twitching.

I'd been working my way through far too much cheese for a single human when I dropped the mini toast in my left hand.

"Who are you talking about?" I think I had an idea and I knew then this wasn't at all about me or my future career.

"Sheila. Sheila Harrison Grant."

15

"According to my research last night, in the State of New York, a doctor can't disclose any information that he acquired while attending a patient in a professional capacity."

I handed Bennett my copy of the page I'd printed from New York State's Civil Practice and Law Rules. Subsection 5.04 was highlighted.

"The question then becomes whether this Elias Phillips attended her in a professional capacity." Bennett's sentence mimicked a professor's Socratic dialog from law school.

"I looked up 'professional capacity,' last night," I said. "It appears that the law isn't much different from attorney/client privilege. When someone pays you or, in the case of medicine, when you're getting services for a fee, then it's clear that whatever you say is confidential."

"I always laugh when I watch lawyer shows on TV and you see one character handing over a dollar for consideration," Bennett said. "It may be a hokey way to show that concept, but there is some truth to that. Otherwise every casual conversation could be seen as some kind of professional relationship and I certainly don't want a cocktail party to be a prelude to a job."

I flashed back to the time Justin and I had done just that. I'd handed over a hundred dollars and he'd helped me cleanly and ethically extract myself from hinky adoption cases. There was so much I adored about Justin, but his unwillingness to be in a relationship wasn't one of them.

Blinking, I turned my mind back to the matter at hand. We were in the back of the black car Bennett had commandeered for our stay. Manhattan wasn't so large that it would take much time to get from our hotel to Phillips's office on what everyone kept referring to as the Upper West Side.

"I think the law might not matter too much here." It's what I'd concluded last night after spending too many hours in the weeds on what constituted professional capacity. "It's going to be a matter of convincing this family friend to help out Juliana Clarke." I took the highlighted paper from Bennett and shoved it into my messenger bag where it could join the fifty-some-odd pages I'd printed out in the hotel's business center last night.

"What approach are you considering?"

"I think we're going to need to go to him hat in hand. Lay out what the stakes are and see where we are from there." I didn't get to say much more because the driver was pulling over in front of another historic-looking building. I craned my head to see that this one was called, The Beresford.

Cleveland had architecturally significant prewar buildings, but New York was an order of magnitude different.

Fortunately, Phillips's practice was on the first floor, so there was no maze of doormen and reception to navigate. The plate glass door had his name stickered on.

"We have an appointment?" I confirmed with Bennett.

He nodded.

This doctor's office was unlike any I'd seen. Tropical fish swam in a bathtub-size tank in reception. The lighting was hidden and decidedly mellow like the music that piped in from invisible speakers.

We were seated with fresh water in hand for no more than three minutes, before a handsome man with slightly graying temples came from a hidden door.

"Peyton Bennett? Casey Cort?" We nodded in unison, then we each shook his outstretched hand in turn.

"Doctor Elias Phillips. Why don't we talk in my office?"

We followed the doctor to his office. The room also had low lighting so as not to obscure the view of Central Park outside the large window.

"You said on the phone that you were acquainted with the Clarke family. How can I help you?"

"How do you know the Clarke family?" I asked, not quite ready to reveal my hand.

"They didn't tell you?"

I shook my head, then turned to Bennett. He was shaking his as well.

"I was Juliana's high school boyfriend." His tone was sheepish. My eyes immediately went to his left hand. It was bare of a wedding ring. I wondered what that story was. He was attractive and a doctor. "I was at Browning. I think we must have met at a party through friends."

I'd look up Browning later. Chapin had been what I'd thought of as a tony girls' school. Browning was probably another. All boys like Cleveland's University School would be my guess.

"If you don't mind my asking," I started. He was nothing like the artists Clarke's sister had described. Something told me he'd predated that era. "When did you break up?"

"I got accepted at Stanford. Before the internet and social media and all that, a long-distance relationship felt impossible. Plus, there was a lot of pressure from friends and family to broaden our horizons, meet new people...all of that."

Phillips's voice held a tinge of regret. If he had feelings for Clarke that were more positive than negative, we could work with that for our own ends.

"I'm sorry, can I ask why you're here? I'm guessing it's not for an ENT or allergy workup."

"No." I opened my bag and fished out a business card. I put it in Phillips's waiting hand.

"Casey Cort," he read, peering at the card. "Attorney at law? Cleveland as in Ohio?"

"Yes. Do you remember an incident in..." I quickly did the math in my head. "...the late eighties, maybe 1989 even. Juliana had come home from Cleveland—"

"With two cracked ribs," Phillips finished. So much for all the worry about privilege. "Wait, is Juliana okay?" I could almost see him filtering through the conversation he'd probably had with her family to see if he'd missed clues. "She's alive? Tell me she's still alive."

"Yes. I don't mean to have scared you. She's alive, but..."

"But what?" Phillips had moved to the edge of his leather chair with his last question. His hands gripped the edge of his desk as he braced himself for what came next.

I turned to Bennett. He could deliver the rest.

"Juliana Clarke is in the Cuyahoga County jail awaiting trial," my co-counsel offered.

"For what?" Phillips's head swiveled between us.

"The murder of Ken Walker."

Phillips sat back in his chair. Rolled away from the desk. He was quiet for long seconds.

"Well, that's the opposite of the way I thought that one would end." Phillips's accompanying nod was slow.

"Why do you say that?"

"I thought for sure he'd kill her if she didn't get out first. I'm surprised she lasted that long. I really am."

"When is the last time you spoke with Juliana?"

"August twentieth. She called for my birthday like she did every year."

"How often did you speak with Juliana?"

"Once a month, maybe." Phillips tilted his head as if trying to count.

I didn't hide my shock. Old family friend or high school boyfriend didn't quite describe what I was sensing between these two.

"Since when?"

"Since we broke up in eighty-four."

Despite the barriers of the days of more rudimentary communication, they'd managed a long-distance relationship. Twenty-plus years' worth.

"What did she tell you about her marriage?"

Phillips closed his eyes. Loosened his renewed grip on the wood. Tented his fingers massaging his index fingers against the bridge of his nose.

"Everything. She shared everything. I knew what was happening and I did nothing. It's my life's biggest regret."

16

I looked up every time a door opened. Each time it wasn't Peyton Bennett. Despite all the false starts, I kept an eye out for my co-counsel, waiting for him to emerge from the dreary day, gray with drizzle. This time when the bell chimed, it was him. He nodded in acknowledgement, then went to the counter at Dewey's Coffee to order for himself. In a couple of minutes he came to the small back corner table I'd chosen for privacy over comfort of the couches in the front, and sat.

"So, you live close to here?" Bennett was making small talk. He never did that. Was an interview with a teen making him nervous, I wondered?

"Around the corner." I gestured toward my apartment mere yards away. "It was a two-minute walk."

Bennett glanced at the clock below the chalkboard menu on the wall.

"Sienna's promised to meet with us at five thirty."

It was five o'clock now. I'd left my office early, though that was becoming more common these days. Growing a tiny human was no joke. I was starting to think training for a marathon might have been easier. At least there would have been time off. Nowadays, I was just too tired to put in the long hours I was used to when prepping for trial.

"Have you thought of how we should approach Sienna?" I asked.

I'd been dreading this interview for weeks. Even though her trial was rushing toward us at the speed of light, Juliana Clarke was still being obstinate.

While Elias Phillips was a definite check mark in the benefit column, Sienna Walker could be a wildcard. She was of age now, but I didn't have any idea what she'd made of her childhood. No impression if she thought her father was a sinner and her mother a saint, or worse, vice versa.

She was the kind of witness that a jury would sit forward and listen to because she would have had a front-row seat to the inner workings of her parents' marriage. Because she had little to gain except an exonerated mother.

"Before we talk about that, can we revisit the discussion we had during that dessert in New York?"

I let out my breath in a huff. He'd finally dropped the other shoe. There had been nearly a month of silence between us on this topic between the night when he'd dropped my first major client's name and now. A woman whose actions had changed the course of my own life in unexpected ways. The halo effect was far wider than I ever expected.

"Go ahead." I extended my hand. It was up to him to continue the discussion.

"I was in love with Sheila Grant," he rushed out. There was a sigh from him. A beat, then, "I wanted to marry her," Bennett finished.

I made my glance at his left hand, the one that was holding chai, obvious. His platinum wedding band gleamed under the coffee shop's halogens. When my gaze slipped to my own sparkling evidence of commitment, I swiftly jerked my left hand from the table and shoved it into my lap.

"I get that, I guess," I started. "I mean, we all have a past. Yours was a little unexpected as it came over dinner, but in this job I've learned to have a certain tolerance for the rich tapestry of humanity."

All those words spoken were there to cover up my utter surprise at his statement. For a whole host of reasons—not the least of which was a wife, three kids, and a mortgage in Moreland Hills—his declaration had been a surprise.

"I'm not saying I don't love Kimberleigh or the life we've built."

"But?" I spoke the word for him.

"But I'd like to speak with Sheila. Contact her if I could."

"I told you I don't have contact information for her. I'm sure that was done on purpose. She didn't tell me she was leaving the jurisdiction. We all know why. Confidentiality protects past crimes, but not future ones. I'm not even sure whether she'd still be on the hook for kidnapping."

"The statute of limitations is twenty years for Ohio. Even considering the parental exclusion to the Lindbergh

Act, the federal kidnapping statute, there is no limitation on that." Peyton spoke with authority. Something told me he'd researched the topic more than a few times.

"All the more reason she'd never contact me. Why do you want to know where she is, Peyton?" I asked.

I hadn't lied when I'd said Sheila Harrison Grant had never reached out to me. It wouldn't be in anyone's best interest for that to happen. But that didn't mean I couldn't find her. Honestly, I'd thought about it on the plane ride home from New York City and concluded that tracking her down would be relatively easy.

"I want to connect with Olivia."

"Olivia Grant, her daughter?" The lights and décor blurred while I did some quick calculations in my head. "She's eighteen now, I guess."

While Olivia had technically been a kidnapping victim of her mother while a ward of the foster care system, now of legal age, she was free to move around without fear of being taken into custody by the state or county.

"Only two months older than Sienna, as a matter of fact. She's out of high school. Maybe even a freshman or sophomore in college."

I wasn't sure if it was pregnancy hormones that fogged my brain, but it took me a full minute to piece the puzzle together. When I did, my eyes snapped back to Bennett's.

"It was December 2001. We were in trial before Judge MacKinnon. So the prosecutor... Damn, I think it was Dick Foster. He had some CFS or CSEA records' clerk on the witness stand. Like nearly every one of my cases before that, they were there to certify that Keith Grant was Olivia's father. I don't remember when taking DNA became standard, but in Juvy the presumption that the man married to the mother was the father wasn't taken as gospel."

I wasn't really looking at Bennett at this point. I was steeped in memory of a time when court felt foreign and unpredictable.

"I remember, I'd kind of tuned out and was thinking of my next witness or the law when Foster hands me the DNA test results. When Olivia's DNA was compared to Keith's, there was no way he was her father. No way that she could have been his daughter. I'd had clients lie to me so many times, in so many ways, and yet I was surprised each and every time. I was naïve back then. Young."

For a brief moment I hesitated. Juvenile court hearings were closed to the public. The files were often sealed. I was likely talking out of turn. Despite the impropriety, I continued.

"So Grant nearly loses it. MacKinnon takes a recess. Vernon Dinwiddie takes Keith Grant, his client out. Maybe Sheila and Keith argued. That part I don't remember.

"Eventually Judge MacKinnon comes back on the bench. She looks down at us at defense table and asks Judge Grant to name the father of the child. If she'd named him, and he'd come to court willing to waive notice, then we'd have finished the hearing that day.

"Ultimately Sheila refused. I stood up in open court and said Olivia Grant's biological father was unknown. It wasn't exactly true, though. In the hall, Judge Grant had said something about him having his own wife and kids, but that Olivia's father had helped her during the confirmation process, which means he wasn't unknown to her.

"He was served by publication, which is legal, but isn't really effective notice. None of that was necessary though, was it?"

I'd spun that long and winding tale because I was trying to convince myself that what was right in front of me could be true. All of a sudden it was so blindingly obvious, I wonder how I could have missed it.

"You're Olivia's father. It's why you hesitated the first time I asked you how many kids you had. You did the same thing my clients do, pause, then give the answer you think is acceptable."

"I didn't mean to deceive you, Casey. I just wanted to meet my daughter."

Deception was my karma.

"You've never met her?" I could have sworn that Judge Grant had intimated just the opposite.

"I met her in the hospital on the day she was born. December thirteen...eighty-eight."

I rocked back in my chair. I hadn't known that one. Had Olivia's paternity been an open secret everyone but her knew? Reflexively my hands went to my own belly, which was extended just a bit with the navel orange-sized human inside. Unwittingly I was wandering down exactly the same path.

"Does your wife know?" That was none of my business, but curiosity had gotten the better of my discretion.

"I've never disclosed that," he said with unnecessary formality.

"So what's your plan? Find Olivia and then what? Go see her and disrupt her life? Shine a light of truth where there has always been darkness?"

"I want her to know that she's not alone."

"She has Judge Grant."

"I may not think any of the stuff that happened to her and Olivia was just or fair or right. But I'm pretty sure that Sheila had a problem with alcohol. I blame myself for that."

"No one's addiction is your fault."

"In theory, Casey. But back then I was living under my own father's thumb. Following in his footsteps. Doing what was expected of me without question. I used alcohol to cope on more nights than I can remember. Sheila was going through her own stuff with Keith and the firm back then. She'd come back to my place instead of going home.

"I'd offer her a drink or several and we'd wind down that way. After a few years, I realized that wasn't going to work long term. Kimberleigh made me reassess a lot. I stopped working so hard. I took the firm's first pro bono cases. I found ways to cope that didn't rely on rum or whiskey."

Bennett closed his eyes for a long time. Shook his head as if to clear it from the fog of memory.

"Sheila went the other way. Her marriage crumbled. Things at the firm got hairy. She didn't have anything or anyone else to fall back on. I can only imagine it was hard for Olivia. I just want to have this conversation I'm having with you...with her."

"Crap," I gasped. The sweep of the minute hand on the coffee shop's clock had my attention.

"What?"

"We're going to be late. We have to meet Sienna now. Good thing she's only a few feet away."

I binned my drink and hustled to the door with Bennett bringing up the rear. I needed to reorient my thinking as quickly as possible because in a matter of two minutes we were at the front entrance to Juliana Clarke's building.

Sienna hadn't traveled to college abroad as she'd planned. She'd deferred while her mother was locked up and getting ready for trial. She'd chosen her mother's con-do over their family house, probably because there had been no murder here. I looked up at the tall brick building, squared my shoulders and pushed my way into the lobby.

While we waited for the elevator, I took a long look at Peyton Bennett. I hoped whatever Sienna Walker had in store for us, it wasn't as much a surprise as the last thirty minutes had been. I didn't think my heart or the tiny person growing inside of me could take it..

17

Nicole
November 26, 2007

"Thanks for coming. Hope you had a good Thanksgiving."
I gave Sienna Walker the warmest smile I could muster
despite putting my foot in my mouth. She's probably had a
crap holiday. Though mine hadn't been much better. In a
different situation, we could have commiserated about
families.

"You didn't give me much choice," she retorted. There
was nothing friendly about her tone. When Juliana
Clarke's daughter hadn't returned the calls from me or our
investigator, I'd left another message, set a time, then had
Darlene Webb pick the girl up from her mother's apartment.

"Are you working?" I asked. "I didn't mean to interfere
if you have a job."

"I'm not working. I was to start school in Edinburgh in September but have deferred instead. I can start midterm in January or next fall. Either way I wanted to be here for my mother."

Did that mean that she'd be on her mother's side? I was a Daddy's girl and had been hoping that maybe Sienna was one as well. But I had no idea whether there had been any abuse in her home, or what she'd made of everything that had happened there. It was like a black box mystery.

It was time to open the lid.

"Here you go," Darlene Webb said as she placed a plastic cup full of water on the conference room table in front of Walker.

"Thank you for this at least," Walker said. From under her curly bangs, she flicked her brown eyes first at me, then at Webb as if we were holding her hostage, then took a sip of the water.

"Your mother's trial is scheduled in two and a half weeks," I said. It wasn't a question, but most people couldn't keep their mouth shut in the face of silence. I waited a beat. Looked at Walker.

"I have it marked on my calendar," she finally said.

Surly.

Alrighty, then. This was going to be like treating her as I would a hostile witness on the stand.

I dropped nice and switched to matter-of-fact.

"We've added you to our witness list. I invited you here because the prosecution is going to want you to testify."

The girl shifted in her chair, then went still a long time before speaking.

"About what?"

"As a rebuttal witness," I answered without explanation. When handling potentially volatile witnesses like her, I found it easier to keep them on an information diet.

"Rebutting what?"

"Look...can I call you Sienna?" I asked. Information diet or not, I still needed to know as much as I ever could what she would or could testify to on the stand. The element of surprise in a courtroom made for great television. It did not work that way in real life. Too many surprises and I could find myself well out of my temporary digs just when I was getting comfortable with the title of head of Major Crimes.

"No, you may not call me Sienna. We're not friends like that."

I flicked a glance toward Webb. Her headshake was nearly impossible to detect, but I got the message. She had no idea what to make of Walker either. I was starting to think that we'd overplayed our hand. Maybe using police intimidation to bring the girl down had been a mistake. It's just that I knew she wouldn't have shown otherwise. I shook my own head. We couldn't go back. Had to work with what we had where we were.

"Okay, Miss Walker, then." My tone was brusque. "Your mother killed your father. She picked up a marble cheese board and bashed your father's brains out. I'm sorry to be frank, but that's what we're dealing with here. Your mother got up, drove over to your house, the one your dad was living in with his new girlfriend, walked into the kitchen. She flew into a rage and hit your father so hard that he died of blunt force trauma. The autopsy report found cracks in his skull. Do you know how hard you have to hit a human to crack a seven millimeter...quarter of an inch bone? For that crime, your mother's going to jail for a very long time." It was the exact kind of speech I delivered to defense attorneys before they convinced their clients to take a plea. Unless a person was a sociopath, they were always swayed by an avalanche of evidence.

"If you have all this evidence, then why do you need me?" Walker asked. She was so much more savvy than I'd anticipated. Somehow I'd expected her to be younger, more naïve, more like a kid who grew up in the Heights. Instead she was acting more like a kid who'd grown up in the Lower Ninth Ward. I didn't answer her and instead moved to another question.

"Have you been contacted by the defense team? Casey Cort or Peyton Bennett?"

"Is that a crime?" was her retort.

"Of course not. What did you tell them?"

"I answered all of their questions truthfully."

"Did they ask you to sign anything, like an affidavit or notarized document that memorialized...recorded what you said?"

"I'm aware of the definition of the word memorialize. The answer to your question is no."

I turned a page on my yellow pad. Clicked my pen a couple of times for effect.

"Do you mind if I ask you a few questions?"

"Yes, I do mind. I didn't return your calls. I haven't reached out to you."

Ignoring that, I ploughed on. Opening a manila folder I'd prepared for this meeting, I slipped two crime scene photos across the table.

"Do you recognize these?"

"You took pictures of my driveway from two different angles. Since my father wasn't murdered in the drive-way..."

"No, he was murdered in the kitchen. By your mother," I reiterated as if that would be enough to sway her. "There is only one car in the driveway. It belongs to Monica Mae Ellis. What's missing in this picture is your mother's car. If your mother was there to pick you up, where is the Volvo?"

"I'm sorry, I have to go. Like I said before, I do mind. I can't imagine your boss or even the Plain Dealer would be thrilled to hear that you thought it was a great idea to harass a girl whose father was murdered, whose mother is in jail. By all accounts, I'm very sympathetic and photogenic. Everyone loves a mixed kid."

It took almost everything I had not to clap back about my own mixed parentage. A wave of guilt came over me like a shroud. Even if I didn't believe in the one-drop rule, I still smarted from the idea that I was passing, somehow pretending to be someone I wasn't, something I wasn't, claiming a privilege that wasn't rightly mine.

Smarting, I took a deep breath, rotated my neck, then stared Walker dead in the eye.

"Why did you come down?" I asked. I was genuinely perplexed. I had thought, or maybe just hoped, that she would be interested in punishing the person who'd killed her father, even if that person was her mother.

Walker didn't break the stare. She sipped slowly at her cup of water. Pointed to Webb.

"She has a badge and a gun. How would you suggest I resist? If you follow the news around here, a young Black person resisting the police doesn't always go well."

I wasn't sure if Walker's comment was general or targeted, but Webb recoiled nonetheless.

"But now that I'm here," she continued, "I can speak to you in person. I don't want to talk to you. I wasn't at the scene of the crime. I haven't been back to my house since."

Some kind of expression took over Walker's face. I couldn't exactly read her. Her fist banged the table.

"Maybe Monica Mae can help you out seeing as I can't get her out of my house. You know what? Maybe you can help me with that. My father died. The house was left to my mother, of course. I'm in charge of my family's assets and I have a woman not ten years older than me claiming squatter's rights. Maybe you can serve an eviction so she can go back to wherever she came from."

When neither of us responded, Walker shook her head slowly.

"No? Well, I guess I'll have to hire an attorney for that. Practically drowning in lawyers these days. Now if you'll excuse me."

Eyeing us again, Sienna Walker lifted the water, drank it down, crumpled the paper cup, then stuffed it in her pocket. Obviously she'd seen too many episodes of those crime shows. I had to wonder, though, why she would think we'd want her DNA and what would be revealed if we'd collected it.

When the conference room door slammed, I turned to Webb.

"Where did Sienna Walker go on the night of the murder?"

18

I scooted back into the huge massage chair after I adjusted the lumbar pillow. Lifting the remote, I set myself up for thirty minutes of full-body motion. I had a copy of Essence and Cosmopolitan tucked next to me. For a Saturday morning, life was good.

"Do you like it warm?" a nail technician asked as she filled the foot basin. Blue crystals swirled with the water pouring from the tap.

"Very warm," I answered. Leaning back, I closed my eyes and enjoyed the sensation of water relaxing the muscles in my feet and mechanical hands kneading my lower back.

For the first time in weeks, I was savoring my time alone, a moment to myself. It wasn't that I didn't love Sinclair, but he needed me so much. He wanted us to have breakfast, lunch, and dinner together. He wanted to text all day just to check up on me.

Yesterday, he'd texted me in the morning to tell me that he'd loved spending the night before with me. When I'd gotten home on Friday night warm with the buzz of our Thursday date night and hoping for a repeat, I was sorely disappointed.

"Seven hours," Sinclair had hissed the moment I'd walked through the door last night.

I'd dropped my purse and briefcase, then tried to wrap my brain around what he was talking about. In that very short period of time, I didn't succeed. It was as if my thoughts were short-circuited by the angry face that was looking back at me.

"What was seven hours?" I asked. I hated the cautiousness in my voice, but I was walking on eggshells.

"The time between my text this morning and your response." He spoke like he was stating the obvious.

"I was at work," I spoke slowly. Maybe I hadn't explained myself sufficiently. "We had a team meeting about the case we're working on. Settlement negotiations are Monday. We have a mediator scheduled," I explained again. I'd sent an email to him somewhere in the day updating him on my schedule. It had been marked as read. The firm required read receipts. I'd hated them until now when I needed verification, proof that I wasn't ignoring him.

"It was a lot for me to be vulnerable to you like that." His voice was plaintive. "The least you could do was respond in kind."

I'd apologized several times over mainly because I couldn't figure out what in the hell I'd done wrong. I wasn't some tween who could text all day. I had a full-time job as a professional. Suddenly, I was seized with jealousy of his wife. I'd have bet my salary that he didn't bother the good doctor who was busy at her world-class workplace, handling important patients with big problems. God, I needed to stop. I could sense my own bitterness. If I didn't get a handle on my feelings of envy, they would eat me alive. I looked around for a distraction, but I'd only brought the glossy periodicals.

The magazines' promises of fixing my dating problems, my hair problems, and my career problems didn't compel me to open their shiny covers. Instead, I closed my eyes and leaned back while my calves were massaged, my heels were scraped, and my cuticles cut.

"Tallulah?" someone asked. The use of my full name made my eyes come open with a snap.

I turned right, but that chair was empty. The nail tech gestured with the powder-blue nail file to my left. I turned to see none other than Doctor Deborah Bloom. Fleeing to New York City or Los Angeles didn't seem like a bad idea all of a sudden. Somewhere I could be more anonymous than in a nail salon on Fairmount. For a long second, I wondered if I'd conjured her from my thoughts. Except the women working our feet were talking to each other. Everyone else was acting like she was real.

"Lulu," I replied. "Everyone calls me Lulu." It was all I could think to say. Running was not an option.

"Not my husband," Bloom said. She minced no words. Went straight for the jugular. Not that there was any way around the fact that her husband had left her and moved in with me.

"He doesn't want to be your husband anymore," I countered.

"Then why won't he divorce me?" Where I expected acrimony, I was only hearing bewilderment. There weren't buckets of salons in our neck of the woods, but I had to wonder if Bloom running into me was purely an accident. I took her in. Professional woman, Jewish, curly dark hair with strands of gray. Mine was curly and lighter, no gray yet. We had more similarities than differences, probably. It was as momentarily sobering as her question. My shoulders lowered at the same time as my defenses.

"What do you mean?" My question was full of genuine curiosity because I'd been wondering the same thing more or less from my own vantage point.

"I filed," Bloom stated with the ring of absolute truth. If I hadn't been sitting in the high-backed chair, she could have knocked me over with a feather.

"You filed? When?"

"Last October."

"Last year. You filed last year?" I searched my memory to see if it came up short. In no uncertain terms Sinclair had told me not once, not twice, but probably dozens of times that his wife was refusing to divorce him. That if he'd filed without getting her on board, that she'd go for blood. Blood he couldn't afford to lose. "He...I don't understand—"

"I told him last October that I was done because obviously he was done. I filed then. It took me until January to serve him."

Ohio wasn't like New York or California that required a lot of steps to getting legal documents to someone being sued. The rules disfavored defendants avoiding service of process.

"He didn't accept or waive service?" This sounded like one hundred eighty degrees from everything Sinclair had ever said to me.

"He claimed he didn't have an address. He wasn't living with me. He wasn't living with you. The law firm where you work are professionals at evading service. Stupidly I thought we'd work it out with a mediator, but that didn't happen, so I hired Madeline Montgomery."

When people hired that alliterative divorce attorney, things were serious. Montgomery was on the high end of lawyers who did a large volume of upper-middle-class family matters. It was who Casey had recommended Sinclair hire. Though now I knew that Montgomery had been conflicted out. He could have just told me that. There were others people hired when they couldn't hire Montgomery. The men almost always hired Gerald Popovic anyway.

"Why are you saying any of this to me?" I was also starting to think her sitting here next to me wasn't a coincidence. Sinclair was in nearly constant contact with her. It wasn't improbable that he'd shared my whereabouts. Probably was the reason he hadn't insisted on a couples' pedicure session.

"I want to be out." Bloom was emphatic. "You want him? You can have him. Maybe you can convince him to just let me go."

"But it's complicated. The house. Your practice. His practice. All that stuff." I parroted every single excuse he'd given me over the last fourteen months.

"But it's not complicated, Lulu. I can call you that, right? The house is mine. My parents bought it for me.

They made sure he never had any claim to it. It was never his. If he waives any right to my medical practice, I'm willing to waive any right to his law practice. I split the bank accounts when I filed. There's nothing to fight over except pots and pans. And you know what? He can have all of them. Tell me what it will take." At the end, her voice was pleading. My head hurt as I tried to accept what she was saying.

"But he said…"

"What?" Bloom asked. "What did he say?"

"That you weren't ready to let him go."

"I was ready to let him go a long time ago. I only stayed for Sarah, and let me tell you, I deeply regret that."

"A long time ago?"

"Maybe he's gotten better in his old age, but he wasn't nice to me. There was nothing I could do to please him. I tried working more. Working less. But when the school asked him to leave, that was nearly the final straw."

"Asked him to leave?" I was starting to think I should take notes. I needed to write some of this down so I could verify it all later or even remember what she'd been saying.

"He had a track record of becoming…infatuated with his female students. The last one threatened to sue for harassment. Willing women…Dean Condit was able to turn a blind eye. That last girl…" Bloom trailed off with a headshake.

"I thought…"

"Oh, honey." I almost felt as sorry for myself as she sounded like she did. "Maybe you can solve that puzzle of his perpetual victimhood. Nothing is ever his fault. Somehow we're all supposed to be grateful to be graced with his attention. Just do me a favor, please. Get him a lawyer. He seems obsessed with your friend Casey. She was supposed to be his attorney, but I don't know what happened."

I nearly fainted in mortification when Bloom's mention of Casey triggered how I'd found out Sinclair was married.

Casey had run into Bloom when she was doing adoptions. Sinclair had said Bloom was sick and that's why he couldn't divorce her. That elaborate lie was the reason I'd given in to Sinclair's pursuit.

Imagine my best friend's surprise when Bloom was a walking, talking—not in any way disabled—surgeon, a colleague of her then client. I'd put that long-ago betrayal out of my mind. But that first lie coupled with what Bloom was saying now and I couldn't figure how I could believe anything Sinclair had said to me over the last year.

"She turned him down. Friend of a friend being inappropriate or something like that."

"What did he do to her?"

"What do you mean?"

"When women turn him down, somehow they have something bad happen to them. Did the bar get an anonymous impropriety report?"

"No..." My brain snagged like a sweater on an ill-placed nail. Only told her potential baby daddies something he shouldn't. I didn't want to believe anything Bloom, the wronged wife, was saying.

Sinclair had given me a different story. An entirely plausible explanation for the exact same sequence of events. But the fact of the year-old divorce filing was leaving the bitter taste of betrayal in my mouth.

While the nail tech was applying a top coat on shell-pink polish, a complete departure from the deep blue or black I used to wear, I tried to remember if he'd told me she'd filed for divorce. Maybe it had gotten lost in translation when he'd called me in Europe last year complaining about the yoke of his marriage and requesting Casey be the one to lift that same yoke.

More than once, he'd emphasized how much he deserved it for his faculty representation of Casey in her losing law school disciplinary procedure. The loss of which had fundamentally changed the course of my friend's life, but did not fit into his great savior narrative. To hear him tell it, he'd saved her from near expulsion.

Not only for that reason, but because of him being my lover and probably being a cheater, Casey had turned that down flat. His request had been reasonable. Her response as much so. Didn't think much about it after that. Now I wished I had.

"You like?" the nail tech asked as she capped the polish in her hand. I looked down at Sinclair's preferred color, a muted version of who I used to be.

"Actually. I hate it. Can I change the color?"

19

Nicole
December 4, 2007

"She's going to have to testify," I explained to Darlene Webb. Trial was slated to start a week and two days from now and I still felt like I was educating Webb at every turn. I just wanted her to chase down information, not ask questions.

"But what about self-incrimination?" she asked. It was a knee-jerk question for anyone with only a cursory understanding of the Fifth Amendment.

"They're going to have a hell of a time doing self-defense if she doesn't. It would be hard for third parties to talk about what happened in the house unless they were there all the time."

"Unless it's Sienna," Webb pointed out.

And that was the sticking point. Sienna was still a black box with its lid shut tight.

"She's on their witness list and ours as well," Webb said.

I hadn't had a single thing to drink last night. Pope's assistant had made a mistake and told me I was scheduled for an appointment at the police station this morning. She was right—I'd been scheduled for a breathalyzer. Without a drink, I was on edge and Webb's observations weren't helping.

"What do you have for me? I don't want to be blindsided. I still think it's possible that her mother is covering for her. If that's the case, then ethically I can't prosecute or I have to turn over anything exculpatory to the defense. And we're getting down to it. Only nine days before trial. So talk to me."

Webb flipped open a notebook. One day I'd have to tell her that meticulous record keeping was a double-edged sword. She probably did it as a hedge against being thrown under the bus like Baldwin had done to her in that shooting case. But it had the opposite effect of tying her down to a story. Today wasn't that day though, so I did my best to actively listen with a sour stomach and pounding head.

"Sienna went to her dad's house to pick up some stuff. She'd been staying there until she graduated, but then she moved out. Her dad was not happy."

"Why'd she move? She's not a kid, so she could go between her mother and father and friends and whatever, right? Most kids wouldn't want to leave their childhood bedroom right before the big transition to college, I would think."

"It was the girlfriend."

"What's her name again?"

"Monica Mae Ellis."

"She's coming in tomorrow, right, so we can prep her. She'll be the last witness from our side."

I often did witnesses in order of how things went down. Witnesses to the crime, the victim, the cops, and forensics to wrap up. But this one had to be different. I needed to end my case presentation with Ellis walking in on the crime scene, bloody murder weapon in Juliana Clarke's hand as the murdering wife standing remorselessly over the body of the husband she was divorcing.

No story of abuse that Juliana Clarke had escaped from with life, limb, and her own condo was going to compete with that for sympathy.

She was alive and he was dead.

That right there was enough to get most of the way toward a conviction. As long as I emphasized that Kendrick Walker had been abandoned for her middle-aged artist crisis, while he had oh-so-bravely soldiered on—and then actually moved on—the twenty-something girlfriend could be batted away like a cat did with a toy.

"Is Sienna Clarke going to be the defense team's reasonable doubt?" I asked. It wasn't the only plausible explanation for her silence, but it was a good one. "She's already shown that she's more loyal to her mother," I continued. "That probably isn't going to change seeing as her mother is her only living parent." Getting through the young adult years without parental support was hard. That I already knew all too well.

"Why she left is a question that I can't answer. Unless you're willing to go the extra mile and swear out an arrest warrant, she's not going to talk. You remember."

I hadn't forgotten our first and last unproductive meeting with the girl.

"So she was at the house..." I prompted.

"From what I can gather, she was there to pick up some clothes. She'd been doing packing and staging at her mother's house since her mother was the parent who was going to fly out to Edinburgh with her to get her settled in school."

"About what time did she get there?"

"My best guess? Five? She'd been hanging out with a friend who's now a senior at University School."

"All her other friends are away at college already." Private school kids didn't hang around town after high school. Guaranteed college attendance is what parents paid for.

"That's the sense I got. So she goes to the house. After that, your guess is as good as mine. Our original theory was wrong. The phone records show that Sienna called her mother at around five after six. Then Juliana's records show a text from her to Sienna around six ten."

"Five minutes. How long does it take to drive from Shaker Square to that house in Cleveland Heights?"

"I tried it this weekend. It's at most ten. But that doesn't take into account leaving her apartment, taking a ride down the elevator, getting her car or having it brought up, or the actual drive down Shaker Boulevard or Larchmere to Fairmount."

"Was she out already or is this part of some premeditation?"

"My best guess is that she was already out. Maybe Sienna had expected her friend to hang around, but when it started taking longer, the friend left. Or maybe Sienna expected her father to drive her back and Monica Mae somehow interfered."

I rolled my neck. I hated open and unanswered questions. They were every trial attorney's enemy.

"What time did the 911 call come in?"

"Seven after seven."

I did the math quickly in my head.

"So we're talking twenty-seven minutes. That's nothing in real life, but a lifetime in a criminal case."

Webb nodded in agreement. When you interviewed crime victims, they always assumed the events had taken minutes, when it was usually only seconds.

"I can see it playing out two ways," Webb started. "Sienna gets into a fight with her father. He follows her to the kitchen or vice versa. The family used that back kitchen door." While Webb was doing her recitation, I sorted through my file looking for the picture of the back of the house. A huge paved parking area led right up to that door. It was pretty similar to how I'd grown up. The front door was for guests.

"He says something that angers Sienna, and she lifts the cheese board and hits him."

"Four times. That's a lot of anger over getting a few clothes or a new girlfriend."

"Maybe there's something to the battered woman thing. Maybe it wasn't Juliana he hit, but the kid. I've seen a couple of cases where kids snap after years of abuse."

"That's mostly boys, though, right?"

"Males commit most of the crimes in this country, but not all. Our women's prisons aren't empty."

"You have a point. You think the mom came in, saw what happened, pulled the weapon from her kid's hand. Then what?"

"Look at the photo in your hand. What cars are there?"

"A BMW sedan registered to Walker. A Subaru registered to Monica Mae Ellis."

"What does Juliana drive?"

"She has a Volvo SUV."

I shuffled through the glossy photos like a toddler with playing cards. Even with them spread out, I didn't see any images of the boxy Swedish vehicle.

"Is the car somewhere else in these photos? In the driveway, or was it parked on the street?"

"It's not on the property or in the garage, but it would have been ticketed or towed if it were left on the street."

That was a quirk of northeast Ohio that I'd had to get used to. Overnight parking was prohibited in many of the Cleveland suburbs.

"What about Sienna? Did she have a car?"

"It was parked at her mom's place. The friend picked her up."

"Who is this friend? What's her name? Where did they go?"

"His name is Bryan Sheffield. University School is an all-boys school in Shaker. They went over to Cedar Lee to watch Into the Wild."

I knew the private schools in Jefferson Parish like the back of my hand. Without kids, schools hardly came upon my radar. I was starting to feel like an old person. I hadn't heard of the movie either. My face must have showed my dismay.

"Independent movie at an art house theater," Webb explained.

Sounded mind-numbing. The kind of thing you did for a guy you had a thing for.

"Boyfriend?"

"Can't tell. I don't think so, though. He didn't read that way when I spoke with him."

That explained the car; riding together made sense. That didn't answer the question of an alternate theory that was starting to take shape in my mind.

"Juliana suspected her kid did the murder, told Sienna to take her car and leave, and she would take the fall. I could see it." The girl would go away to school and Juliana would use a battered women's defense to get off. That left no one going to jail for the obvious crime of murder.

I could see it playing out that way as plain as day. The question was, whether the defense saw it.

20

"Do you want to argue?" I asked Peyton Bennett. In about an hour, we were going in front of the judge on our pretrial motions. What she decided this morning would define how the trial would go. The determination of what evidence could be presented and what couldn't be heard by the jury could make the difference between a guilty verdict and an acquittal. The law was one thing, trials were another, because in a courtroom, the judge was God.

"This is your playing field. I think you should go on ahead."

"Have you gone in front of her before?" I asked. Judge Essie Cox had been on the bench for nearly five years, but I'd never appeared in her courtroom. In every case, one of thirty-four judges was assigned at random. Some I'd had many cases in front of and others, like Judge Cox, none. As it was, our assignment was random. Our original judge had taken a sudden leave of absence for medical reasons.

"No. This will be my first. She recused herself from all of our other cases."

My mind raced. Judges only recused themselves for conflict of interest and even that was rare.

"Recused?"

Peyton must have noticed panic on my face because he waved his hands in a dismissive motion.

"Abundance of caution, I think. One of our former partners used to be married to her. When she got elected, she made a blanket policy to hear no cases where the firm was representing one of the parties. She said there may be an appearance of impropriety because she could have, however tangential, a financial interest in the case outcome."

While Peyton was explaining, I did the mental gymnastics in my head. I guess if her husband was a partner and profits were divided among the partners, some win or loss in Cox's courtroom could affect income or bonuses. Since Cox was entitled through marriage to that money, it could be a problem. I didn't think any ethical board or disciplinary counsel would require any judge to go that far. I tried to piece together whether that made her fair and impartial, which was a good thing, or an unyielding rule follower which wasn't.

"And nothing from Juliana?" I asked. Bennett had gone to see our client alone just yesterday. We'd tried all manner of ways to get more information from our client, but she remained tight-lipped. Her behavior was such a departure. I couldn't stop most clients from talking. The only other client who had been as reticent was Jarrod Carter.

And he'd been hiding an entire sex trafficking ring from me. I wasn't interested in another bombshell like that one.

"I think there's something to your theory about Sienna," Bennett said. "It's really the only explanation for her being so tight-lipped, for being so unhelpful in her own defense."

"Does she understand that by filing this affirmative defense, claiming that she's not guilty by reason of insanity, that essentially she's admitting that she committed the crime. The issue will be why. It's a justification, not a denial."

"I did explain all that to her when I saw her on Monday," Bennett said. We'd decided that it was best if he go alone on the last visit. I'd worried that I was Juliana Clarke's barrier to honesty. Maybe I'd been wrong. Maybe she hadn't been hiding her actions, but those of her daughter. I turned to Bennett, held my hand up, palm facing the ceiling.

"Let me go in and have one last go at her, then," I decided. "She should be up in the holding cell."

"Can't hurt. Can only help."

I walked from the defense table to the hidden door on the side of the courtroom. I knocked until a sheriff's deputy answered.

"Casey Cort," I announced. "I need to meet with my client before the judge comes on the bench." I learned early in this job to assume compliance. If I asked for permission, it gave someone the opportunity to say no.

He hesitated a beat too long. Got my back up.

"She's here, right? Juliana Clarke. Defendants have a right to be present at all hearings."

"Counselor, it's not that. The rules only permit the defendant to meet with one person at a time."

I swiveled my head as I looked in all directions. The doorway was small enough that I'd have noticed if Bennett had walked in front of me or even behind me. Wasn't him. I started shuffling through the possibilities in my head.

When a defendant was in county custody, there were a number of professionals they encountered. Court psychiatrists, probation officers who offered opinions on bond as well as sentencing, medical personnel. None of those made sense today before a motions hearing.

"Who? Who is meeting with her?"

"Prosecutor."

If he'd pulled out his gun and shot me dead, I couldn't have been more surprised.

"Are you kidding me? She's represented by counsel. Interrogation of my client without counsel is a constitutional violation. Take me to the back right now before I have to get the judge involved."

Judge Cox would certainly back me up, but I wanted to minimize damage as quickly as I could. If the one time Juliana Clarke decided to open up was to Nicole Long, it could torpedo our defense.

I nearly ran in my low flats to keep up with the deputy's long strides. He hadn't lied. The holding cell was more like a visiting room. One bench ran along a wall with a table in the middle and a bench along the other wall of the six-by-six room.

There were loops bolted to the wall where they cuffed prisoners when there was more than one. Juliana was in the far bench in a conservative navy dress. It was always difficult to get the court to allow defendants to wear their own clothes, especially when there was no jury. Judges would swear up and down that they weren't biased against defendants in prison orange and wrist and ankle shackles.

I didn't believe it.

I looked closely and there she was, Nicole Long on the opposite bench facing the far wall. She was in a black suit that made her skin seem paler than usual and her inky hair stand out.

"You can't speak with my client without counsel. You know better."

"I know I can't ask her anything that will incriminate her," Long said turning toward me. "I'm interviewing her as a witness."

"A witness to what?"

"Murder."

21

"Come out of there. We need to talk," Cort demanded. The normally soft-spoken attorney wasn't now.

When I zeroed in on my opposing counsel, I noticed something I hadn't before.

She was pregnant, for one.

I searched for other clues. Besides a pretty noticeable bump, there was a new sparkly diamond ring on her finger. But she hadn't said a thing, and I certainly wasn't going to ask.

The deputy looked between us like we were going to get into a cat fight and he was a ready and willing audience. I wanted to smack him. I was better than that, and even if I wasn't, I wouldn't take on a woman growing a human inside her.

"Fine," I agreed.

I stood and strode through a hall door which my county key card opened and went into a small conference room. I knew without looking that my opposing counsel was following closely behind.

"What in the hell are you doing? I know prosecutors break all the rules, but are you for real?" The attorney's face was getting red. In the two cases we'd tried against each other, I'd never once seen her angry. I didn't want to chalk it up to hormones, but I did have to wonder about this personality transplant.

"I didn't break a single rule."

"Then..." She was shaking her head like I'd lost every last one of my marbles.

"I was doing exactly what I said I was doing. I was interviewing her as a witness to murder."

"Witness? Did something happen in the jail? Or you have exculpatory evidence you haven't shared? Or—"

"I might have if you hadn't interrupted."

"Do you think Juliana Clarke didn't kill her husband?" Cort's voice was incredulous.

"The evidence points to her guilt," I equivocated.

Cort plopped herself into a chair. Swiveled it. Stopped mid-swivel. For long moments, she looked lost in thought, making no attempt to speak or move. In my family, someone would have made a comment about the smell of logs burning. I refrained. Done with whatever she was considering, suddenly she leaned forward. Put her elbows on the faux grain wood veneer.

"What we need to discuss is off the record. I want to talk to you, because this process should serve the truth not only punishment. But before I open my mouth, you have to promise not to use anything I say against my client. Can I trust you? Can we have that kind of conversation?"

My need to win at all costs was warring my belief in justice. It was more a battle than skirmish. Justice edged out, barely.

"Five minutes," I decided on the spot. "I can do this for just five minutes."

"Go." Cort pointed both index fingers at me in two hand guns.

"You expect me to speak?" That hadn't been my idea of conversation. I'd been expecting some kind of confession from Cort.

"The other option is having a very long conversation with Judge Cox about the egregious violation of my client's constitutional rights. Your choice."

This Casey Cort was different from the attorney I'd met years ago. That Casey had been easily intimidated. I didn't think her threat was an empty one. A call from Judge Cox to Lori Pope would put the nail in my career coffin. I decided speaking to Cort was the less worse choice.

"We think it's possible that Sienna Clarke may have murdered her father. Possibly in defense of her mother." Before Cort could get her panties in a bunch about prosecutorial misconduct, I rushed on. "But we've hit a dead end. Sienna refused to speak with us, and we had no way to compel her. Monica Mae Ellis, the new girlfriend, wasn't in the room at that time. Kendrick Walker is dead. We all know dead men tell no tales.

"That leaves Juliana. I was in the holding cell to try to impress upon her the importance of the truth. To let her know that if her defense fails, then she'll be in jail for a long time. She'd be lucky to get out and meet her grandchildren."

"What did she say?"

"You'd be proud," I admitted. "She exercised her right to remain silent. I'm not going to ask you to violate your client's confidentiality. But I am going to ask you this one question: Is there any information that you've acquired that would lead you to believe that your client is not guilty?" Cort's knitted brow let me know that I needed to be crystal clear. "Not 'not guilty'"—I air quoted—"but actually innocent?"

Innocence was not a word that we used often in criminal court. Cases ended with a guilty verdict, an acquittal, a plea, or more rarely, a dismissal of charges. Never in my career had I considered that the defendant may not have actually committed the crime. That idea went against every firmly held belief I had about our criminal justice system.

Cort inhaled deeply, then exhaled.

"Unfortunately, no."

22

"What's pathetic?" I asked. "You're the judge, honey. What do the cards say?"

Sinclair flipped over the three red Apples to Apples cards, then read them aloud.

"My Past? The Midwest? Jerry Springer?" Sinclair looked between each of us: me, Cara Guzman, and Ron Pinheiro. It was a motley crew.

Usually, card games were the kind of thing I'd either be doing with my family on a Sunday night or with Casey and her parents or her neighbors. Right now, none of those folks were really speaking to me.

When Sinclair suggested a game night, I was at a loss as to who to invite. But he'd taken care of it. Cara Guzman was an associate who was a couple years behind me at work. Ron was an odd choice, but I didn't say a thing. The moment Ron had walked through the door into the apartment, he'd said he was free because Casey was preparing for her murder trial starting in a few days. I wanted to know if he'd met Casey's parents or if they'd set a date for a wedding, but I shied away from prying into stuff that wasn't my business…anymore. Sinclair had seen to that.

I'd hugged both of them, trying not to feel sadness at the fact I wasn't with people I was closer to. When Sinclair had seen my pout, he'd pulled me to the kitchen and told me I needed to change my attitude. That I had to think of this impromptu gathering with colleagues as broadening my circle. Expanding my horizons. My smile was a little tremulous. I could feel my lips trembling, but I tried to hide it as best I could.

Instead I turned my attention to hostess duties, putting out hot passed dishes and two different kinds of wine. I tried to keep up with the small talk as we ate hot cheese- and meat-filled bites, sipped prosecco, and traded work gossip. When conversation petered, Sinclair pulled the Apples to Apples game from my shelf and proposed a few rounds. I tried not to let my nerves get the best of me when I cleared away dishes and refilled wine. I'd never really played any board or card games with Sinclair. He always turned down my offers to play. Instead, he'd shared stories about how he'd swept all the chess pieces from the board when his little brother had checked his king or how he'd stopped playing games with his daughter when she got the best of him at Monopoly.

We were in the final round of the game. It had been if not fun, at least uneventful. From the side glances and stifled yawns, it was time to call it a night. When it was my last turn, I plucked a silly card from my options. Best to go out with a laugh.

"Who put which cards in?" Sinclair asked.

Cara raised her hand. "I own up to The Midwest. I'm so sorry," she said as she looked between Ron and me, the two who'd been born here. "But, Richard, everyone knows there's no love lost between you and the states here in the middle."

Ron and I laughed.

Sinclair did not.

"Who's responsible for Jerry Springer?" he asked.

Ron raised a hand.

"Everyone thinks his show is pathetic, that's for sure. His single life highlight was mayor of Cincinnati," Ron explained. "Lowlight was either his arrest for prostitution or the TV show. Either way, I think he's perfect for that card."

I liked Ron's sensibilities. He'd make a great law firm partner. I didn't think he'd make a great partner for Casey, though. He wasn't sparky. Casey needed someone who challenged her. I shook my head of my uncharitable thoughts. Again this was none of my damned business. My boyfriend had been quiet for a beat too long.

Sinclair looked at Pinheiro. Nodded sagely. When he did that while also stroking at his chin, it made him look more like a professor and less like a peer.

"My Past? Lulu? That has to be you."

The moment Sinclair held up the card I'd submitted, I got scared. Every shred of humor I'd seen in the choice was gone. My thoughts scattered, but everyone was expecting a response. The filter between my brain and mouth evaporated in an instant.

"Um, I was thinking your marriage," I sputtered out. When Sinclair's mask of civility started to slip, I changed tack. "Well, not exactly that. Maybe the fact that you're divorcing. Sorry. That was a bad choice. I just didn't have any other good cards."

Ron's phone buzzed, breaking into the awkward silence I'd left after I'd stopped trying to explain my horribly passive-aggressive choice. Ron got up from the spot he'd occupied around the coffee table and paced back and forth by the front door.

"Hey, it's getting late," Ron said after he finished his call and put his phone in his pocket. "I think I'm going to need to head out."

"I haven't picked a winner yet," Sinclair said.

Ron stood and moved toward the coat rack.

"You know what? I should get going too," Guzman added. She made motions to leave as well. "I need to get up early for a conference call with the Sixth Circuit in the morning. You know how the clerks can be down there."

"Speaking of Cincinnati," Ron piped in. "It's like a completely different state down there. I once crossed a Sixth Circuit clerk. Took me years to redeem myself. So I get it. Let me help you with your coat," Ron offered to Guzman. In a moment, the two of them were standing by the door wrapped in coats and scarves against the December cold.

"Congratulations, Lulu," Guzman gushed, her hand firmly on the doorknob. "It's so great that a woman made partner this year. You'll be great. Hopefully we can work together on something soon."

"Thanks so much," I said. I wanted to be happy with partnership. Something I'd worked so hard toward for ten long years, but without sharing the news with those most important to me, the whole thing was anticlimactic somehow.

Sinclair had said it wasn't all it was cracked up to be. That I might be much happier at home with kids. Deborah hadn't been as good a wife when she'd bought into her private practice and added it to her hospital work. I nodded my gratitude for my guests' well-wishes, then showed them into the hall. Something propelled me to take them down the stairs, through the vestibule, and out front despite their protests.

With that, both attorneys were into their cars. My walk up the stairs was slow, deliberate. Sinclair was standing just on the other side of the door when I pushed it open again.

"Ruined another party." He planted hands on hips. "Couldn't help yourself, could you?"

"I don't think I ruined anything, honey." I kicked off the sneakers I'd jammed my feet into. Started picking up the cards. Jammed the glossy cartoon apples backs into the appropriate molded slots. Fitted the cover on even though they weren't properly sorted.

"It's late. I told you a party on a Sunday might be awkward. It's when people usually recharge for Monday morning. They left because they're working tomorrow."

I took plates, dirty and clean, to the kitchen. Scraped everything into the garbage. Loaded the dishwasher. Sinclair followed me into the kitchen. Every step was a stomp. I didn't need to turn around to know he was there.

"My past. How did you think that would sound?"

"I picked up what had been in front of me," I said. I pressed the start button on the dishwasher. Pushed everything else down the disposal. Flipped the switch that ground the food remains until the drain cleared. Corked the wine before I turned around. "We were at the end of the deck. My only other options were a morgue, clowns, and gravity."

"You were trying to embarrass me. Is this because of what Deborah said to you? All these weeks later, and you're still angry about your faulty memory? Did she say something else about me that you didn't tell me? A scorned wife isn't a reliable source."

I wasn't ready to admit that exactly. I wanted to be over it. I wanted to believe all his excuses, but I was starting to think everyone was right. That I was just the other woman, and not an especially smart one at that. I still believed he was going to leave his wife. I mean he'd left her...mostly.

"I don't know why you didn't tell me that she filed. It's something that's so important to our future. It makes me think you didn't want to end your marriage. That you really don't want to be with me. You can't hold on to her and to me at the same time."

"What are you talking about? I told you she filed when I talked to you last October. Maybe you couldn't hear me over the boats on the Elbe in Dresden."

My mind raced back to that noisy riverbank. One ship's horn had been going at the same time pleasure book ticket takers were shouting. Chatty tourists had completed the sound landscape.

"That's not true. I could hear you just fine," I said. And I had been able to hear him through the Blackberry's speaker despite all that.

"That's absolutely not true," Sinclair insisted. His face was so sincere that I had the shortest moment of doubt. "I told you. It's why I needed Casey's help. Otherwise, why would I ask about hiring your damned friend who couldn't even save her spot on the law review masthead."

I let the dig pass, working hard to keep my eyebrows from my hairline. Didn't point out that he was the one Casey and I had hoped would save my best friend from career derailing humiliation.

"Then what are you talking about? What specifically would I be mad about that Deborah told me?"

"That she's not over me. That she's still in love. Not ready to let me go."

"Sinclair, she filed. She's ready. I'm ready. Maybe you're the one who's not ready." It was the absolute first time I had the guts to say what I'd been thinking for more than a year. He said he wanted me. He'd moved in. But something was holding him back. I wasn't enough or Deborah was too much. Either way, I wasn't getting what I wanted which was him loving me unencumbered by the past weighing him down.

Sinclair lurched forward. I backed up against the sink. He grabbed my wrists in his hands. He turned my palms up, then down.

"You're not wearing my ring."

"What ring?" I asked.

My mind spun out. Sinclair had never offered nor given me a ring of any kind. The only ring exchange I'd witnessed recently had been when Casey had gotten a ring from Ron. I sifted through my memories at warp speed making sure I hadn't conflated events or forgotten something. Coming up empty, I didn't have a choice but to wait until he spoke.

"You don't get to dictate my life until you're wearing a ring." Sinclair's grip was tight when he shook my hands. "Only then can you weigh in."

"I thought you wanted to marry me," I was embarrassed at my whine, but couldn't help myself. "That we were partners—"

"As of January, we will be partners, law firm partners. I'm surprised you passed the vote. Almost no one in the room had any confidence in you. It was only me and Ron who were able to turn the tide against you."

"The tide?" Over the eleven years I'd been at the firm, unwavering support would have been my take if asked. Maybe I needed some kind of drugs or more coffee because nothing was as it seemed.

"All those changes I had you make were to avoid exactly this thing happening," Sinclair said, his voice soft, and if I was brave enough to think about it, a little bit condescending. "Unfortunately, it was too little too late."

I didn't address that issue. I had made partner, so something had worked. Sweeping away the innuendo, I kept a firm grasp on the reality of the result. I'd think about how to navigate the politics of the choosing process later. Sinclair was a master of derailing the conversation. I wanted to get back to it. Figure out how our relationship, how the two of us were going to shake out because us standing there was feeling like an ending not a beginning. I had to choke back the bile rising as I saw my worst fears of being abandoned, realized.

"Is this it, then? Are we done? You go back to Deborah. I stay here?"

Sinclair moved even closer. His grip on my wrists tightened considerably.

"You can't leave me." His voice was a hostile entreaty. "I love you."

"Let go. That hurts." It did, though I was sure he didn't mean it that way.

"I would never hurt you." Sinclair's voice was soft, warm and yet it made me shiver.

"I'm not kidding," I pleaded. "You're really hurting me, Sinclair."

"I thought I told you to call me Richard."

"I think you need to go." All the fight went out from me in one big whoosh. "I can't do this anymore. My friends were right. My family was right. I was wrong."

So, so wrong.

The immediate clarity was edifying and horrifying in equal measure. As I stood there, literal prisoner to this gray-haired married man, I didn't even recognize myself.

"Why can't you accept that I love you?" Sinclair asked. As he held me tighter, the pain increased. "I can love you enough for all of these other people you insist on having in your life. If you just let me. But you won't let me. Why can't you realize that I've been nothing but good to you?"

Pain burst through the left side of my head. For a long minute, I wasn't even sure what had happened. Then I looked at my hands. Sinclair was holding my right in his left. But his right hand was free, balled into a fist. A bruise was rising on his knuckles.

I shook my other hand free, brought it to my temple. A lump was starting to form. When I took my hand away and looked at my fingers, there was blood there. Bright red blood.

"Oh, sweetie, I'm so sorry." Again his voice was filled with sympathy, his eyes soft with compassion. "Look what you made me do."

23

I looked up at the three-foot-diameter bronze wall clock that hung above my inoperable fireplace. In five minutes it would be midnight. I closed my eyes. Opened them. Had a look again at the clock. How six hundred dollars for a clock had seemed like a good idea, I'll never know. I closed my eyes again, this time in relief.

Money wasn't my biggest problem—anymore. Like promised, Justin had wired me my portion of the Brighthill settlement. I put aside about half for federal state and local taxes. I'd written a check to pay off my loans. I paid my parents back for the car.

Financial freedom was new and it felt good. I could buy overpriced decorative clocks for days and not feel the pinch of it. Not that I'd make that mistake again.

Expensive accessories didn't matter right now. A client facing prison time always kept me awake for more hours than necessary. There was fierce irony in the fact that I couldn't sleep right before trial when a client probably needed me at my well-rested best.

We'd start choosing Juliana Clarke's jury in four days. Four days until I had to cross-examine police officers and crime scene investigators. Clarke had four days to lay all her cards on the table and tell the truth.

Either she'd spill the beans about Sienna being the real killer or she'd admit that there was abuse. Or she wouldn't say anything at all and some random group of twelve of the county's registered voters would have to sort it out for themselves.

My sigh was deep, long, and very much audible, if my cat's twitching ears were any indication. I needed more time to prep and I needed more time to sleep.

At week nineteen of this pregnancy, I was feeling more energetic than the first trimester, but I didn't think I could possibly pull an all-nighter. I'd bet all the money I had left that Peyton Bennett wasn't losing a lick of sleep in his Hidden Hills mansion. There was some relief in knowing I could rely on co-counsel if I completely fell apart.

As gently as I could, I lifted Simba from my lap. He was good and pissed off when he woke up. The cat gave me an evil yellow eye before he stalked to the bedroom. I knew that after I brushed my teeth, washed my face, and put on my pajamas, that Simba would be curled in the very middle of the bed in stark defiance of me, his sleeping companion.

"Casey!" a voice yelled. The chain rattled on my living room door.

The files I was holding fell to the floor as I rushed to the door. I did not want whoever was shrieking to wake my neighbors. I slid the chain and twisted the locks. Lulu was standing on the other side holding a wad of gauze up to the left side of her head.

"What happened?" I asked after I took in the makeshift bandage and a trickle of blood. "What are you doing here? It's late." The last was unnecessary, but I was very surprised she'd show up and at such an odd hour to boot. Her betrayal, even if inadvertent, had been too grievous to forgive easily.

"I made partner," my friend said.

I kind of had to wonder if I was dreaming. Nothing about the woman in front of me made sense. She was in a pencil skirt and cashmere but sheepskin boots, all wrapped in the multicolor patchwork coat Sinclair had forbidden.

"And you came here to tell me this. At midnight? On a Sunday?"

"No."

Either pregnancy hormones were making me fuzzy or I was just tired.

"So congratulations are in order, I guess. What's wrong with your head?"

"Sinclair couldn't go home," Lulu answered. Her voice was quavering, hovering around a cry.

"Excuse me?"

"Can I come in? I know things are fucked up between us. But I don't have anywhere to go. Please." That last word held so much sorrow that I stepped back from the door, an unspoken invitation. Lulu came through without hesitation and pushed it shut with a firm shove. There'd be no cat Houdini routine today.

Without a word, I turned away and padded to the bathroom, fished a clean washcloth from the built-in linen cabinet, dampened it, and then brought it out to her. She'd curled up in the corner of my couch.

"Do you need this?"

She nodded. Removed her hand. The gauze came with it. She had a quarter-sized lump and a cut that was still oozing just the tiniest bit of blood. Her eyes closed with relief when she applied the washcloth.

"You're starting to show," she said. "Ron was at our place tonight."

Ron and Justin and all of that was off-limits where she and I were concerned. I pushed all that out of my mind and focused on the facts in front of me.

"Lulu. It's quarter past midnight. I have meetings with Peyton Bennett and our expert witness in the morning. Jury selection starts on Thursday."

"Sinclair had nowhere to go."

"What do you mean nowhere to go? He has a house and your apartment."

"This...he...I got hurt. Neighbors called the police. I asked them to get him out. Send Sinclair home. The police recognized him. He couldn't go home because Doctor Deborah Bloom has a restraining order. She didn't mention any of that. So he's staying in my apartment, that I pay for. Deborah Bloom's house is her own, turns out. She's changed the locks, and he can't go back there. So I'm here. I know it's late, but I didn't want to bother my parents. I didn't want them to see me like this. I..."

For a long minute, I filled in the missing words from her sentence fragments. I flashed to the stories Calandra Clarke Young had told Bennett and me during our visit. Then Elias Phillips came to mind. I shook my head. One thing was spilling over to another. Unless I sought more clarity, I was going to conflate things.

"What happened?" I spoke the two words as slowly and compassionately as I could.

Lulu's eyes teared up. Her lips trembled, yet she was mute.

"Did..." I didn't want to ask it, but I couldn't not. "Did Sinclair hit you?"

She collapsed into herself on the couch, buried her face in her hands. Her nod was barely discernible.

"Why?"

"I don't know. Because he thought I humiliated him in front of Ron and Cara."

"Guzman?" I don't know why that question. I think I was afraid to ask more about the other just yet.

"We were having a little dinner party to celebrate, you know. We were playing a stupid game and I tried to make a joke. Only Sinclair didn't find it funny."

"Then he hit you."

"I think so. I don't know. I was in the kitchen putting stuff away. We were arguing about Deborah and his divorce and next thing I knew, I was standing there hurting."

"The police?"

"Maybe the arguing was loud. I don't know. I've never had police at my house before. It was embarrassing. Sinclair was really sorry. He said he didn't mean it. But the police didn't really care. They said it was policy that they couldn't leave the two of us together. I suggested he go home."

"But..." She was here and not home.

"One of the cops sort of squinted his eyes. Looked at Sinclair and asked for his ID. Then the officer took Sinclair's driver's license and pulled that big radio thing off his hip and stepped outside. He came back and said Sinclair could go anywhere, but not to Deborah Bloom's house."

"Did she change the locks? I mean, if no one has filed, there isn't really a separation, I would think. It's as much his as hers..." I trailed off because I realized I wasn't making much sense.

A restraining order trumped everything. From what Lulu had said when she'd come through the door, we were in protective order territory, not the normal push-pull of who got to stay in the house during the divorce.

"That's maybe what started the argument. She filed," Lulu said. She pulled off her coat, slid from the couch to the floor in a dejected heap.

"When?" I asked. I knew Sinclair to be a liar. I already knew he was a cheater which was lying in a different form.

"While we were in Germany. At the time of filing, she went for a temporary restraining order and now it's permanent," Lulu said. The recitation of facts had her on a more even keel. I decided to stay with that for a moment.

"What was the underlying basis for the order? They don't hand those out like lollipops at a pediatrician's office."

There was a single retired judge who had been appointed to hear domestic violence petitions that came with a divorce filing. He was old school. He'd been known to quote from the Bible about wives submitting to their husbands. If a victim didn't look victimized enough, he'd dismiss their petition without so much as a backward glance. That made me sad for Deborah and worried for Lulu.

"Domestic violence. The police said that she kicked him out because he punched her in the face one time too many."

My mind went so many places. I'd met Deborah. She'd been a colleague of a client. Bloom had seemed so strong and self-assured. She was a doctor for goodness' sake. Then I turned an eye toward my friend. I'd have said the same about Lulu. She had a loving family, a strong personality, a great career. Maybe even the same about Juliana Clarke if I'd met her in any other context.

Suddenly I wanted to kick myself. Instead I scooted over and took my very best friend in the biggest hug I could manage. All along, I'd thought of these women as perpetrators of betrayals, of murder. Maybe this is what victims looked like. I pulled back, took the discarded washcloth and wiped at my friend's tears.

All I had to do was convince a jury of what I now knew to be true. If the wool could so easily be pulled over my eyes, I had one hell of a battle ahead.

Nicole
December 17, 2007

I was alone at counsel table. Normally, Lori Pope would insist on one attorney mentoring another, especially in a case like this, a murder trial. Or at a minimum a second chair to make the likelihood of reversible error as miniscule as possible.

My boss's trust in me obviously didn't extend that far. I took a fortifying sip of the coffee on the table in front of me. Without anyone next to me, I'd been so bold as to add a slug of bourbon.

I'd already white-knuckled it through weeks of surprise breathalyzers. I'd bet that Pope wouldn't complicate the opening of a trial with a drug test. As I took another steadying sip, I was happy I'd been right. My boss got the satisfaction of a completely sober interim head of Major

Crimes. I got the liquid courage I needed to be the thin line between Clarke's freedom and her punishment.

"Ms. Long, your opening argument," Judge Essie Cox directed from the bench. That was my cue. I stood, buttoned my blazer, smoothed down any flyaway hairs not caught with bobby pins. Took a deep breath, then walked over to the jury box where twelve members and two alternates sat waiting for me to tell the story.

They were predisposed to be convinced that the woman sitting at the far table—her own hair in a chignon that mirrored mine—was guilty of a heinous crime. Innocent until proven guilty was an interesting constitutional notion, but most people thought an arrest and badly lit mug shot equaled guilt.

Even with the scales of justice tipped just a little bit in my favor, I hesitated at the uncertainty of not only my skill at argument, but the uncertainty of result. I took another sip of my beverage, felt any remaining nerves calm. This is where I excelled. Oh-so-slowly walked the few steps to the jury box. I knew they wouldn't take their eyes off me. I took a deep breath, then spoke in a clear voice that carried to all four corners of the wood-paneled room.

"Ladies and gentlemen," I started, then paused until I was sure that fourteen pairs of eyes were on me. "I want to talk to you about a moment in time.

"Gavin de Becker, a violence expert and the author of The Gift of Fear refers to a violent incident—that singular moment in time—as a line between foresight and hindsight.

"The defendant, Juliana Clarke, voluntarily left an eighteen-year marriage to Kendrick Walker. Her attorneys are going to say that she had no choice but to kill him.

That her husband's cruelty and abuse made her do what she did. But all of that is hindsight.

"First, the prosecution is going to show that there isn't much evidence of this so-called abuse. But even if, let's suppose it's true, that Kendrick Walker's alleged creepy psychological manipulations were somehow the cause of his death at the hands of his wife. The same one he vowed to love and honor. It would be no excuse.

"I submit to you that Juliana Clarke went to her former family home with murder in her mind. She had the foresight to premeditate a murder.

"She or her defense team will give the flimsy excuse of having to go from her condo in Shaker Square to the family home in Cleveland Heights to pick up her daughter, Sienna Walker."

I gestured vaguely to Sienna Walker who was sitting on the pew-like bench behind her mother in a button-down yellow oxford and chinos. The jurors, led like puppies on leashes, turned their heads away from me toward the girl. I wanted them to see a full-grown adult, not some adolescent in need of protection.

"The same daughter who is eighteen years old and a graduate of Hathaway Brown. Who has her own car. Who had a friend who'd dropped her off there.

"For all her supposed intent in driving over to Cleveland Heights, the evidence will show that Juliana Clarke never chauffeured her daughter home. She never got too far past the back door.

"She walked into her old kitchen, picked up the marble cheese board, then bashed her husband's head in. She didn't hit him a single time, which is what you'd think a woman would do to her aggressor. Hit him once to disable him, then get the hell out.

"This was a man who was killed in a murderous rage. She hit him not once. Not twice as he staggered away in surprise and pain. But at least four different times. Then he fell against the marble counter, bashing in the back of his head this time.

"No, that's not quite right. The evidence will show that Juliana Clarke didn't just hit her estranged husband, she bludgeoned him."

I paused a good, long time. Let that sink in. Then I hit the side of my right hand against the palm of my left five distinct times. The sound of flesh hitting flesh was the only sound in the courtroom.

"To. His. Death."

I turned away from the jury. Took a deliberate walk toward counsel table. Drank a sip of water. Part of it was needed. Part of it was theater.

"When Kendrick Walker's murder is keeping me awake at night, I do wonder what Juliana would have done if she hadn't been found. But she was—found, that is. Monica Mae Ellis will testify about what happened when she walked into Walker's kitchen and found Juliana Clarke on the floor, weapon in hand, blood everywhere.

"Mrs. Clarke has never said she didn't commit this crime. That's a tacit admission that she killed him. Her defense? He'd hurt her before and he might hurt her again. She was not in imminent danger when she walked into that Cleveland Heights kitchen. There's no reason she couldn't have stayed safely in her home hating her soon-to-be ex-husband from afar. But she didn't do that. One flimsy excuse and she was somewhere she shouldn't have been.

"You will hear from the responding officers, who found Juliana Clarke hovering over the body of the deceased with the murder weapon in hand. You will hear from crime scene experts who will confirm that Walker's death occurred just as I've stated. You'll hear from a Cleveland Heights detective who will confirm that there are no complaints of domestic violence and that we exhausted all other possible avenues to solve this murder by considering any other possible suspects.

"I will prove to you, beyond a reasonable doubt, that Juliana Clarke murdered Kendrick Walker in cold blood. I ask that after hearing all the evidence, you return a verdict of guilty so the defendant gets the punishment she deserves because divorce is the solution to a bad marriage, not murder."

25

Casey
December 17, 2007

The morning had whirred by in a blur. I gulped coffee when I didn't think the jury was watching. My focus wasn't where it should be. It was split between Lulu, who had been sleeping on my couch when I'd tiptoed out, and the woman beside me at counsel table. I'd pulled her aside for one last confab. Peyton had done the same. After my bid to get some kind of story from her, Juliana Clarke glanced over her shoulder toward her daughter, Sienna. They shared a look I couldn't interpret. Then Clarke had turned back to me.

"Use your best judgment," was all she had said.

"I may have to call you to testify. It's usually necessary in self-defense cases without witnesses to vouch for you. Do you understand?"

She'd merely nodded, then turned her head forward, her gaze fixed on the court reporter plugging in the electronic machine that had long replaced the one that spilled tape like a busy cash register.

Nicole Long was surprisingly steady on her feet. Her opening statement had been eloquent. As Peyton Bennett and I had agreed before, we exercised our right to save our argument until the close of the prosecutor's case. I found that jurors would not remember the huge jumble of words. I wanted them to hear out theories on Juliana Clarke's innocence when they knew more about the case and the players and were more receptive to some kind of refutation of the prosecutor's evidence.

I looked down at my notes. It was going to be my turn in a few minutes. Long was winding down with her first witness, the police officer who'd discovered Clarke kneeling over Kendrick Walker's body, marble cheese board in hand.

My glance toward the jury was quick. I needn't have worried that they were interested in anything going on at defense table. They were too busy paying rapt attention to officer Geoffrey Cummings. Before I had time to get a good look at my notes, Nicole Long was speaking to me.

"Your witness," she said toward defense table.

"Which one of you will be cross-examining the witness?" Judge Cox asked.

"I will, Your Honor," I said, and stood. My first day outfit was a gray silk suit. I smoothed down everything and took my notes to the lectern.

"Mr. Cummings, I'm Casey Cort. Peyton Bennett and I"—I gestured toward defense counsel table—"represent the defendant, Juliana Clarke. I'm going to ask you a few questions about that night, Sunday, September second of this year."

Cummings nodded. The introduction had a twofold purpose. One was to reintroduce our side to the jury. The first time the jury would hear either of us speak, we'd be tearing down the testimony of the prosecutor's witnesses. I wanted them to hear me speak normally in a calm voice. Wanted them to view Bennett and me simply as people doing a job, not as accessories to murder.

The second purpose was to disarm Cummings. Prosecutorial witnesses were usually attacked from the get-go. I was starting with honey over vinegar.

"How long have you worked for the Cleveland Heights Police Department?"

"Eight years."

"In your eight years, how many times have you encountered a dead person?" I asked, eschewing the words "murder victim" that Long had spouted more than once.

Cummings paused to think.

"Three."

"Would it be fair to say the nature of the other two deaths weren't violent?" I was taking a bit of a stab in the dark, but there were few murders in Cleveland Heights. It was nothing like its neighbor to the north, East Cleveland, which had probably held the title for most murderous city in the county more than once.

"That's fair, I guess. One was a welfare check. The woman had been dead at least a week when we found her. The other was a man who'd died of a heart attack or stroke. We called the coroner for the first, an ambulance for the second."

"This would have been your first violent death, then?"

"Yes."

"Had you seen that much blood before?"

"No. Only in training videos. I was surprised at how much there was."

"Did you enter the house through the front door or the back?"

"The front."

"What made you go to the kitchen?"

Cummings paused a long moment. Nicole had given him a copy of one of the police reports filed to help the officer refresh his recollection of the night some three and a half months ago. He looked down at the two sheets of paper stapled together in the top left corner. I'd read that report more than once and knew the answer wasn't there.

"Mr. Cummings?" Judge Cox prompted.

"I don't know. Maybe the 911 call?"

"That sounds like a question and not an answer," I said. "Are you sure of that?"

"No."

"Was there screaming or noise coming from the kitchen when you entered the house?"

Cummings's eyes rolled back unseeing as he filtered through his memory.

"Not that I recall."

"So is it fair to say, you're not sure what prompted you to go to the kitchen, but you went anyway."

"Yes, that's fair."

"Okay." I paused for a moment considering my next question. "Who was in the house when you got there?"

"Your client. The deceased."

"Who called 911?"

"I don't know."

"My client didn't call. The deceased didn't call."

"I'm not sure."

"Did you canvass the neighbors?"

"Yes."

"What did they observe about that night?"

"No one heard anything out of the ordinary."

"Thank you, Officer Cummings." To the judge and jury, I said, "No further questions."

I took my seat, relieved that my cross had gone off without a hitch. It wasn't fireworks like television. It was about building the blocks of a defense one brick at a time.

I drank more coffee during the preliminaries of the next witness, Hazel Mathis, the crime scene investigator. This one would be Peyton's to cross-examine.

Long came back to the prosecution table. That was odd since she wasn't coming to retrieve any documents or notes that I could see. There was a pause while she took a large sip of her own coffee.

"Ms. Long?" Judge Cox inquired when the prosecutor was slow to return to the lectern.

"Ms. Mathis, how did Kendrick Walker die?"

"Blunt force trauma to the head."

"Can you expand upon that?"

"There were five separate skull fractures. Four in front and one in back. The trauma on the back of the head is consistent with hitting his head while falling. The front ones are consistent with being hit with a heavy object."

"Did you have occasion to examine the cheese board recovered from the scene?"

"Yes."

"What was your conclusion?"

"That it was the weapon that caused the injuries to the deceased."

"Your witness."

Bennett rose, buttoned the slim-fitting bespoke suit that was fashionable without being flashy, and walked to the lectern.

"Ms. Mathis, what was the approximate height of the perpetrator?"

For a moment the witness looked out of sorts. I saw her eyes dart between the jury and the prosecutor as if an answer were coming out of the sky.

"Five five, maybe. Since the defendant was found with the murder weapon in hand, we didn't investigate the possibility that there were other possible suspects."

"Would it surprise you to find out that the expert the defense hired concluded the perpetrator may have been as tall as five foot eight?"

"Objection," Long sounded.

"Basis?" Judge Cox asked.

"Calls for speculation."

"Sustained."

"No further questions," Bennett concluded.

The fact that the witness didn't answer made little difference. The jury got the information we wanted to impart anyway. Bennett and I had debated long and hard over this approach. He thought we were best served by sticking with and doubling down on the battered women's syndrome defense. I'd wanted to keep the possibility open of a different perpetrator because our client's cooperation wasn't guaranteed. I'd won the debate.

"Let's call a break," Judge Cox announced, "before our next witness."

The jury looked grateful for what was really an elaborate way to give them time to go to the bathroom.

"I need a minute," I said to Bennett. Securing my cell, I moved out through the gallery to the hallway. Before I did,

I snuck a look at Sienna Walker and her mother who were standing and talking in hushed tones after the jury had been escorted out. Sienna Walker was a good three inches taller than her mother. I looked down at the floor beneath defense table as well as the carpet beneath the gallery seats. Neither woman was wearing heels.

Once I was away from any jurors or trial witnesses, I dialed my own home phone number. It rang three times before Lulu answered.

"Geez, you need to get a cordless. I can't believe I'm standing in the hall like it's 1957."

"It's the morning break," I said ignoring the dig. "How are you?"

"Umm…"

"Lulu. Seriously. I only have a few minutes here. I really need to know that you're alright. I have to go back and try a murder case."

My friend's voice dropped to a whisper.

"Sinclair is here."

So much for her staying away from a guy with fast fists.

"What!" I exclaimed. "Do I need to call the police? The Cleveland police. I'd have to tell them about the other night's Cleveland Heights call." I looked up, took in my surroundings. "There are officers here for the trial. I could have one of them put in a call."

"I'm okay," Lulu insisted.

"Are you saying you don't want me to call?"

"I'm saying that he's okay right now. He brought me flowers. He's going to hire a lawyer and go forward with his divorce. He bought me a ring."

I shivered as a weird déjà vu rippled through me. If something or someone didn't intervene, she could be on the same path as my client in the courtroom not thirty feet away. I had no desire to be sitting next to her at a defense table twenty years from now.

"Open my back door."

"What? Why?" Lulu sounded confused.

"Just do it."

I heard the locks twist and the hinges squeak as the seldom-used door opened.

"Now what?" Lulu asked.

"Step outside. Don't worry, the cord stretches far enough."

"Jesus. I feel like I'm in high school pulling the phone into the closet."

"Slip the cord around to the right side of the door and pull it shut. There's a gap there big enough for it not to get smushed."

"Should I ask why you're so good at this?"

"Is the door closed?" I asked. I ignored her question. It was embarrassing to admit I'd had to have conversations outside my own apartment to spare the person inside from the full brunt of my feelings.

"Enough. The cat will stay in."

"Simba's not going anywhere. He's too fat and lazy and dependent upon me for that. I want to talk to you in private."

"Fine. I told him I'd agreed to hold down the fort and that you'd had business calls forwarded here. I have a minute."

"How big is it?" I asked.

"What?"

"The ring?"

"That's crass."

"We're well beyond propriety, Lulu. Answer this, then. You've always said that you wanted a ring like that girl from Dawson's Creek."

"Katie Holmes. Five carats, oval shaped with a rose gold halo."

"Or that woman from the Housewives show."

"Eva Longoria. Five carats, emerald cut set in platinum surrounded by two hundred forty-eight smaller diamonds."

Lulu was not unclear on what she wanted. She'd told me enough times that I remembered some of the details. I had to imagine that she'd been nearly as clear with her lover.

"What did Sinclair get for you?"

"A...uh...dainty fourteen-carat yellow gold band with a half-carat, maybe quarter-carat baguette. He says it's understated, more suitable for my personal style, for my new role as partner. Anything else he said would alienate everyone at the firm."

"Do you like it?"

"It's not my taste."

"Accept the ring, Lulu. Do whatever it takes to get him out of my apartment, then send him downtown. I'll have Ron confirm when he's in his office. Then get to your apartment. Hire a locksmith. Change the locks. Get someone to pack up his stuff. Send it to Deborah's house."

"He's not allowed there."

"The protection order is against him, not his stuff. If he's hiring a lawyer, then his attorney and his wife's can work it out."

"He says he's really sorry."

"He hit you, that's not love and there's no apology in the world that can make up for what he did. It's simply not acceptable. Ask Deborah Bloom if you must. Lulu, I love you. But I'm about five minutes out from going back to a trial where the ending turned out a lot differently. I don't want that for you. If you listen to nothing I say again ever, please hear this. The only safe path for you is one that points away from Sinclair."

26

I took the Altoid mint from my mouth and pushed it into a tissue before stuffing the same into my bag. When everyone was assembled, Judge Cox looked down at me.

"Counselor. Your next witness."

"I call Darlene Webb to the stand."

The detective made her way to the witness chair. Despite my suggestion, she was not in her best suit. She still looked like she was wearing hand-me-down clothes. When we'd been preparing her testimony, I'd told her the jury would be looking at her as a person of authority. She and I obviously had very different ideas about what that looked like.

As quickly as I could, I glossed over the preliminary questions about her time and experience as a police officer and detective. She didn't have the gravitas of years of experience to lean on, so I didn't.

"Detective Webb, can you tell me about your first contact with the deceased and the defendant?"

"I was the homicide detective on deck the first weekend in September. I got a call from dispatch saying that uniformed officers had been called to the scene of a suspicious death."

"Let me stop you there. What constitutes a suspicious death?"

"One that's not natural causes or a car accident or the like. Something that was likely at the hands of another person."

"Thank you for that. What happened when you got to Kendrick Walker's house on Shelbourne Road that Sunday, September second?"

"I radioed my arrival from the car. The officers on scene told me to come through the back door to the kitchen."

"Had they sealed the crime scene by the time you arrived?"

"No?"

"Why not?"

"Because the defendant, Juliana Clarke, was still in the kitchen. They were having a hard time getting her to let go of the cheese board in her hands, or getting her to move from the body. The medical examiner hadn't arrived on scene yet."

"Is that what you witnessed when you arrived?"

"Yes."

"Then what happened."

"The medical examiner arrived. Pronounced Walker dead. Only then did Mrs. Clarke move away from the body and drop the weapon she'd been holding. After that, the crime scene techs took pictures. Collected evidence. Officer Cummings made the arrest and took Clarke into custody. I remained at the scene."

"What was your investigative protocol?"

"Secure the scene. Make sure there was no evidence contamination. Assure chain of custody. Do a preliminary interview of witnesses. Try to establish a preliminary timeline."

"Did you follow all of those procedures in this case?"

"Yes."

"Let's turn to witnesses. Who was in the house at the time of Kendrick Walker's murder?"

"Mr. Walker, the victim. Monica Mae Ellis."

"Is she the one who called 911?"

"Yes."

"Anyone else?"

"Sienna Walker, the child of the deceased and the defendant had been there earlier in the evening."

"What time did she leave?"

"I don't know exactly, but she wasn't there when I arrived."

"The medical examiner puts the time of death around seven p.m. The 911 call was at precisely seven oh seven. Sienna's last text that evening was received at six ten."

"Given that fifty-minute window, did you investigate the idea of outside suspects?"

"No. We narrowed it to three."

"How did you eliminate the other two?"

"Sienna wasn't at the scene. Monica Mae made the 911 call. The defendant had the murder weapon in her hand."

"Thank you. The defendant through counsel has notified the court of her intention to claim a self-defense of battered women's syndrome. Were you aware of that?"

"Yes. You made me aware of the filing."

"Did that change the nature of your investigation?"

"Yes."

"How?"

"I made an exhaustive search for police reports, hospital reports, and witness statements over the last twenty years to corroborate those claims."

"Did you include the city of Cleveland, city of Shaker Heights, and city of Cleveland Heights in your investigation?"

"Yes."

"Did you search both public hospitals like MetroHealth and private like Cleveland Clinic and the research institution University Hospitals?"

"All three."

"After investigation of police, hospital, and neighbors at the four addresses they lived in Cuyahoga County, what evidence did you find to support the claim of self-defense?"

"None."

"Your witness."

Peyton Bennett walked to the lectern I'd just vacated. I had no idea what to expect from the older white-shoe lawyer. He reminded me so much of the kinds of men my father associated with at church and at the club. This was the fourth time I'd been up against Casey. She was a known quantity I was sure I could best, especially without the handicap of co-counsel throwing the case. He was an unknown quantity. Big firm lawyer didn't always equal good.

"Ms. Webb. I'm Peyton Bennett here today representing Juliana Clarke. Would you mind if I asked you a few questions about the case at hand?"

I saw Webb's shoulders come down from around her ears. Bennett was going to do charming and gallant. I tried to catch her eye before she played right into his hands. It was not to be. Bennett had caught and held the detective's attention.

"Yes, that's fine," she finally answered.

I wanted to shake my head, but the jury was like an all-seeing eye. Instead, I took a sip of my now cold, but fortified coffee. That helped settle my nerves.

"Bear with me, Detective Webb. I may have a lot of gray hair, but I'm still new to criminal trials, so I may refer to my notes often."

Webb nodded, charmed. I wanted to shoot lasers from my eyes to Cort's co-counsel. Webb was a people pleaser. She'd bend over backwards to help him build his case. If we hadn't just come back from a recess, I'd have asked for one. At this point, if I did, the judge would recognize it for the ploy it was and probably out me in front of the jury. I stayed silent, downing all but the dregs of my spiked drink.

"Okay. Let's see." Bennett paused, unbuttoned his suit jacket, extracted a slim case from the inner pocket, took out small silver reading glasses, polished them with a little gray cloth, then slipped them on his nose. "You testified that the crime scene wasn't cordoned off when you arrived."

"Yes."

"So none of that 'Police Line Do Not Cross' or yellow 'Caution' tape was around the house?"

"No."

"Hmmm. You said that my client over here in the blue dress, Juliana Clarke, was over the body when you saw her?"

"Yes."

"Was she kneeling or standing?"

"Kneeling."

"From your experience, could she have killed him? Wait a moment. He was five foot eleven and one hundred eighty-two pounds in the reports. Do you think my five-foot-five client, who is only one hundred thirty-five pounds, by the way, could have exerted the force necessary to lethally hit him?"

"Objection, Your Honor," I said. "Calls for speculation."

"Point of clarification, Your Honor," Bennett interrupted. "I asked about Detective Webb's experience."

"He's right, Ms. Long. Overruled." To Webb, Judge Cox said, "You can answer the question."

"In my experience, I haven't seen anything like this. But she didn't deny killing him."

"Did my client make any admissions to you?"

"No, she exercised her right to remain silent."

"Then she hired me, right? I would have advised her to continue to exercise her Fifth Amendment rights. Fair enough. So let's talk about your experience. How long have you been with the Cleveland Heights Police Department?"

"About a year. I came in as a detective, having just passed the exam."

I tried to keep my sigh silent. Webb and I had discussed how to talk about her...inexperience...but she was ignoring my advice.

"Congratulations. So before Walker was murdered, you were there about nine months. Would that be fair?"

"Yes."

"Before that you were with the Cleveland Police Department?"

"Yes."

I held my breath hoping beyond hope he didn't bring up Marc Baldwin. My butt was at least an inch off the chair ready to argue that one. Revealing that to the jury would be far more prejudicial than probative. Even if Judge Cox instructed the jury to disregard the mention, something as explosive as Webb being the partner to a cop who'd shot an unarmed Black man would surely stick with the jury. Probably taint their perception of Webb's testimony.

"How long? What was your title before you left?"

"I was a patrol officer."

"Congratulations on your promotion."

"Thank you."

"We know that my client, Juliana Clarke, didn't answer your questions. Did you interview Sienna Clarke Walker about what occurred the night of Kendrick Walker's death?"

"Yes." Webb referred to her notes. I'd instructed her to do that anytime she needed a moment before giving an answer. "She came in November twenty-sixth."

"After meeting with her, did you glean any additional information about what occurred that night?"

"She was reticent to speak with Ms. Long and myself. She did not provide anything helpful or additional information."

"At any time did you suspect her of murder?"

Webb hesitated too damned long. We'd talked about this and still she got hung up.

"We considered her," she finally said. "But eliminated her from consideration."

"When did you eliminate her from consideration?"

"Last week."

"So from September second through the middle of December, you considered her a suspect?"

"Yes."

"How tall is Ms. Walker?"

"Five foot seven or eight."

"Interesting. Did you interview Monica Mae Ellis?"

"Yes."

"How tall is Ms. Ellis?"

"About the same height as Sienna Walker, five seven or eight."

"Can you please tell the jury Ms. Ellis's relationship to the deceased?"

"She was his girlfriend."

"How did she come to be at the Shelbourne house on the night Walker died?"

"She was a resident there."

"So, Mr. Walker wasn't divorced from my client, but he had a live-in girlfriend."

"Yes."

"Did you consider Ms. Ellis as a suspect?"

"Briefly. We had to verify the claims of everyone who'd been in the house."

"Were her prints on the murder weapon?"

"Yes, as were Sienna's and your client's."

"They must like cheese a lot."

The jury tittered. They too were charmed by Bennett. Juries were never charmed by me. Bennett's little joke served to pave the way to a change of subject without it being abrupt. If he weren't opposing counsel, I'd have been impressed by his technique.

"You testified that you made an exhaustive search of hospital and police records to check on the validity of my client's self-defense claim," Bennett said. "Do I have that right, Detective Webb? Again, congrats on that promotion."

"Thank you. Yes, you're correct that I did make an exhaustive investigation of any claims of domestic violence. I found no evidence."

"Interesting. Did you ask Sienna Walker about growing up in the Clarke-Walker home?"

"She didn't disclose anything about that."

"When you were training in either the Cleveland Police Department or in Cleveland Heights, did you cover the issue of intimate partner violence? Given your short tenure at each department, any training should be top of mind."

I'd have hated to be in an argument with Bennett; he was the master of the subtle dig. His touch was light enough to give him plausible deniability should anyone ever call him on it. That facility with language was probably what had made him successful at the practice of law.

"Yes," Webb answered. "Domestic violence calls and our response was covered at both departments."

"So you wouldn't be surprised to learn that domestic violence is something that's often a secret? Maybe secret's not the right word. Rather it's often not spoken of. Would that jive with your training?"

"Yes."

"Are you also aware that when police come out to domestic violence calls, they often leave without filing a report. Especially if the victim, often the woman, recants?"

"Yes. It's unfortunate. I've been on calls like that myself. I think it's a shame that the women don't press charges more often. I think it would make things easier for them down the road."

"Yes. That's true, but it's a thorny issue because the statistics show that women are often in more danger after they receive protective or restraining orders. I think that statistic may have been in the Gavin de Becker book the prosecution mentioned in her opening argument. Alas, that's another issue for another witness. So no reports or information about the Clarke-Walker relationship before you came upon the scene. Okay. Bear with me."

Bennett shuffled through a sheaf of papers, most of which I'd have bet my bottle of Maker's Mark 46 didn't pertain to this case, but were merely for show.

"Were you aware that Juliana Clarke and Kendrick Walker lived in Philadelphia, Pennsylvania?"

"Yes, before their marriage, I think. They met in school there," Webb answered.

"You're right. They met at the University of Pennsylvania in the West Philly neighborhood. Let me show you this document."

Bennett handed a document to me and the judge. It was marked as defense exhibit one. I was about to object, but my boss, Lori Pope, walking into the courtroom distracted me. I became immediately unsure. Both sides had to share any evidence that was to be presented at trial. I wanted to say that I'd never seen this one before, but for a beat I wasn't sure. In the time I could have objected, Bennett had already approached the witness with another copy of the document.

"Can you please read the highlighted words at the top of the page, Detective Webb?"

"Philadelphia Police Department."

"And below."

"Incident Report."

"Whose name is listed under the heading 'Suspect Data'?"

"Walker Kendrick. James is under middle name."

"Does the date of birth and descriptive data match with the deceased?"

"Yes. It's the same birthday. Same height. Same race. His weight was lower."

"We all were thinner in our twenties, I suspect. On page two in the summary section, can you please read the officer's notes?"

"Objection, Your Honor." I shot up, finally finding a place where I could break up Bennett's presentation. "This is hearsay."

"Judge Cox." Peyton's voice was so damned calm, it made mine sound shrew-like. "We're not offering this report for the truth of the matter asserted. That we'll do later during the presentation of our case with proper foundation, of course. This is only offered in rebuttal to Ms....excuse me, Detective Webb's earlier assertion both in direct and cross-examination that she'd done an exhaustive search of police reports involving the deceased and my client."

"Overruled, Ms. Long. You can answer the question, Detective Webb. The jury is instructed that this isn't offered as proof of domestic violence between the parties, but rather as proof of whether the detective's investigation was as thorough as she said."

The moment my butt hit the chair I regretted my objection. It only underlined what seemed like Webb's incompetence to the jury.

"What was the question?" Webb asked, clearly flustered.

"Can you please read the brief two-sentence summary section."

"Victim Clarke called emergency dispatch in response to an assault by Walker."

"Thank you, Detective Webb," Bennett said. I thought I heard something akin to smugness in his voice. There wasn't a thing I could object to about that.

"Did you interview Mrs. Clarke's parents or sister?" he asked next.

"No."

"Would you be surprised to find that she'd disclosed the true nature of her relationship to them?"

"No."

"In your training, did you learn that often victims disclose to family and friends and even neighbors if not police?"

"Yes."

"During your investigation, did you interview Elias Phillips?"

"No."

"Would it surprise you to find out he's a family friend and also a physician who tended to Mrs. Clarke?"

"No, I guess not. I mainly focused on what I could investigate within the state of Ohio. I didn't check Pennsylvania or New York."

"Well, I guess our federal system gives us fifty states and at least five thousand counties. It's understandable that you wouldn't go beyond this county's boundaries. Thank you so much for your candor, Detective Webb. No further questions."

I stood. My mind scrambled for purchase for a way to rehabilitate the witness. I couldn't grab on to anything. I was going to have to leave the damage done. After all, their client had been standing over the body with the murder weapon. I had that. For the moment it would have to be enough.

"Redirect, Ms. Long?" Judge Cox asked.

"No, Your Honor. The prosecution rests."

"Well, then. This trial is off to a swift start. I thank all counsel for their efficiency. Let's adjourn for the day so I can attend to other matters. We'll reconvene tomorrow morning at ten a.m."

The judge instructed the jury in all the usual protocol, admonishing them not to discuss the case with each other or outside of the courtroom. Not to watch the news or read the papers. I downed the last of my drink. I was afraid to look over my shoulder to see if my boss was behind me. I needed to get to my office or get home and prepare like hell for tomorrow. I was The Riot and I needed to keep this one, this slam-dunk case, in the win column. While the jury was shuffling out, I popped three curiously strong mints into my mouth, then bit down on them—hard.

27

To say I'd been surprised when Casey had asked me to come to court today would have been a massive understatement. That said, I'd made a huge effort to rearrange my schedule. If she needed support, I wanted nothing more than to be there for her. Especially after all the havoc wrought in the last few months by Sinclair—and by extension, me.

As the jury lumbered in, I took in the gallery. Spectators were sparse. Aside from me, a few people I assumed to be from the prosecutor's office, and two or three probably related to the defendant, the rest were court watchers. Mostly retired folks who found their entertainment from the personal tragedies on public display.

"Call your first witness."

Judge Essie Cox's eyes were trained on the defense table. I glanced at my watch. It was quarter to eleven. I'd gotten here as quickly as I could, but it looked like I'd missed the defense's opening argument.

"The defense calls Elias Phillips to the stand." That was from Casey. I kind of wanted to stand up and whoop. There was my best friend, once unemployed and reviled by the legal community, standing up ready to question a witness in her first murder trial. There she was with a white-shoe lawyer as her second chair. If I wasn't here to see it in person, I might not have believed it.

For a long moment while the witness was being sworn in, I considered that. Whether I'd been taking my friend for granted. Whether I'd not seen her for who she really could be. Had I condescended to her by referring tiny matters her way? Maybe that's why she'd invited me. I tried not to stew in humiliation with how bad a friend I'd been.

Casey strode to the lectern, yellow pad firmly gripped in her left hand, the gold pen her parents had given her in her right. The baby bump in front of her leading the way. I swiveled my neck first right, then left. Neither Justin McPhee nor Ronaldo Pinheiro were here to support her. Maybe they hadn't prioritized her in their lives. Maybe neither would be a good father. I vowed right then to step up and fill whatever gap they might leave. I wanted to be the best auntie possible.

The guy who came to the stand was handsome without qualification, though it was clear that he was in early middle age. His hair was still mostly dark blond. His eyes a clear blue. His jaw was square. His clothes and his comfort in them suggested he'd never gone wanting for anything.

"Mr. Phillips, thank you for traveling here from New York City. Can you please tell the jury and the court how you know the defendant?"

"Juliana Clarke and I were friends in high school," Phillips answered.

"Did you attend the same school?"

"No. I went to Browning. It's an all-boys school on Manhattan's Upper East Side. Juliana went to Chapin, which is an all-girls school about twenty-two blocks north. The schools had dances and activities together, like school plays."

So they were from the same milieu. If these two had gotten together, married, had babies, none of us would likely be sitting here right now.

"Did you date?" Casey's voice was so kind, where once it had been strident. I wanted to confess all my sins to her. She'd gotten really good at developing a sympathetic court persona. I had to wonder if it were experience or pregnancy that had introduced subtlety into her presentation.

"I guess you could say we were high school sweethearts. But we broke up before we went to college. It was before the internet really, and long-distance relationships weren't a thing."

"What's your educational background?"

"I went to college at Stanford. Then medical school back in the city at Cornell."

"Did you reconnect with Juliana once you got back to the city?"

"Yeah...yes. I was a year ahead of her, so she was still in college in the city when I came back for medical school."

"How would you characterize your relationship after college?"

"We were just friends. We had coffee, dinner, that kind of thing. I was engaged at that point. Then she was dating Kendrick Walker and in and out of the city because she was in school in Philadelphia."

"Thank you. Let's turn your attention to 1987, about twenty years ago. Did you have occasion to run into Juliana Clarke?"

"I'm not sure if 'run into' is the right term."

"Then, please tell the jury in your words what happened that year that was significant enough to have lodged in your memory."

"I was on call at New York Pres...Presbyterian Hospital one night when I got paged. I thought it was a patient coding, but it was Calandra Clarke."

"Can you please tell us who Calandra Clarke is?"

"She's Juliana's younger sister. She was at Chapin behind Juliana. We weren't friends, but I knew her."

"So you receive a call from Calandra."

"Right. She wanted to know if I could stop by the apartment. The Clarke family's apartment at The Osborne, she meant, after my shift. They had a...I think she called it a situation."

"Did you go?"

"I handed over my patients and left my shift early. There was something in Callie's voice that, I don't know, felt off."

"Objection to the witness's characterization."

"Sustained," Judge Cox ruled. "Mr. Phillips, we'll need you to testify only to what you saw or witnessed with your senses. There's no need to speculate on people's feelings. The jury will disregard."

"What happened when you arrived at the Clarke apartment?"

"Juliana's mother kind of ushered me in. She wanted to know if I could help Juliana. I told her it wasn't like some old black-and-white TV show or something. I didn't carry a medical bag with me. But I'd certainly have a look at Juliana, and if medical intervention was necessary, I'd steer them in the right direction."

"By steer them, you meant...?"

"I'd tell them if she needed to be admitted to the hospital and which facility may be best depending."

"Got it. What happened next?"

"I went to Juliana. She was in her childhood bedroom. I asked her what was wrong. She said that she'd been hurt in a fight with Kendrick Walker."

"Objection. Hearsay."

"Sustained. Counselor," Judge Cox admonished.

"Mr. Phillips. You can only answer about what you said or saw. Did you examine Mrs. Clarke?"

"Yes. Based on her answers to my questions, I did an exam."

"What did you conclude from your examination?"

"That two of her lower ribs were fractured."

"Did you recommend she go to the hospital or otherwise seek out medical care?"

"I did. It's what I'd have recommended for anyone in my family. She refused."

"What did you do after she refused?"

"I gave her advice on what to look for—extreme pain, shortness of breath, this kind of crunchy sound when she moved. But I told her that the fracture didn't feel too bad from my examination and it would probably heal in a year or less. I had her mom call their family doc for a prescription for some pain meds, stuff that's over the counter now, and recommended bed rest."

"In your opinion, what was the source of the injury?"

"It presented like someone had kicked her in the chest or hit her with something hard."

"Objection, Your Honor. He can't testify that Kendrick Walker kicked her. He wasn't there to witness any violence between the defendant and the deceased."

"I didn't suggest that, and neither did the witness, Your Honor," Casey said, one hundred percent correct. Long had jumped the gun on that one. "We stayed well within the bounds of the evidentiary rules."

"That they did, Ms. Long. Overruled."

"When was the next time you lent your expertise to help Juliana Clarke?" Casey asked Phillips.

"A couple of years later, I got the same kind of phone call as before. But this time from Juliana's mom."

"Did you do another examination?"

"Yes. Juliana had flown in from London and she was complaining of pretty bad foot pain."

"What did you conclude?"

"That she'd broken a toe. Her injury was consistent with her story about being injured on the London underground train. I'd seen the same kind of thing from our own subway system in New York."

"What did you do?"

"I taped up her toes. Using one toe to splint another to prevent injury."

"At this point, what was the source of these injuries?"

"She said they came from Kendrick Walker."

"Objection."

"We're not offering it for the truth of the statement, Your Honor."

"Then why are you asking Mr. Phillips these questions? These would be more appropriate for the person who is claiming to have sustained these injuries," Judge Cox pointed out.

This put Casey in a corner. The constitution made it clear that a defendant was never required to testify on their own behalf. But the practicalities were that a jury would be dying to hear if and when Kendrick Walker had hurt the defendant. Also it was probably going to be necessary for the defendant's battered woman syndrome defense. There was only so much others could testify to.

"If you'll let me ask my next question, Your Honor, I think my intention will become clear."

"Ask the question."

"Mr. Phillips, while you were talking to Juliana during these two visits and during the other times from 1988, through 2006, what did you conclude?"

"That someone was hurting her. That the injuries weren't the kind that could be self-inflicted."

"Did you give her advice?"

"I gave her lots of advice."

"Like what?"

"I told her that she didn't deserve to be hit or pushed or shoved by anyone. That if that was what was happening, then she'd be best served by leaving a relationship like that. That her family was supportive, and even if she didn't want to lean on them, she could stay with me."

"Did she agree to that?"

"Unfortunately, no."

"Did you give her other advice?"

"During my ER rotation, I met a psychiatrist who was advising a patient who presented as a victim of domestic violence. He sat with that patient for hours trying to convince her to press charges. When she didn't though, he gave her another piece of advice."

"What was that?"

"Objection, Your Honor," Long said. "We're in the weeds here. What's the relevance?"

"Two questions, Your Honor."

"Go ahead, Ms. Cort."

"What did this psychiatrist recommend?"

"He gave this woman a stack of white three-by-five index cards. He told her to use a single card to make a note of each time she was physically hurt by her boyfriend. Then he said to use an index card every time she was insulted. He said to use a card each time she was put down or he drove crazy or threatened their pets or whatever."

"Why was this psychiatrist's recommendation significant?"

"When I was taping Juliana's toes together, I gave her a stack of index cards."

"Did you give her the same instruction as that doctor in the emergency room?"

Phillips nodded. "I did. She was reluctant to take them, so I modified the instruction a bit."

"How?"

"I told her that she did not need to keep the cards. The psychiatrist's idea was that this woman would mass a stack of cards and realize that maybe she should leave when she looked at the stack. Juliana was too fearful to keep notes in the house she shared with Ken Walker, so I told her that she could send the cards to me."

"Did she? Did she send you those cards?"

"Yes."

Casey walked to the defense table and reached into her litigation bag.

"Objection, Your Honor. None of this was included in discovery."

"Approach," Judge Cox said, but she didn't cover the microphone. No one said anything, so like the jurors, I kept my eyes on Casey.

"Casey, you did not turn this over to the defense."

"Not true, Your Honor. I sent a copy of the note cards to the prosecutor's office in late October or early November."

"Ms. Long?" Judge Cox sifted through the court's file. "I have them here."

"One second, Your Honor."

Long strode to the prosecutor's table, her back stiff with anger. She sorted through some stuff. She lifted some photocopies and waved them.

"Step back, Ms. Cort." Casey came away from the bench. "Ask your question," the judge ordered.

"Mr. Phillips, again I ask you. Did she send you those cards?"

"Yes, she did."

Casey retrieved five stacks of small envelops from her bag. She made five different trips from the defense table to Elias Phillips on the witness stand. She put a stack in front of him each and every time.

"Your Honor, these are marked as defense exhibits A through CCCCCCCCC. That's nine C's."

"Mr. Phillips, can you please tell me how many cards you have in front of you?"

"I never counted."

"Do you think it would be fair to say that there are at least two hundred cards there?"

"That's fair. She sent about one a month for the last eighteen years."

"One a month for the last eighteen years? That's a lot." I had to give it to my best friend's skill. Her repetition of his answer as a question was like underlining, boldfacing, and italicizing the point.

"Did you open all of the envelopes?"

"Yes."

"After opening and reading the contents, what did you conclude?"

"That Juliana should probably have left her husband."

"Did you share that with the defendant?"

"I did."

"What was her response?"

"That she loved her daughter more than herself. That she was going to stick it out for the sake of her daughter."

Before Casey could turn it over to Long for cross-examination, I stood and strode from the courtroom. For a long moment, I lingered in the hall while the muted voices slipped through the space between the double doors, and at that moment I got it. Casey thought I was like Juliana, that I was somehow the same as this woman who'd been subject to years and years of abuse. That Sinclair was at all like Kendrick Walker was laughable. My heart filled with shame. I'd been so bloody stupid. So damned naïve.

Without a backward glance, I stalked away from the courtroom and pulled my phone from my bag. I'd walked away from love and now I needed to do anything in my power to get it back.

28

"The defense calls Doctor Edmund Holland to the stand."

Bennett stood, buttoned, and waited patiently while our expert witness came into the courtroom, walked through the gallery, and took a seat on the stand. He was a picture-perfect expert. Male. Salt-and-pepper hair. Gray suit. Blue bow tie. The kind of person who appeared on 60 Minutes or as a pundit on cable news, innocuous but seemingly authoritative.

After Dr. Holland was sworn, my co-counsel took his place at the lectern.

"Dr. Holland, can you please give us your educational background?"

"I completed my undergraduate degree in biology at the University of Michigan in Ann Arbor. My master's work was in clinical psychology at Indiana University at

Bloomington. I completed my doctorate work there as well."

"Can you tell the jury about your post-doctoral work?"

"I completed a two-year program in family forensics at Washington Square Institute of Psychotherapy and Mental Health in New York City."

"What is family forensics?"

"It's a specialty area that focuses on the place where family psychology, forensic psychology, and the legal system come together."

"Would it be accurate to say that certification gives you the expertise to testify about family dynamics?"

"Yes, specifically in two areas. The first is child custody disputes. The second is family violence."

"What training have you had specifically about intimate partner violence and what the Ohio statutes refer to as battered woman syndrome?"

"I completed both Michigan's and Ohio's Integrated Domestic Violence Court Training Programs."

Bennett turned from Dr. Holland to face Judge Cox full-on.

"Your Honor, pursuant to Ohio Rule of Evidence 702, I submit that Dr. Holland be qualified as an expert witness as it pertains to family psychology and battered woman syndrome."

"Any objection from the prosecution?"

"We stipulate to his expertise, Your Honor," Long said.

"Thank you for keeping this running smoothly, counselors. You can examine the witness, Mr. Bennett."

"Dr. Holland, what is battered woman syndrome?"

Our expert got comfortable. Wiggled his butt back into the stiff wooden chair. From our prep sessions, I knew that

Holland was about to deliver a long-winded explanation littered with technical terminology. I hoped Bennett was able to break it up and keep it interesting for the jury. We didn't have a television editing suite or cable news host to keep it engaging.

After working together for these last weeks, I would be the first to say that Bennett was a good lawyer. His main flaw, at least in this arena, was that he was missing a certain level of street smarts. Bennett's cases had mostly been complex litigation in federal court. Common pleas was a different beast. Juries got bored. Judges got bored. Keeping it moving had been my main contribution to his courtly and professional style of trial lawyering.

"Battered woman or women's syndrome is an umbrella term psychologists use for a range of symptoms abuse victims suffer."

"What causes this syndrome?"

"A history of abuse at the hands of her partner. Usually it's a long history. I haven't seen a woman strike out or strike back after a single incident. It's something that develops over years."

"What develops?"

"BWS is really a subcategory of post-traumatic stress disorder."

"What we used to call combat fatigue?"

"Yes, also shell shock. PTSD was first identified in 1980 in the third edition of the Diagnostic and Statistical Manual of Mental Disorders. What we call the DSM three."

"Would it be fair to say that was a legacy of the Vietnam War and veterans suffering once home?"

"Yes. That was the genesis of its inclusion by the American Psychiatry Association which publishes the manual."

"How do battered women fit in?"

"It's the same in a lot of ways to domestic violence victims and soldiers. Exposure to continued violence and also the threat of that violence wears on a person, and in this case, women. First, she's hit. There's the physical impact, but also the trauma associated with being hurt by someone who loves you or claims to. Often women feel the need to protect their children, but aren't successful.

"Like troops in the jungle, they are always on the alert. That constant state of arousal wears on a woman, her psyche and her nervous system. Then there are the intrusive thoughts and memories of the violence that occurred. Being hit or beaten or watching your kids or pets being abused has an almost irreversible impact on the brain.

"On the other end, though, are the coping behaviors, numbing emotionally whether that's through the use of drugs or alcohol or something else, like food. Often these women don't have a social safety net because the batterer has usually isolated them from their friends and family."

"In light of the framework of the diagnosis that you shared, did you examine Juliana Clarke?"

"Yes, I met with her."

"Would you say that she displays the same symptoms or traits that you've described?"

"Yes, to a degree. Though she appears to be quite dissociative and numb."

"Why is that?"

"It appears to be this particular victim's coping mechanism."

"Is that still harmful to the victim?" Bennett asked.

"Yes. It's less harmful to others than alcohol or drug use are. But it still affects the child or children as well as the victim herself."

"Let's turn to the self-defense aspect of battered woman's syndrome. Why might a woman act out when there is no specific and immediate threat?"

"It goes back to something I said earlier. Very often women in abusive relationships are hyperaware of cues that indicate they or their children may be harmed. It's not something that someone outside the relationship would necessarily see."

"What are some examples?"

"The man coming home drunk or maybe silently drinking in the living room. That may be a cue for him becoming violent when he reaches a certain level of intoxication. It may be something like him coming in and slamming doors or stomping. That may be an indication of anger and impending violence. It can sometimes be as subtle as a look."

"After speaking with the defendant, do you know what the trigger may have been on the night of September second?"

"Juliana heard her husband say something to their daughter, Sienna, about her mother coming to rescue her. That kind of phrase usually presaged violence."

"In those situations where violence feels imminent for the victim of abuse, what happens?"

"In these kinds of cases, the victims, finally pushed to the brink—and everyone's brink is different—lash out. They do what they can to stop the violence they think is coming their way."

"Even if, in that moment, the perpetrator may not have been violent?"

"Even then. There are cases where the abuser falls asleep and is killed. But this is not that case. Juliana heard threatening words. In this case, she was pushed back, and not necessarily physically, toward the kitchen counter where she bumped her hip. Given her past experiences, it wasn't a leap to believe that he'd hurt her or her daughter again."

"Thank you, Dr. Holland. Your testimony has been illuminating. Your witness."

While Bennett gathered up his stack of papers from the lectern, only to be replaced by Long, I turned back to the gallery. Lulu wasn't there. I'd wanted her to hear not only from Elias Phillips, but from Dr. Holland as well. I wanted her to know that what was happening to her, had happened to her, could have long-reaching effects if she didn't do something right now to shut it down.

I did not want to be representing my best friend on a murder charge, or worse, the nightmare of being called to identify her body should Sinclair's behavior follow its path to a likely conclusion.

29

Nicole
December 18, 2007

"Dr. Holland, thank you so much for your illuminating testimony. You testified that women who experience domestic violence can be triggered to act out violently based upon their history of abuse. Is that correct?"

"Yes."

"You've been published in quite a number of journals, yes? And one such journal was Frontiers in Psychiatry, is that correct?"

"I had an article about expert testimony in child custody cases."

"So we're in agreement that it's a legitimate and well-respected journal that is at the forefront of publishing research on trauma and trauma responses, is that a fair assessment?"

"Yes, I'd say so. It's a preeminent publication." Dr. Holland almost preened. I wanted to say something about how pride goeth before a fall, but I didn't think he'd be interested in my interpretation of biblical quotations from the Proverbs.

"So I was over at the Cleveland Clinic library a few weeks ago," I started, trying to use my folksy Southern tone that usually appealed to juries. "I was having a look at this journal and I came across an article that talks about PTSD and its likely causes. Let me read you the first line: 'Over seventy percent of the general population report experiencing or witnessing a traumatic event that would qualify under criterion 'A' one of the diagnostic criteria for post-traumatic stress disorder as defined by the Diagnostic and Statistical Manual of Mental Disorders.' Would you say that statistic is accurate?"

"Yes, but that's all events including exposure to seeing death, being threatened by the possibility of death, sexual violence, and of course interpersonal violence of the kind I testified to earlier. But not all of the people who are exposed develop PTSD."

"Well, let's talk about that. What percentage of the American population is estimated to have some form of post-traumatic stress disorder or PTSD?"

"Somewhere between two and fifteen."

"So let's do some rough back-of-the-envelope math. The population of the United States stands at about three hundred million give or take. Two percent of that is six million and fifteen percent is forty-five million. That's a lot of people running around with PTSD. If we just take Ohio, that's a spread of two hundred thirty thousand to one million seven hundred twenty-eight thousand. Still a huge number. Let's just narrow it down to Cuyahoga County. Now we're talking from twenty-six thousand to one hundred ninety-five thousand. That's a lot of walking wounded people for sure, wouldn't you say?"

"I guess I'd have to agree with that."

"Since I do work in the county prosecutor's office, I do have access to murder statistics. So far this year in this county there have been a total of one hundred six murders. The year isn't done yet, but let's just assume a few more holiday killings for good measure because someone thinks the ham is too salty." I waited a beat. Nothing from the jury that sounded like laughter. I moved on. "Here's a copy of the stats from the Ohio Office of Criminal Justice Services. You're used to reading statistics, would you agree with the number I've read?"

"Yes, that looks to be accurate."

"Currently, I'm the acting head of Major Crimes in Cuyahoga County's prosecutor's office, so I have more exposure, shall we say, to the reasons behind homicides than most people. Would you be surprised if I told you that nearly one hundred percent of the perpetrators of these crimes had some kind of traumatic background?"

"No."

"What kinds of traumas, in your experience as a forensic psychologist, do killers suffer?"

"It runs the gambit. Physical abuse at the hands of their parents or caregivers or even sometimes their siblings. Sexual abuse from family or strangers. Witnessing violence inside their family or in their neighborhoods. Exposure to particularly gruesome traffic accidents. Also exposure to violent media, traditional and now even online can play a part."

"So if I'm beaten or raped or exposed to the sight of something like you described above, I can suffer from PTSD?"

"Yes, that's fair."

"What does that look like, PTSD exposure?"

"The victims suffer from re-experiencing the memories as if they were happening in the moment, also flashbacks. Sometimes nightmares. They may have a stronger than usual startle response. They're often hypervigilant, like looking around every corner for a bogeyman where none might exist."

"And?"

"They work hard to protect themselves, like ways to forget about what happened. Sometimes they compartmentalize or disassociate, or even have amnesia. Also there's substantial substance abuse among these folks, from alcohol abuse to use and addiction to more dangerous or at least illegal substances."

"That sounds awful. I genuinely hope that some of these people get the help they deserve, truly. Unfortunately that's not the sole aim of our criminal justice system. So if a vast majority of the killers I mentioned earlier, just over one hundred, also have this kind of background, how many would you expect to be able to get away with murder?"

"Very few, if they're guilty."

"How many, do you think, could effectively argue that the trauma suffered entitled them to a not-guilty verdict by reason of self-defense?"

"Probably fewer."

"The answer, at least for this year, stands at zero. Despite all of what you said above being true, we have a system that requires people to be accountable for their actions no matter the background that brought them to the point of killing. Do you agree that's fair?"

"It may be fair, but it may not be right."

"But for over two hundred years that's the constitutional system we've agreed to. No fu rther questions, Your Honor."

30

Casey

December 19, 2007

"The defense calls Juliana Hope Clarke to the stand," I said, then stood. Today I was wearing a maternity dress. I'd almost stretched another suit around my belly. The ones from my heavier days would have done the trick. Bennett had insisted though, that jury sympathies would be with a visibly pregnant lawyer—and by extension to our erstwhile client.

Along with my rose blush dress, my only jewelry besides tiny gold studs in my ears was the cross my parents had given me for Holy Communion. I fingered that as I stood and got comfortable. If there was one thing I disliked about criminal practice, it was an unpredictable client.

Unsophisticated clients tended to keep quiet, so afraid of punishment they were once they realized how far they'd walked into the justice system.

Guilty clients understood better than most their need to exercise their constitutional rights and protections. But the Juliana-type clients were the most unpredictable. I never knew what would come out of their mouths despite hours of preparation and buckets of warnings.

Rubbing the smooth metal of the crucifix, I sent up a quick prayer to a God I wasn't sure existed. Then I got on with it because no matter what happened today or tomorrow or whenever the jury came back with a verdict, it wasn't my life on the line. When this murder trial was over, I'd go home, have my baby, and plan the next crucial steps of my own life.

After my client was sworn in and I dispensed with the preliminary questions, I looked her in the eye for a few long seconds.

"Mrs. Clarke, may I call you Juliana?"

"Yes."

"How did you meet Kendrick Walker."

There was such a long pause, I wondered if my client was going to mutiny right there on the stand.

"We met in architecture school in Philadelphia."

"What year would that have been?"

"1984."

"What brought you together?"

"There were about six hundred students in the program. Two hundred for each year. Our classes were structured, meaning that we didn't have any choice of what to take, so we were all in class together every day of the week. The classes were mostly huge, but we had small discussion groups in our history and theory class. We met there, I guess."

"When did you start dating?"

"After some party, I think. I mean, this was over twenty years ago. But my best memory was that our design studio professor had a party at his house. Ken kind of cornered me and talked to me the whole night. Then he asked me out for the next weekend."

"Did you want to go out with him?"

"I don't know. I mean, I hadn't had a boyfriend since college and I may have been a little bit lonely. He wasn't exactly my type, but my friends said I needed to expand my dating pool because I wasn't able to have a successful relationship with my 'type' of guy."

"Was he not your type because he was Black?" I had to ask that one. I did not want the jury to think she was racist.

"No. God, no, that's not it at all really. I mean, he was tall and good-looking and all of that. Other than Elias Phillips, I'd only dated artists. Visual, musical, a guy from the Tisch school who wanted to make movies. Ken was this guy from Washington, D.C. His mom was a public-school teacher and his dad worked for the federal government. It was just a lot different from my own upbringing. I'd always imagined I'd marry someone more like me, I guess."

"How would you describe the beginning of your relationship?"

"It was kind of overwhelming in a way. I'd never dated anyone who, I don't know, pursued me."

"What do you mean by pursuit?"

"He called me every morning even when we had class together. He called me every night before bed. He constantly complimented me. Brought me flowers. Took me to dinner. Said that we were soul mates and twin flames. Even when I wanted to take things slow, he didn't listen.

"I thought I was being swept off my feet. He gave up the lease to his apartment and stored his stuff at mine over that first summer. When we got back to school the second year, he never got an apartment. He talked about how much money we could save on rent if he just moved in. I let him."

"Would you say the beginning of your relationship was good?"

"Back then I would have, I guess. In retrospect, of course not, no."

"What makes you say no with hindsight?"

"It was all a façade...a manipulation."

"Objection, Your Honor. She's characterizing a dead man's actions."

"Sustained," Judge Cox ruled. "Ma'am, the court is a bit like an episode of Get Smart. Just the facts, please."

One older juror laughed. The rest, I suspect, didn't get the joke.

"What makes you use the word manipulation?" My question got the word out twice and that's what was important.

"In the beginning, I felt like I was on a pedestal. Like I could do no wrong. He always complimented me on how beautiful I was. How smart I was. How ridiculously talented I was. Those were his words, by the way. How I was smarter than everyone in our class and how successful I'd be."

"But that stopped?"

"On a dime. It was kind of like someone had flipped a switch. One day I was the best thing since sliced bread and the next it was like he couldn't stand the air I breathed."

"How so?"

"I wasn't as pretty as I used to be. My hair was limp and greasy-looking. I was putting on too much weight. I wasn't as talented as I liked to think I was and maybe I should just go back to being a starving artist because architecture was the marriage of art and design and I was excelling at neither. Maybe I thought I was smart because my father was a college professor, but he was the one with the brains, not me."

"That sounds horrible." It wasn't a question, but I knew Long wouldn't object. She would come across like a monster.

"It was truly demoralizing because in between each insult, and they weren't in a string like that, he would tell me that he loved me. That he wanted the best for me. That this was all just constructive criticism which would help me be a better person."

"What else bothered you?"

"He was always accusing me of flirting with other students in our school, or guys on the tram. He would sometimes go through my notebook or backpacks to see if I was getting notes from other guys."

"School notes?"

"No, love notes."

"Okay, let's turn your attention to May of 1987. Did you and Ken both graduate from the architecture program?"

"Yes."

"Where did you go after that?"

"We came here to Cleveland."

"Why?"

"Ken got a job offer with Fernsby. It's an internationally known architecture firm. We'd hoped to be placed in London or New York, but this opportunity for Cleveland came up and we...he took it."

"Did you want to come to Cleveland?"

"I was a little worried about being so far away from my family in New York and my support system, but Ken said it was too good an opportunity to pass up."

"How so?"

"Fernsby was one of the final firms in the running to build the Rock and Roll Hall of Fame. They didn't get that commission, but it was just at the beginning of the downtown Cleveland building boom, so it made sense."

"What about you? What kind of job were you planning?"

"I had an offer to work at I.M. Pei and Associates, but it was in New York City and Ken didn't want to do long distance."

"I.M. Pei, as in the actual designer of the Rock and Roll Hall of Fame in addition to many famous buildings across the world?"

"Yes, he's one of the most well-known architects in the world. He started out at our school in Philadelphia and has a soft spot for the students there."

"What were you to do instead?"

"It was kind of important to Ken that I support his career. So we agreed that I could pursue my painting and he would work to make this new Fernsby outpost a success."

"Can you please tell the jury about the incident that led to you seeking refuge with your family in 1987?"

Clarke leaned forward, opened her mouth as if to speak, closed it. She looked like a scared rabbit. We'd come to, I guess, the part that she never wanted to revisit. Probably never wanted to rehash in front of a prosecutor trying to put her in jail, the jury who would decide her guilt, and the family who would witness her shame.

"Your Honor, can we take a brief recess?"

Judge Cox, thank the Lord, was not without empathy. She promised us fifteen minutes, which in essence would mean a half hour. Judges were slow. Juries were slower.

Juliana Clarke returned to the defense table. The jury stood and went back to their jury room. Nicole Long wasn't moving from counsel table, which was entirely too close to ours. There was no place for private conversation. On the other hand, no sheriff's deputy was going to allow me to take my client to the hallway where she could roam free and escape the confines of custody.

"I need the attorney room," I said to the deputy that looked the most friendly.

I'd never have said it out loud, but I was glad that my client was an unassuming white woman, because he nodded after only a moment's hesitation. I glanced at Peyton Bennett, fully expecting the questioning rise of his eyebrows. My headshake was as definitive as I could make it with minimal head movement. This was one I think I needed to do alone. Clarke and I were in a choreographed dance that only the two of us could complete.

Hand on her upper arm, I marched my client to the hall, then immediately into one of the rooms designated for private and confidential conversation. The moment the door was closed, I spoke because there was no more time.

"There's no second chance. I cannot imagine how hard it is to talk about this. To talk about your life. To talk about how your husband may have hurt you in secret, or in front of your daughter. I have a friend who is going through this exact thing. Not to be glib, but it looks like a hellish thing to be in and get out of.

"All that said, your life is on the line here. You getting up there on the stand and telling the truth can be, might be, even will be the difference between you walking out of here by Christmas or you spending much of the rest of your life behind bars. That's somewhere you've been for months, so I'm sure by now you understand it's not pleasant and will not be more so in Dayton or Marysville. If you want to spend time with your daughter and truly get on with the new life you were trying to build, I strongly suggest that you tell the truth. You need to say everything that you haven't so far. This will be your only chance."

Clarke simply nodded. I opened the door and a deputy was there to escort my client back to the courtroom. I paused a beat and gathered myself. I did a quick internal pep talk convincing myself that I hadn't bitten off more than I could chew, that I was up to the job. That with a client who did nothing more than tell the whole truth and nothing but the truth, I could win this case and for once see justice served.

"You're doing a great job up there," a voice said.

I'd been so in my own head that I'd missed my friend Lulu's presence in the hall.

"I thought you'd left."

She shook her head. "I took a few days off work. I made partner, remember?"

"Oh my gosh, that's right. Congrats. I never—"

"I didn't give you the chance. No matter. That's something for later. They can't fire me. The holidays are coming up. Hanukkah was last week, but I don't think anyone's paying close attention. I needed the time to figure out what comes next. You invited me, so I came to see it through."

I didn't have more than a minute, if the noise coming from behind the tall wood doors was any indication, but I felt like I had to say something. What that was, I couldn't even begin to formulate words for. It was like I'd used them...was using them all to defend a client who was acting like she really didn't want defending.

"Thanks. It means a lot to have your support," was what ultimately came out of my mouth. Those overly formal words weren't the exact right ones, but it was all I had.

"You need to get back."

Five minutes later when everyone was exactly where they had been before the break, I asked my question again.

"Mrs. Clarke, can you please tell the jury about the incident that led you to seek refuge with your family. From 1987."

"We...Ken and I had been in Cleveland for like two weeks. We had this apartment on Mayfield Road. That night, it was a Monday, I'd finally finished unpacking, but hadn't really had time to cook. So when Ken got home, I suggested we go out for dinner."

"Where did you go?"

"Wings N Things. I...I don't know if it's still there, but it was on Coventry. We lived a five-minute walk from Coventry Village."

"What happened once you went into this eating establishment?"

"Actually, you can eat there, but it was really a two-level sports bar. So we ordered wings, then went upstairs because it was quieter. There were dart boards and a pool table. Ken thought we should play."

"And did you...play?"

"Yes. I was solids and he was stripes. I went first and sunk a few balls. Then I fouled because I'd overcompensated and the cue ball bounced. It landed on Ken's foot."

"Was he injured?"

"The way he howled you'd have thought so, but no. He didn't require medical care then or later."

"What happened next?"

"So he goes to sink a shot because the foul meant it was his turn. He missed, so it's my turn again. I sink all my balls and the eight ball."

"I only have a limited understanding of the rules of pool, but was it fair to say that you won?"

"Yes. So I offer to do a best of three after we eat, but Ken didn't answer. When the waitress put down the food and beers on the table and went downstairs, he picked up the pool stick. I was like, oh, can't we eat first? Then he swung the stick and it caught me in my midsection. I lost my breath."

"Was there anyone there who saw that?"

"Not that I remember. I looked at him and his face was so calm."

"Did he say anything?"

I pinned Long with a look daring her to object, to throw a greater spotlight on her victim's bad behavior. The prosecutor's blink was slow as she thought better of it. I turned back to my client.

"He said that I'd made him do it."

"What happened after that?"

"I stood up as best I could, making sure I could breathe and then I kind of hobbled downstairs and went home. I called my dad. He and my mom and my sister came and got me. I don't know how they did it, but they were there the next morning with the car."

"Did you go with them?"

"They packed up my stuff, like in bags and a couple of the boxes. They loaded it in the car and drove me home."

"Did Ken say anything?"

"He'd come home with all the food bagged up that night. I'd just laid myself down on the couch—a futon, actually. I'd put it down and I just lay there. He asked if I was mad. I didn't say anything. It was just quiet when my parents were there. He mostly stayed in the bedroom. Though I think he did ask if they needed help. But it was just a lot of tense silence."

With our client on a roll, I got her to talk about how her parents had rented an apartment and offered to help her with a fresh start. As I paused to take the testimony in a different direction, I snuck a glance over my shoulder at Lulu. I could see there was a time—this crucial moment—when a victim of violence could probably make a clean break. It was a very narrow window. Juliana Clarke hadn't taken it. I hope Lulu did.

"How long did you stay in New York City?"

"Not that long. A few weeks maybe."

"Isn't it the case that your family found an apartment for you, so that you could stay in New York and start from scratch?"

"Yes. They did. It was in DUMBO." Realizing for the first time that maybe the jury had a different perspective, she explained, "It's a part of Manhattan near the Brooklyn Bridge. It was an inexpensive neighborhood at the time."

"Did you ever move in?"

"No."

"Why not?"

"I was going to. I was ready to break it off. I'd even convinced the architecture firm to renew their offer. When I called Ken to ask him to ship the rest of my things, he was so full of apologies. He spun out this story about how he'd messed up, but that we were destined to be together. That he really couldn't tackle a new city without me."

"So you went back?"

"Yes."

"What was your family's reaction?"

"They were shocked, worried. They really tried to get me to come back to New York for the next few months."

"You didn't go?"

"Ken said we needed to make things perfect. That we needed to put down roots. He needed to prove he was serious."

"What did that mean? How did he prove he was serious?"

"He went out and found a house. Put down a deposit for a place in the Onaway neighborhood in Shaker Heights. It was a huge gesture."

"Did you move again? You had just moved."

"He took care of everything. Found a tenant to sub-lease. Closed on the house. His only stipulation was that I change our number after we moved."

"Why?"

"He said my family was interfering with our future happiness."

"So you went along with it?"

"Yes."

"And everything was hunky-dory after that?"

Clarke's head tilted this way, then that. "Yes, until it wasn't."

"What happened to break your spell of happiness?"

"We flew to London for a few weeks while Fernsby was trying to get this commission for a building there. I was upset that Ken didn't have time for me. He was working seven days a week and more than ten hours most days. After the first few weeks, I'd seen all the friends from high school and college who lived there, but they had their own jobs, their own lives.

"I'd already visited most of the museums that interested me. I wasn't painting because Ken said it would be too messy in the corporate apartment, and there'd be no way for the oils to dry and for me to get them home anyways. So there wasn't anything to do. I kept pestering him to give me a day. Just a single day for him to play hooky and go to the British Museum."

"Did he agree to go?"

"Grudgingly. Ken was kind of fuming the entire time we took the train from Knightsbridge to the stop near the museum.

"When we got to the stop, he pulled me kind of abrupt-ly to get off and my boot got stuck in the gap between the train car and the platform. He was impatient and didn't look back. Fortunately some people helped me so I didn't lose my leg. I was in excruciating pain all day, but Ken just gave me the silent treatment. When we got back to the apartment, I waited until he went back into the office and then got a taxi to Heathrow. I called my parents and they somehow got me a ticket to JFK."

"So you went back to New York City again?"

"Yes."

"And your parents were willing to help you, even though you hadn't spoken to them in many months?"

"Yes."

"Did you stay in New York this time?"

"For a few days, maybe a week or so. Elias, he came and taped up my toe. He said it was broken. He begged me to stay. He was engaged by then, but he offered to break up with his fiancée if that's what was needed for me to give him another chance."

"But you didn't."

"No, but...I wish I had—not broken up his relationship, but mine."

"What happened after that?"

"Ken flew in from London. He showed up at my parents' place with something like two dozen red roses and an engagement ring straight from Tiffany's on Fifth Avenue. He apologized. Said he knew he'd done wrong. Was ready to go all in."

"He proposed marriage this time?"

"Yes."

"You said yes?"

"I did."

"How long after his proposal did you get married?"

"Two or three days? The time it took to get back to Cleveland."

"What day did you get married?"

"Friday the thirteenth."

"How many other incidents would you say there were over the twenty years of your marriage?"

"I don't know."

I went to defense table. Bennett, having been prepared for my dramatic close to Juliana's testimony about her history, handed me the stacks of notecards.

"These are the notecards Elias Phillips testified that he received from you starting in 1998 and ending in 2006. Did you write the note on each card?"

"Yes."

"Can you open any of these cards and read it?"

Clarke picked up an envelope on the top of a random pile. The envelopes had all neatly been cut open by something sharp. I imagined Elias Phillips's library fitted with a fireplace and an engraved opener. She fingered it while the courtroom sat in anticipatory silence.

With a sigh that sounded over the microphone as a hiss, she slipped her fingers inside the envelope. A white three-by-five notecard came out.

"May twenty-second, 2002. Ken says him slamming my fingers in the glove compartment was accidental. He was angry because I'd adjusted the car vent away from him. He said the driver gets to choose the air and temperature. Last week, when he was the passenger, he said the passenger gets to choose. My fingers are only bruised. They'll heal in a week or two."

"Can you choose and read another?"

"Objection. Your Honor, may we approach?" Long asked, ending her silent streak.

Judge Essie Cox covered her own microphone. I came from behind the lectern. Long was at the bench before me, though I was closer. I was thinking she was drinking way too much coffee.

It was only when I got closer and saw her chewing on a mint like her life depended on it, that I had a niggling thought coffee wasn't the only thing fueling her.

"Ms. Long?"

"Your Honor, I'm going to object to this line of questioning."

"This line, Your Honor," I interjected, "my client's very self-defense claim is based upon her being a battered woman. We have here before us contemporaneous writings that confirm the very basis of the defense."

"While that's true," Judge Cox hedged, "this is nothing more than cumulative evidence. If the defendant were to read every single one of those cards, not only would it eat up precious court time right before the holidays—"

I winced at her use of the holidays. I could not imagine any court record where an appeals court would find that Christmas trumped a person's constitutional rights. The ruling coming would be bad and good in equal measure. I silently hoped an appeal wouldn't be necessary. Which it wouldn't be if we won an acquittal from the jury.

"—it would be prejudicial. What jury wouldn't find abuse when she read two hundred more examples like the one she just picked."

"I think the prosecutor's argument proves the point. I need each of these read out so that, one, there's no doubt in the jury's mind that abuse did occur between my client and the deceased, and two, her later actions were therefore legally justified."

"Ms. Cort, you had me until the last sentence. It will be up to the jury to decide justification. That said, I understand your need to prove your affirmative defense, but Rule 403, subpart B does give me the discretion over matters like this. The defendant reading the notecards into the record during testimony would be cumulative and therefore prejudicial. However, I will allow their admission into evidence over any later prosecution objection for the jury to consider during deliberation. Now step back."

31

In that pink getup, Casey Cort moved like an Energizer bunny that had lost its batteries.

After Judge Cox had ruled in my favor and prohibited the defendant reading some two hundred notecards documenting her mistreatment, Cort removed the envelopes and placed them on counsel table, ten at a time. Took her twenty trips to move the evidence. I knew if I objected, Cort's process would grind to a halt and draw even more attention to the cards.

I practically had to sit on my hands to keep my mouth shut. Finally, with the envelopes moved to a towering stack on defense table, Cort continued. I tried not to get up and shove them somewhere because I knew one swift push from the courtroom door and they'd go flying everywhere, drawing more attention where I didn't want it.

Finally, Cort continued her direct examination of her client.

"Mrs. Clarke, do you need water?" Cort asked.

"No, I'm okay."

"Let's turn your attention to the night your husband, Ken Walker, died."

"Okay."

I looked directly at the jury. Not an eye was on me. Each and every pair was trained on Juliana Clarke.

"What prompted you to drive over to your house? The home you shared with Ken Walker for sixteen years."

"My daughter, Sienna, sent a text saying she needed a ride home."

"Can you read the text you received to the court?"

Cort handed Clarke a printout of the phone's text message conversations from the night of the murder. I pulled out my copy.

"Daddy's being crazy. Please come get me," Clarke read.

"By home, did you mean the apartment in Shaker Square?"

"Yes."

"Why did your daughter move out with you as opposed to staying in her childhood home?"

"Objection. Calls for speculation," I said. I did not want the jury to continue to hear how horrible Kendrick Walker was. Sympathy for my victim gave me a much greater chance at a guilty verdict.

"Sustained."

"I'll rephrase. When did your daughter move in with you?"

"When her father's new girlfriend moved in."

"What time did Sienna send the text?"

"It says here"—Clarke studied the paper in front of her—"six oh three p.m."

"What time did you text her about your arrival?"

"Six ten p.m."

"While parts of Cleveland Heights and Shaker Square are not so far apart, seven minutes is an awful small window. How did you get there so quickly?"

"I'd been painting at Horseshoe Lake Park. I was losing the light and had been packing up my trunk."

"What happened next?"

"I slammed the trunk door and drove over. It's only a two-minute trip or so. I pulled into the drive at the back of the house and waited."

"How long did you wait?"

"About five minutes, I guess. When Sienna didn't come out, I texted her to let her know I was there since she might not have expected me so soon."

"Did she come out?"

"No, but I could hear raised voices."

"What did you decide to do?"

"I was worried about Sienna, so I turned off the car and went into the house."

"You still had a key?"

"The back door was open. I stepped through the mud-room and into the kitchen."

"What did you see when you walked into the kitchen?"

"Ken and his new girlfriend yelling at my daughter. All three were standing on different steps. They were accusing her of stealing."

"What did you do?"

"I told Ken that my daughter wasn't there to steal her own stuff. She was just there to get some things she wanted to take to college that she'd forgotten. Sienna was having a hard time packing for school when half of her stuff was in one place and half in the other."

Though I knew better, I couldn't help but shift forward a little in my seat. We were coming to it now. When defendants went to trial, I was usually in the dark as to what really happened. Anyone who made it in front of judge and jury had exercised their right to remain silent. If they hadn't, we usually had a confession and a plea, and they walked themselves right into jail.

There was a pause before Casey asked the next question. Even though I could only see her back, the shift in her body posture was not about pregnancy, but very much about the import of what was on the cusp.

"What happened after you spoke with your estranged husband?"

"He started yelling at me, accusing me of parental alienation. Saying that I was trying to turn Sienna against him."

"And?"

"Then his girlfriend comes all the way down the back stairs, which end directly in the kitchen near the back door. Anyway, she's yelling all the way down the stairs and at this point I seriously regret coming in because it was going to be nothing but the kind of drama Ken thrived on. So Sienna went into the study. I'm not sure why, but Monica—that's the girlfriend—was following behind her. I turned to Ken and told him it was inappropriate that any of this was going on when all our daughter had wanted to do was get her own..."

Juliana Clarke trailed off into quiet. I glanced at the jury and every single one of them, including the two alternates, were on the edge of their government-issue tweed swivel seats. Casey Cort was either an unacknowledged genius or she was shying away from the question that could determine her client's innocence or guilt.

"Mrs. Clarke, I know this is very hard, but can you please tell us what happened next."

"I'd done this dance before with Ken. He was going to continue to be angry no matter what I said, so I just backed down. Told him he was right and we were wrong and would just leave."

"And then?"

"Then he shoved me against the counter so hard that I bumped my hip and slipped. I don't remember what happened after that."

"Why don't you remember what happened immediately after your apology?"

"Because after I hit my hip, I slipped. I'd been wearing espadrilles and either my shoes were wet from being by the lake in the park or the floor was wet. Either way, I hit my head and I think I passed out."

"Think?"

"This felt the same as every other time he's hit me hard enough that I lost consciousness. When you come to sometimes it's hard to figure out that you were out."

Casey Cort paused and let that sit with the jury. It was a huge blow. I wished I could have stood up and objected, somehow thrown a grenade of some kind into the proceedings, just to tilt the scales of justice a little more my way.

"What did you observe when you came to?"

"That my hip hurt. That my head hurt. That Ken was lying on the floor near me. That there was that stupid marble thing a college friend had bought for our wedding, and it was on the floor with blood and something else on it. I didn't want to look too closely. I noticed everything was quiet, too quiet. Then Sienna was there and I told her to get in my car and go home, that I would handle whatever."

"Do you remember lifting the marble and striking your husband in the head?"

"No."

"Do you remember him hitting the counter like you did or the floor?"

"No."

"Mrs. Clarke, did you kill your husband?"

"I don't know."

"Your witness," Cort said striding back to defense table.

This was going to be the most important moment of this case, and it was looking like it was going to be the most important of my career as well. I took my time. Gathered my notes, strode to the podium ready to spin things a little bit more my way.

"Mrs. Clarke, there are quite a few notecards that were introduced into evidence. Can you tell me why you didn't call the police after that single time in Philadelphia?" I'd gone straight for the notecards. They were going to be the proverbial elephant in the jury deliberation room and I was ready to shoot it dead before it stole all the attention.

"I didn't feel comfortable calling the cops."

"If your husband was this abusive guy with not just one, but hundreds, by your count, of incidents where he hurt you, police intervention certainly would have been warranted."

"He's a Black man. When I called the police that first time, the cops were not friendly. The idea of this Black man having a relationship with me, a white woman, did not go over well. Obviously there's nothing in the report about that. Who would include it? But it gave me that sort of lynching vibe you get when watching videos about the American South at a certain time in history."

Part of me wanted to object, but of course I couldn't. She hadn't done anything objectionable other than slowly torpedo my case. The other part of me wanted to stop passing, to let the jury know that I was, according to the one-drop rule, a Black woman who'd lived in the South most of my life. There was no place for that either.

"So your discomfort was the problem?"

"Also Ken specifically asked. He said we could handle everything ourselves. I was angry with him for how he treated me, but I did not wish him death at the hands of the police."

I wanted to object to that characterization of the police. But with Casey Cort and Darlene Webb in the courtroom, they would be the first to call me a liar. I had to wonder if the specter of Marc Baldwin would forever hover over my career. That was a problem for later. For now, I had to convince a jury that damning evidence of abuse wasn't exactly that.

"You testified that you had cracked ribs after an incident at a chicken restaurant in Cleveland Heights. Is that correct?"

"Yes."

"You also testified that you'd been moving during that same time. Is that correct?"

"Yes."

"Did you have movers or did you do it yourself?"

"We rented a moving truck and drove it from Philadelphia to Cleveland."

"On what floor was your apartment?"

"Third."

"Was there an elevator in this building?"

"No. It's a prewar walkup."

"How many boxes do you think you carried?"

"Fifty? I don't know. A lot."

"Did some have books, or were otherwise heavy, or awkward?"

"Sure. We were moving from graduate school, so there were lots of textbooks. I have no experience packing and made some too heavy."

"So we have you lifting heavy boxes up three floors over quite a few hours. Would you be surprised to learn that heavy lifting or continuous repetitive motion can cause a fractured rib?" I paused long enough for Clarke to realize it was a question.

"No, I guess," she finally answered. Again the answer wasn't at all important. I wanted to give the jury an alternate possibility for her injuries.

"How do you know that it was the pool cue that cracked your ribs?"

"Objection, Your Honor," Casey groused. "Unless Ms. Long is going to call an expert on this issue, this question is way out of bounds."

"The pool cue cracked in half like I'm sure my rib did," Clarke answered before the judge did.

"Ms. Clarke," the judge scolded. "When one attorney makes an objection, I'll need to rule before you answer the question. Sustained."

Clarke nodded. A red flush was hovering around her cheeks. I thought that she may have finally been provoked to anger. I'd made my point. I'd have to trust that my question sowed seeds of doubt in Clarke's defense. I decided to leave it there. I wished I had something else that would make the defendant lash out at me or the judge, but I was fresh out of ideas.

"No further questions, Your Honor."

"Mr. Bennett, Ms. Cort, how many more witnesses do you plan to call?"

"One, Your Honor."

"Ms. Long, at this time, do you think you'll have rebuttal witnesses?"

"Possibly one or two, Your Honor."

"Thanks, all of you counselors. Let's call it a day. We'll reconvene tomorrow at ten and the defense will call their final witness."

32

Peyton Bennett stood and buttoned the jacket of yet another bespoke suit. I kind of had to wonder how many he had. He was wrinkle-free despite being jammed in the too-small elevator with the rest of the masses of attorneys, defendants, and cops.

For once, I didn't look like I'd gone a round with someone. Now that I was visibly pregnant, most courteous people gave me a wide berth. It was nice getting upstairs without damp hair.

Standing in my shoes was getting uncomfortable, so I waited until the bailiff and judge came through. The jury wouldn't be far behind. Once the twelve solid citizens and the two alternates were seated, Judge Cox looked at our table.

"Your next witness."

"We call Sienna Clarke to the stand," Bennett said.

I turned toward the gallery as the bailiff opened the doors and stepped out into the hall to let the girl know it was her turn. Juliana Clarke's daughter had been excluded from the courtroom during much of the witness testimony. Preserving influence-free testimony was part of the process of a fair trial.

My feet were already hurting, but I stood with Bennett while we waited for Sienna. He was doing the questioning today, so I'd have a good forty-five minutes off my feet. At most there'd be another day of witnesses and arguments and then the case would go to the jury. From the comfort of my office, I could wait for the verdict in shearling boots and within spitting distance of a bathroom. Babies were hell on the bladder.

"Jimmy?" The judge's use of the officer's name was a question.

"She's not here, Your Honor," Jimmy replied. He looked like he'd rather be doing anything but delivering this kind of bad news to the judge.

My head whipped around to look through the doors. The hallway was nearly empty save for a few white-haired attorneys in blue and gray wool. There wasn't a single woman I could see from where I was standing.

"Mr. Bennett? Ms. Cort?"

"May we approach," I said before Bennett could get a word out. I wasn't interested in airing anything in front of the jury. I didn't want them to jump to a single conclusion though I'd already jumped to many.

Bennett, Long, and I made our way past the lectern, and stood below the judge. Cox wrapped her hand around the foam ball of the thin microphone. The court reporter scooted closer.

"Where's your witness?" The judge peered down at us, her face showing her annoyance.

"Can I speak with our client, Your Honor?" I asked, knowing that we were on her bad side first thing in the morning. That did not bode well for the day. Maybe I could get something out of Juliana Clarke that would fix the situation before it got too out of control.

"Is there a subpoena?" Judge Cox asked.

"Yes, of course," I said. Bennett had thought that me issuing a subpoena for Clarke had been overkill. Having been burned years ago with a disappearing witness, I always issued subpoenas when possible because as a civilian, I did not have the power to compel anyone to show up in court. When squirrely witnesses knew a warrant under their name could be issued, and they could be arrested for a no-show, a subpoena nearly eliminated the problem. Today was the exception, and an unexpected one.

Glad that Long was at the bench, I didn't have to worry she would overhear this exchange. I bent and looked my client in the eye.

"Where is your daughter? She's been here since the start of the trial. Today she was supposed to testify on your behalf."

"She's in Scotland." Juliana Clarke's eyes were wide with fake innocence. She didn't even blink.

"Excuse me?"

"Second semester starts on January seven. That only gives her a couple of weeks to settle in. Her life has been disrupted enough."

"That's it. You let her get on a flight out of the country when her testimony was absolutely necessary and crucial to your defense."

"Ms. Cort, I'm going to send the jury out," Judge Cox announced.

I turned and gave the judge a curt nod. Once again the court officers were going to have to smooth things over with doughnuts and juice. I wasn't looking forward to the sugar-addled jury that would come back.

"Where is the witness?"

I turned my entire body toward the bench. The judge was no longer covering the microphone. The court reporter had stepped back so that she was once again in her comfortable and unobtrusive spot.

"Edinburgh, Scotland."

"I'm sorry. Did you say Scotland as in the United Kingdom?"

"The very one, Your Honor."

"Was she aware that she was slated to testify on her mother's behalf?"

"The subpoena was duly served. It should be in the file," I dodged.

Judge Cox flipped open the official file the court kept in the clerk's office when there was no trial or anything pending before the judge. She thumbed through some papers and nodded when she came upon what was likely the proof of service from the county sheriff.

The judge looked from me to Bennett to Clarke.

"Fifteen-minute recess, Your Honor."

"I'll go talk to the jury," Cox said as she swiveled in her chair and walked through the door to the area the courtroom clerk, jury deliberation room, and judge's chambers occupied.

It took an act of Congress to keep my brows in place when Bennett shot me a look. Judges treated juries like voters—which they were. It was the primary qualification for service in Cuyahoga County. Schmoozing probably got any judge a good twenty to thirty extra votes which, given the low voter turnout for down ballot races, was enough to tip a local election in an incumbent judge's favor.

When Long took her coffee and left the courtroom Blackberry in hand, I used my full voice.

"What the hell?"

"You were going to use her," Clarke shot back.

"Use her?"

"I may not be a lawyer, but I'm not stupid. You think there's a chance that Sienna did the deed. You were going to sow the seeds of reasonable doubt this morning."

I lowered my head for a second. What Clarke said wasn't entirely untrue. Bennett and I had prepared extensively for the daughter's testimony. We prepared for two different stories. One that she'd seen or heard her mom commit murder with a story that wasn't favorable to our client but would bolster her self-defense claim.

In the alternative, we'd prepared to ask a series of questions that would leave us the option of arguing actual innocence and reasonable doubt to the jury at the close of trial.

All of a sudden, our options had dried up like a puddle in the hot summer sun.

"Is there something we should know?" I asked Clarke point-blank. We'd all danced around the question of Sienna for weeks.

"My daughter is safe. That's all that's important. It was very hard for me to testify, but I did what I had to do. That will have to be enough."

Hands tied, I raised two fingers letting the courtroom deputy know that we were ready to continue.

I pulled Bennett aside.

"So we rest?" I asked him as if he had some ace up his sleeve.

"Don't see a lot of alternatives," he answered. I guess he didn't have a trump card.

"Did you know she was going to send her daughter away?"

He shook his head.

"Juliana played that one close to the vest."

"Feels like déjà vu."

"How?"

"Sheila left right before I won her appeal."

"Yes, well. Clients are unpredictable."

I nodded, but didn't agree. My poorer clients were one hundred percent predictable. They showed up and swallowed their medicine like children. They mostly did what I said, and I ushered them through the system as best I could with whatever scenario they had.

The ones with money and a level of sophistication never trusted me. Grant had run. Jarrod Carter, a.k.a. the Sledge Hammer, had blackmailed the prosecutor without informing me of any of it. It had worked for them, but left me on the back foot. Like in the past, I was going to have to scramble to figure things out, snatch victory from the jaws of defeat—only this time my client was looking as guilty   as   sin.

33

"The defense rests?" Judge Cox asked on the record.

"We do, Your Honor," Peyton Bennett confirmed.

My best friend did not look happy. I'd come late after arranging for a locksmith, then delivering a new set of keys to my landlord.

If anyone had asked, I'd have said I was at trial to support my friend. The truth was, however, that I needed the distraction of someone else's problems to make me forget my own. I was here to make one hundred percent sure that the difference between this Clarke woman and me was as stark as the difference between the rain forest and the desert.

Sinclair had not called me back. All of my calls had gone straight to his voicemail. His set of the shiny new brass keys hung heavy in my pocket. I'd set a two-week deadline in my head. If he reached out, then he'd get a second chance. If he walked away from the greatest love of his life—his words, not mine—then I'd heal my broken heart the best I could and move on.

Judge Cox turned from the defense table to Long who was alone at the prosecution table.

"And the State?"

"We have a single rebuttal witness, Your Honor. We call Monica Mae Ellis to the stand."

I had to blink twice when the witness came through the double doors. Monica Mae was a younger version of Juliana Clarke. I craned my neck and stared at the jury and the gallery wondering if everyone else saw it. Kendrick Walker had a type. The new woman was merely a younger version of the one who'd left him. For a moment I had a glimpse of myself versus Deborah Bloom but dismissed it because she and I were far more different than these two.

The deputy swore her in. I had to wonder what this woman would say. What was she there to rebut? What in the heck had happened to the defendant's daughter? I'd have thought not wanting your mother to go to jail would be the most important thing in a girl's life. Maybe it was more problematic. Maybe the daughter blamed the mother. So many complicated relationships to navigate around a story of violence. I didn't envy a single one of them.

"Ms. Ellis, how did you know the victim?"

"I work as an architectural draftsman at Fernsby," Ellis answered.

Oh my God, and practically the same job as well. Talk about carbon copy. Well, either that or Walker had preyed upon a subordinate at work and had taken advantage of the power dynamic. Both scenarios felt like a punch in the gut. I squirmed in my seat.

"Is that how you met Kendrick Walker?"

"Rick? Yeah. He was the one who hired me. I was pretty grateful because it's kind of a guy's world, you know, but he was willing to take a chance on me."

"When did you two become romantically involved?"

"After she up and left him one day. No notice or nothing. He was really sad at work and some stuff was slipping through the cracks. I kind of went in and picked up the slack before the other partners noticed. He was the sole support of his wife and his daughter, who was first in private school, then was going to be in college. If he lost his job, lots of people were going to be screwed, so I stepped in to help. It was like he was in a fog of sadness and grief, then one day it was like Rick looked up and noticed how much I was helping him."

"When did you move into his house?"

"I'd only just gotten my degree when I moved here to Cleveland. I'm from Pittsburgh. Anyway, I kind of moved into an apartment here without really looking around. One day the landlord says that he wants to move back into the house I'm renting with like no notice. I was telling Rick and he said I should just move in with him. I could save money and we could see if our relationship had legs, you know?"

"How long had you lived there by September of this year?" Long asked using a pen to tick at her notepad. I imagined, like any lawyer would, she was going through a checklist of questions and topics to cover making sure nothing got left out. With a trial there was no second bite at the apple.

"Like nine months. My landlord pulled that crap during the holidays last year. That was some shit. Excuse me, everyone. I have a potty mouth."

And a penchant for drama, I thought.

"Right, so you'd moved in most of your personal items? Is that fair to say?"

"I don't know about that. Rick kind of wanted to keep the house as it was. So like I could put my clothes in the guest room closet. He was kind of waiting for Juliana to get all her stuff. He also had like furniture in every room, so I just put the junk I'd bought on Craigslist."

"Did Sienna live with you during the time you were at the house on Shelbourne Road?"

"She was kind of in and out. Like she was there that first Christmas. I don't think she liked the way her dad doted on me though. He like bought me some really nice jewelry from Tiffany's and a designer handbag from Kate Spade. He'd gotten her the same bag in a different color and like a charm bracelet from the jewelry store. I think she didn't like that my blue box was bigger than hers. She yelled abuse at him and stormed out. She didn't really come back for more than a night or two after that."

"Were you home the night that the victim was killed?"

"Yeah, of course. It was Sunday. It wasn't like I was going out anywhere. There's nothing to do on a Sunday night anyway in Cleveland. It's supposed to be a city on the rise, but I think Pittsburgh is doing a better job."

I almost felt bad for Long. Monica Mae was...extra. They may have looked alike, with an obvious twenty-year age difference, of course, but where Clarke was all polish and New York sophistication, Ellis was...not.

"What time was it when Sienna came over?"

"I don't know. Give me a second. There was no Steelers or Browns or Ravens game. It was the week off between preseason and the full season. I think I was just flipping through cable. You know, a thousand channels, nothing to watch. Rick had been out on some site doing a visit. He'd only gotten home like ten minutes before his daughter walked in. She didn't call or knock or even use the doorbell. Just came right in like she owned the place."

"Would five thirty be a fair assessment?"

Ellis shrugged.

"It was still light out. The news hadn't come on."

"When did you see Sienna in person on that Sunday?"

"So I was watching whatever. I think it was skating, by the way, ice-skating...figure skating. Something they put on when there was no football and NASCAR was done. Some skinny girl is like twirling like a dervish and one of the judges said something. Not judge, announcer. Anyway, I couldn't hear what they said. They whisper like talking would disturb the skaters when you know they're in a booth."

"Sienna? You saw her?" Long asked. Keeping a dog on a racetrack was easier than this.

"Right, so like she's stomping around upstairs. I thought at first it was Rick, but he came in asking me if we had the little onions he likes to have in his drink. It's called a Gibson, his drink. It's like a martini but with an onion. He thinks the thing I like to drink with gin and cranberry and lime is too sweet."

"She was stomping?" Long was trying to bring it back. It was going to be, I could see, a struggle.

"Yeah, and when he asked me about the tiny onions, I realized it wasn't him. So I was like, I think Sienna's here otherwise we have a burglar and I need to get my gun."

"You carry a gun?"

"Of course. My daddy said no woman's safe without a pistol in her pocketbook."

"Sienna was upstairs?"

"I was like, Rick, go check on all that commotion. Make sure it's the girl and not your ex or, you know, a burglar. No one in the Heights seems to lock their doors. A couple of neighbors just wandered in to say hello a while back. I said to Rick, you check and I'll get the jar of onions you couldn't find. I swear to God, men wouldn't be able to find their ding-a-ling if it weren't attached."

Half the jury laughed out loud at that, the female half.

"Did Kendrick Walker go upstairs?"

"He didn't come back. I put his onions on the counter. Got the gin out from the freezer and a glass. I was even thinking of making the drink. But Rick was so particular and would throw it out when I didn't make it right that I didn't bother. I told him if I couldn't make it like his wife had, he could get back together with her and I'd make myself scarce or he could mix it himself. He went with doing it on his own. I was proud that I got him trained like that real quick. Told him I wasn't the kind of woman to wait on him hand and foot. Not like that one. She was a doormat. If she'd stood up for herself—"

"Your Honor," Long interrupted her own witness, the bid to the judge, a plea.

"Ms. Ellis, you weren't here for the other witnesses' testimony, so I'll tell you what I told them. Please answer the question asked and confine your answer to that. Ms. Long?"

"Did you go upstairs?" the prosecutor continued.

"Eventually. It was like fifteen minutes and...wait. That's it, right. I already said too much, didn't I?"

"You're doing fine," Judge Cox soothed.

"What happened when you went upstairs?"

"I heard Rick and Sienna talking, so I walked in to say hi to the girl. I mean, we're not friends or anything, but to not acknowledge her wouldn't be right and my parents raised me to do what's right."

"Then what?"

"She yells at me to get out of her room. She was all like, 'you may think you own this place, but this room is mine at least for a few more days.'"

"Look, I'm not Sienna's mother or anyone's mother, but backtalking to adults points to poor parenting." Her glare at Juliana Clarke lacked subtlety, but so did everything else she did, so it shouldn't have come as a surprise, though it did. "I was telling her that she needed to adjust her attitude while she was in her father's house."

"What did the victim do?"

"He sided with me. Rick pointed out that I'd been nothing but nice to her, which was true. He said that I'd stayed out of her way and that she was being crazy unreasonable. Then Sienna gets even more salty. She tells Rick that she'll never be back after she leaves for college. That at least she has a place that she feels welcome. Obviously she was talking about her house." Ellis didn't point to Clarke, but she might as well have.

"Did you or Kendrick Walker say anything in response?"

"Of course. That girl was being ri-dic-u-lous." Ellis drew out the last four-syllable word with an eye roll and lip curl. "He pointed out that not only was he paying for the floor under her feet, but that he was paying for Juliana's Shaker Square condo as well."

"So they were arguing?"

"Yeah, about whether Juliana was having an affair and why she'd leave her husband and child and house behind. Then Sienna points to me and says that her mother's not the bad one, he is because he's got me as a girlfriend. I got hot at that one. I mean we really love...loved each other. I wasn't just some rebound girl."

"And then what?"

"He was talking about cutting Sienna off, money-wise. She finished packing up whatever she'd come for, zipped her duffel, and yelled that she was calling her mother because she hadn't driven her own car over."

"Would you say they were both angry?"

"Of course. It was an argument. He was trying to put his ungrateful child in her place and Sienna wanted to just say what she wanted with no consequences. I didn't see her text her mother, but her phone dinged. Then she got cagey with her bag. I kind of had to wonder what she could have forgotten that she hadn't picked up in one of her other trips. So I pulled at her duffel."

"Why?"

"I just wanted to have a look inside to make sure she wasn't taking something of mine or that her mother hadn't sent her in on some kind of spy mission."

"After Sienna's phone sounded, did you notice Juliana Clarke entering the house?"

"Kind of? Rick ran downstairs and started yelling. I figured it was her. He was mad because obviously she'd turned Sienna against him, against us. Then Sienna comes down with the bag. She kind of looked at her mother and father and screamed at them to stop yelling at each other. They were already getting divorced, so there was no need for all that."

"Did Sienna leave then?"

"No, she ran into her father's study. I went behind her. She had no business being in there and I was really starting to think her mother had sent her over to collect financial documents or some kind of evidence to use against Rick in the divorce. I needed to make sure Sienna or Juliana wasn't going to do anything to hurt him."

"Then what?"

"I don't know. They were screaming. I was trying to get Sienna to leave. Then all of a sudden there was quiet. I went into the kitchen and Juliana had that fancy party thing in her hand and Sienna ran out the back door. Then the police were there."

"Thank you, Ms. Ellis, no further questions."

34

"Ms. Ellis, let's take a closer look at the events on the evening of September second. Would you be okay with that?"

"What do you mean closer?"

"By that, I mean we need to get more specific information for the jury on how we went from a teenage girl packing to someone dying. Do you understand now?"

"Sure. Yeah."

"You testified that you went upstairs to the second floor of the Shelbourne Road house to greet Sienna, is that right?"

"Yes. I already said that. Since you all think I talk too much, I don't want to just repeat what I said before."

"It's not repeating that I'm asking you to do. I'm just asking questions to clarify the issues for myself and for the jury. I need them to know exactly what happened that night. Do you understand?"

"Got it. I'll just answer. You all get tired of Monica Mae, one of you will say something."

"Thank you for your understanding. What was the mood of Sienna and Kendrick Walker when you got upstairs?"

"Objection, speculation."

"Your Honor. Can we let the witness answer? It's entirely possible that one of the parties expressed their feelings out loud. Also, given Monica Mae's experiences in her twenty-eight years of life, she's likely to have witnessed the broad tapestry of human emotion. And if she doesn't know and can't answer, she can state that."

"I can answer," Ellis answered before the judge could rule. "The girl, Sienna, was being kind of bratty. Rick, her dad, he was pretty angry."

"Did he say why he was angry?"

"Because his daughter was acting entitled to his money but had picked the mother over him."

"Had he ever used those words, suggesting that Sienna had made a choice between her parents?"

"Yes. Why wouldn't he use those words? He'd been putting a roof over her head and food in her mouth for nearly eighteen damn years and first thing she moves out and into her mom's condo at the first sign of trouble."

"Had you witnessed other arguments between Sienna and her father?"

"Yes."

"What were they arguing about?"

"Her mom's boyfriend. Her mom wanting spousal support. Her not treating me right."

"Let's take these one at a time, shall we. Why was Kendrick Walker talking to his daughter about his mother's dating?"

"He did not want to pay for her if another man was lying up in her house."

"Do you know if Mrs. Clarke ever had a boyfriend?"

"No. Rick hired a detective. There was no boyfriend, at least by the time the guy was surveilling her."

"The second thing was spousal support. What was the argument around that? Sienna had no power over whether a court could order support."

"He wanted her to convince her mom to get off her ass and get a job. He said he'd supported her for nearly twenty years. She could do it for the next twenty. I get it, I mean, I got a job and I don't have half the education she does."

"And what is your job, specifically?"

"I do drafting work for Fernsby."

"So Kendrick Walker not only hired you, but supervised you as well."

"Yes, that's right. Don't you go thinking I slept my way to my job, okay? I got my associate's degree and do great at my job. Rick always said so."

"The last disagreement concerned Sienna's relationship with you. How would you describe your relationship to the deceased's daughter?"

"Fine on my end. I was cordial. Stayed out of her way as much as I could, though I was living in the house."

"Did you ever witness any violence between Kendrick and his daughter?"

"What do you mean by violence?"

It took nearly an act of congress to keep my eyebrows from my hairline. Violence felt like it was akin to pornog-

raphy, a person knew it when they saw it. But if this witness, and by turns this jury, needed explicit, then that's
what everyone would get.

"Did he ever hit her?"

"Hit her, no. Smacked her when she ran her mouth.
Yes. But it was deserved."

"Did you think it was okay that he hit his daughter?"

"It wasn't like he was stomping her. Now that would be
something to get up in arms about."

Something caught in the back of my head. A little seed
was sprouting. I had to decide right then and there whether to water it.

"Did you come downstairs to the kitchen before or after
Juliana Clarke came into the house?"

"After."

"What did you see?"

"Why you asking that? You already know what happened."

"Your Honor?"

"Ms. Ellis. Unless I say otherwise, you have to answer
the questions asked."

"First you all say I talk too much. Now you're asking
me to answer the same questions more than once. Fine.
This is your house, Judge Cox."

"Yes, and therefore my rules. Ms. Cort?"

"That's funny, your name. You get a lot of ribbing for
that?"

I ignored the witness talking out of turn and trickled
water on the seed instead.

"What did you see when you came down the stairs?"

"Rick and Juliana over there were yelling. She was saying something about Sienna. He was mad about the girl moving out."

"Next you followed Sienna to the study?" A little more water.

"Yes."

"What did you hear from the kitchen while you were in the study?"

"I don't know...the screaming got bad. I was worried that someone was going to get hurt." A little more and I had a sprout.

"So you went back to the kitchen?"

"Yes."

"What did you see?"

"You know...I...uh...why do I have to talk about this?"

This was the crux of it. Either I was going to have two leaves and a real plant or the seed was going to die in the ground. I went for the plant because my client had nothing to lose and everything to gain.

"I apologize if this is hard, Ms. Ellis. My client here is facing a long time in jail if she's convicted. Please think about a few minutes of talking versus years of confinement."

"Fine. Rick was being an ass, okay? He'd been on some site visit, on a Sunday. I have half a mind to think he was doing some other girl or his wife. Obviously not her, though.

"He was pissy when he couldn't find the onions. He was complaining that I couldn't do anything half as good as his wife over there. You know how sick I get hearing about Juliana Clarke? You'd think she was shooting rainbows out of her ass. Anyway, there was something about how they were arguing that made my stomach feel queasy, you know, like I'd had too many fast-food tacos."

"What did you see when you got in there?"

Monica Mae Ellis closed her eyes. I knew then that she was back there. Seeing, smelling, experiencing the night just as it had played out. Something tingled in my stomach. Intuition was telling me that some truth was right around the corner. This time it was like waiting for the sun and time to do their work on the seed in the ground. I paused, the jury waited. Finally, she started again. Ellis's eyes were still closed.

"When I got in there, Rick was in her face, the wife's. She wasn't saying anything. She was real quiet. He'd been yelling so much that I hadn't realized she wasn't anymore. He got this queer look in his eyes, like the lights had gone out or gone on or something. He was only five foot ten, but he had to be at least a hundred eighty pounds maybe. He wasn't all fat, but he wasn't all muscle either. He gets this look..."

Monica Mae Ellis's eyes popped open, but I'd have bet dollars to doughnuts that she couldn't see a thing that was happening in the present.

"He stiff-armed her. The wife goes flying into the kitchen counters. She folds like she doesn't have any bones or anything. Bumps her hip. Loses her balance. Hits her head. Then she's on the floor and out like a light. Her eyes were closed. Her body looked like some weird full-sized Raggedy-Ann, but with blond hair.

"Rick had never taken off his shoes. Boots. The construction sites all require steel-toe boots. He only wore them on site visits, never to the office or anything. His were black though. All the other guys, they had tan boots, but that was too common for him.

"So he looks down at her, then he lifts his boot like he's going to kick her when she's down. I yelled foul play, and he stopped for a long moment and looked at me. It wasn't love for either one of us though, I could see. Rick didn't look quite right."

"What did you do next?" I said that at nearly a whisper. I didn't want to do anything that would interrupt this telling or pull her away from the truth I suspected was on its way to the surface.

"I was so mad. I mean, she didn't deserve to leave her marriage and get a free pass to a house and a life of a lady who did lunch. But she didn't deserve to be stomped either. I don't know what happened. Next thing I know I had that cheese board thing in my hand. It was stupid, that thing. I don't know who's serving cheese on a little stone board. I took the glass cover off, picked it up by its metal handle and swung as hard as I could until I was sure that he wasn't going to stomp the hell out of her."

"Why did you do it?" This question was in my full voice. "Why did you kill Kendrick Walker?"

"My daddy told me that no man should hurt a woman. He also said a person wasn't worth anything if they let something happen and didn't go to a helpless person's defense. And my purse was too far away, otherwise I'd have shot the bastard. Thought he could just treat a woman any old way. Didn't know who he was messing with. Monica Mae don't play."

"No further questions."

The courtroom was silent. That plant was turning its leaves and flowers up to the full sun.

"Counsel, in my chambers now," Judge Cox said while simultaneously pounding her gavel.

In less than three minutes, Bennett, Long, Cox, and myself were in chambers. The court reporter barely had time to extend her machine's feet before Judge Cox started speaking.

"I'm going to assume none of you knew what Monica Mae Ellis was going to blurt out on the stand."

"No, Your Honor." Long's voice sounded defeated. "As you could see, asking a question and getting a straight answer from her was a challenge. Upon questioning by the uniformed officers, Detective Darlene Webb, the prosecutor's office investigator, and myself, she maintained she'd walked in to discover the murder weapon in the defendant's hands. The defendant never refuted that assertion. In fact, she lodged an affirmative defense. At no point did the prosecutor's office shirk its duty."

"And yet, Ms. Cort here was able to get to the truth in a few short minutes?"

The people-pleasing part of me wanted to take up for Nicole Long. Tell the judge that Bennett and I and even the defendant had suspected Sienna Walker. That it was only when Ellis kept throwing out too many words did I begin to suspect her verbosity was a cover-up for what she wasn't saying and that I suspected that she was ready to relieve herself of the burden of a lie that could have put our client behind bars. Instead, I remained silent.

Judge Cox, who had been so keen and engaged during the entire trial, suddenly looked world-weary, her face a carbon copy of judges who'd been on the bench long enough to become cynical and apathetic in equal measure.

"Ms. Long, are you going to pursue charges against Ms. Ellis?"

"Of course, Your Honor. This murder cannot go unanswered."

"I'll direct one of the county sheriffs to arrest her and take her into custody. She'll be processed here. I trust your office will handle the paperwork so that she gets over to arraignment."

Long nodded.

"Off the record," Cox said. The court reporter's hands lifted from the keys as if levitated. The judge continued, "I'm not here to tell you how to do your job, but maybe you can suggest to your boss that she strongly consider Ellis's actions in the light of her right to defend others because a good defense attorney is going to rip your office a new one over this. Now, let's get this case over with and get the defendant home for Christmas. Maybe she can fly to Scotland and celebrate with her daughter."

We all hustled out of chambers. Juliana Clarke's face was a question mark. I turned toward the bench without speaking to my client. Instead I waited for the jury to settle and the judge and court reporter to situate themselves. Bennett could handle Clarke from here on out. I'd been called in as a pinch hitter and had done my job.

"Do you have a motion?" Judge Cox pointedly looked at defense table.

I stood from my chair, not bothering to make the walk to the well of the courtroom. I'd project my voice from back here.

"We move for a dismissal of all charges against the defendant."

Judge Cox's "Granted," was so swift I wouldn't have heard it if I wasn't paying attention. "All charges against the defendant, Juliana Clarke, are hereby dismissed with prejudice. The defendant is free to go."

To the jury, she said, "Thank you for your service. You are hereby dismissed. Have a happy holiday and new year."

Sometime in the last half hour Nicole's boss, Lori Pope, had appeared in the back of the courtroom. Long was packed and out the door with her boss, Darlene Webb, bringing up the rear in minutes. The jury scurried away almost immediately, probably to finish up last-minute holiday shopping. The deputies took Clarke back to the jail downstairs to process her release.

That left only me and Bennett in the courtroom.

"You did a masterful job," he said, as I packed up the stacks of notecards in envelopes and the other evidence I'd stacked on the defense table.

"Thanks. Once I decided to treat this as I would any other trial, I was much more able to see the case for what it was."

"The minute Sienna Walker played no-show, I was convinced it was she who'd killed her father in defense of her mother."

"I think Juliana was convinced of that as well. It's such a shame. Kendrick Walker feels like a one-man wrecking crew who took a heavy metal ball to at least three people's lives."

"Tragedy strikes in the oddest places and leaves so much carnage behind, a lot of which is heaped unfairly on recipients."

Once my trial case was packed, I dug my hands through my messenger bag.

"This is for you," I said. I handed Bennett a sealed envelope. This rectangle of paper was not embossed with my practice name and Public Square return address. It was a generic one I'd picked up for ten cents in an office supply store downtown.

"What is this?"

"What you asked for. An address in Pittsburgh."

"Pittsburgh?"

"Don't ask me anything else. I can't say much in any case. It's my gift to you. They have no heads-up, so please be empathetic and kind in your approach. She's already lost one father."

Bennett nodded and slipped the thick paper into the left breast pocket of his suit jacket. I could only hope that he brought Olivia Grant more answers than questions.

35

My due date was in exactly four months. In one way, that seemed like an eternity, and in another, it felt like I could snap my fingers and spring would be here along with a newborn.

Christmas Day, I'd decided over the previous weekend, was going to be my day of reckoning. Denial had been my go-to for long enough. It was time to face the music.

I answered the door decked out in an emerald-green maternity dress.

"Wow. You're really pregnant," Justin said when I let him in.

"Yeah, I get kind of shocked too when I look in the mirror or try to turn over at night like I used to, only it's a bit more work than I'm ready to put in."

"Merry Christmas." He leaned in to kiss me. That zing of attraction was still there. Still strong. I took a deep breath at the same time I took his coat.

"Hot apple cider?" I offered. My own mug was steaming on the coffee table. It was a shame I couldn't have anything stronger to fortify me for what was to come. But I'd already exceeded my allotment of pregnancy alcohol. Plus I'd never been a late-morning drinker.

"Smells great, but I'll have water."

I'd already made myself comfortable on the couch after I'd hung his coat. I pushed my right palm against a decorative pillow getting leverage to rise.

"I'll get it myself, Casey. I'm sure I can figure it out."

And he did, disappearing into my kitchen only to reemerge seconds later with a tall glass of seltzer.

"You wanted to talk about all of this," he said gesturing to my swollen abdomen filled with someone's baby.

Like an opening argument, I'd practiced what to say. I'd rehearsed in front of the mirror, then in front of Greg and Jason, and finally in front of Lulu. By the fifth time I'd stopped blushing and stuttering over every third word.

"I don't know who the father of this baby is. I'm very sorry about that. Never in a million years did I expect to find myself in this position. Because of the possibility, though low, of harming the baby, I'm not going to get a test before birth. I will promise, however, that I'll do it right after he or she is born in April."

"You don't know the sex?" His question was an unexpected one. I hadn't accounted for it during my rehearsals.

"I opted not to find out. The surprise will be my reward for giving birth."

"Is someone helping you with that? You know, birth coaching and all that?"

I waited a beat, hope filling my heart as I waited for Justin to volunteer. That hope was in vain. The room was deadly quiet until I spoke.

"I don't know. Maybe my mom or Lulu. The classes won't start until February or March," I said, leaving another opening for him to step into.

"I wonder if it's like TV with all the breathing and panting," Justin sidestepped the invitation.

A birth plan was on my list of "things to get to," as soon as I could. The idea of figuring out how you wanted to give birth seemed so foreign. I imagine the women of my mother's generation weren't given much choice, if any.

"The baby's not what I wanted to talk to you about."

"It wasn't?"

My headshake was swift, definitive.

"When I met you, I was at a low point in my life. Unemployed and unemployable, I'd just decided to hire myself. Even with that decision, I was swimming in a pool of uncertainty. While we were at that domestic relations GAL training, you steered me toward juvenile court. Those cases were tragic in so many instances, but those two-hundred-fifty-dollar checks kept my practice afloat in the beginning. We had amazing and sad drinks. You made me laugh when things were so down. Then you got me out of the adoption business when Hudson got hinky. So you were there at my lowest, but at my highest too when we got that settlement for Brighthill. It solved nearly all of my problems in an instant."

"We've been in and out of each other's lives for years," Justin confirmed.

"Then things changed. You and your raging pantsfeelings made the first move. We went from acquaintances to friends to something more. In June, you told me not to fall in love with you. That's the one thing I couldn't do, Justin. I did fall in love with you. I'm still in love with you. I love you. I know there's not one single conventional thing about us, but despite all of that, I want a future with you. I'd like to raise this baby together and pursue a relationship."

I winced at the last. It sounded weird and formal, but it was the best I could do. It wasn't perfect, my delivery, but I was still proud of myself nonetheless. I'd done the hard thing. The ball was now in Justin's court.

"You're wearing an engagement ring," he observed. I'd thought of that. Tried to take it off until I realized my finger was too swollen and gave up.

"I'm not married. I haven't told my parents that someone proposed."

"That someone being Ron Pinheiro."

"He wants me, Justin. But I want you. The choice is yours." As I said the last, something twinged inside of me. This would be the last time choices in my life were in someone else's hands.

The last time I'd ask someone, beg someone to choose me, love me. Despite the vow I'd act upon tomorrow, or maybe as a New Year's resolution, I waited for him to choose me in the excruciating seconds that turned into minutes.

"I like you, Casey," he started. Justin didn't need to finish, his answer to my bid was obvious in those four introductory words. In high school I'd made the mistake of taking an acting class as an art elective. I was awful at it, acting, but our teacher had a policy of starting any critique of our scenes or monologues with a positive. That came down to the standard refrain of, "It was good, but..." His tone mirrored my teacher's perfectly.

"But," I interrupted, suddenly in a hurry to be disappointed.

"But I don't like you in that way. This was always something casual for me. I should have been more sensitive to your feelings because women always feel more, always think it's more than it is," he said, dumping me and my feelings on the pyre along with specters of countless other women I couldn't see.

My, "Thank you for your honesty," was stiffer and even more formal than my declaration had been. But I was doing everything in my power to stop my hormonal self from crying.

"About the baby..."

"We'll cross that bridge when we come to it, Justin," I said. There was a fifty-fifty chance this man, whom I loved, who didn't love me, would be in my life for the remainder of it. I didn't cherish the prospect of the constant reminder of his rejection.

"So..."

"So, merry Christmas, I guess." My shrug was my probably failed attempt at nonchalance. "I have to go see my parents today. With the murder trial and everything, it's been a while. Are you going to your parents? Will your sister be there?"

"Yeah." He nodded. "I should get going and head over."

"You should." I stood too quickly and had to brace myself against the couch while I waited for the blood to get to my head in sufficient quantity to chase away the dizziness.

"You okay?"

"Fine. Just pregnancy stuff. Fortunately, it's all temporary. Let me get your coat."

"I can do it myself," he said.

"I insist." I strode over and plucked his overcoat from the hook and handed it to him along with the scarf I'd safely stored in the sleeve. While he wrapped himself in the wool, his unique smell of woodsy cologne and him wafted by my super sensitive nose. I battled dizziness a second time, but had my bearings by the time he was pulling on his gloves.

He turned toward my bank of living room windows. The curtains were open wide. I'd hoped to get some of the weak morning sunlight, but that was long gone, replaced by clouds and light flurries.

"Maybe we'll have a white Christmas."

I opened the door while shooing the cat away with my naked foot.

"Maybe."

"Can I—" But before Justin could finish asking, he was already kissing me like he loved me, like he didn't want to stop, like it was going to be our last time. When he pulled back, I took a giant step away from the man that was my kryptonite.

"I'll see you around," I said.

Justin's response was a nod and a salute before he started down the forty-eight steps to the building's vestibule and front door.

A covey of kisses, I thought. Justin would have liked that one.

I downed the rest of my cider, emptied the bladder my baby was sitting on, and executed plan B.

In an hour, Ron Pinheiro was at my door, suited and ready to go to my parents' house. While I sat and eased dress shoes onto my growing feet, Ron slipped off his coat and took a seat on the new easy chair I'd splurged on. My single reward for getting Juliana Clarke off.

Without a lamp or a small table, it was an awkward place to sit, but I didn't want to stock up on more furniture until I made plans. I'd been in this apartment for more than a dozen years. I didn't think a tiny baby needed more, but I was thinking that maybe I wanted more for her or him, for me, for...the us that Justin and I were going to be.

"So, I want to be clear," I started. "You're walking into a situation. I haven't told my parents that I'm pregnant or that I'm engaged. It's all been so fast and I didn't really have a moment between preparing for a murder trial—"

"Congrats again on that, by the way. You scored a major victory. I wouldn't be surprised if you got even more offers from every firm in the city, white-shoe, top criminal, the big family law practices."

"Thanks," I said. The mention for this trial had been a small one on page three or four of the Plain Dealer. Nonetheless it had been read by a few people at least.

Miriam Shively had called to renew her offer. Bennett had said there was a space for me at his firm when I was ready to get back to work in the summer or fall. There were quite a few big decisions on the horizon, but I was focused on the ones that affected me the most.

"Like I was saying, I didn't have time to see them. I know we were supposed to go there in October, then Thanksgiving, but it was..." I trailed off. I couldn't say I'd avoided them because I was unsure of him and me, that I wanted to sort out my feelings for Justin before I committed to a certain future.

"Don't worry, Casey. I completely understand. We're not twenty-five. I think that our parents have to acknowledge that we're adults and are living our own lives as it were. I know they'll be shocked, but they'll adjust as will mine."

"Before we get in the car, there's one other thing I need to tell you."

He sat again, this time with his coat fanned out around him. I was getting hot. He had to be melting in his own formal clothes. I should have started with the revelation when he'd walked in the door. I'd been so deliberate this morning, that by now I just felt like everything was messy, secrets spilling everywhere.

"There's nothing you could say, Casey, that will scare me away. I want you to know that."

I almost laughed because I was going to tell him the one thing that would scare away ninety-nine point nine percent of men.

"I don't know who the father of the baby is," I blurted out before I lost all the nerve I'd stored up for a day of confessions.

Ron's blink was so slow, I knew that I'd lobbed the one thing he hadn't been prepared to catch.

"Um...okay. I don't even know how to ask."

"The other...candidate, for lack of a better term, is only someone I was seeing casually. We were never serious. It was just a habit that I didn't know how to break."

"Chicago Seventeen," Ron referenced. I smiled through the sweat prickling my upper lip. I think that was going to be our first shared joke.

"Does he know?"

I nodded.

"And?"

"Nothing. And nothing. I told him I'd get a paternity test after the baby's born."

"Why?"

"Why...what?"

"Are you getting a paternity test? He wants nothing to do with you or the baby and I want everything. Why don't we get him to relinquish his rights now and move on as a family, the three of us."

"But...aren't you...?"

"He sounds like a bit of an asshole. My love for you is not conditional, Casey. We weren't exclusive then, but we are now, right?"

I nodded again as more sweat trickled through my breasts. At nearly twice their original size there was a lot of places for water to collect.

"My behavior at the beginning of our relationship wasn't the best. I was gunning for partner afraid to make any missteps. Now that's done and squared away. I'm a full equity partner, so my job is all but guaranteed. My billable hours are much lower than they were when I was an associate.

"I got my life back and now I want to spend it with you. If I haven't told you how amazing you are, I want to now. You're smart, and kind, and funny. You're loyal to your friends, love your family and this cat." He scratched Simba behind the ears while my cat purred like Ron was his new best friend. "You've built this amazing career from nothing, and you want a family. That's enough for me, Casey. I love you and am all in if you are."

I almost cried because they were the very words I'd always wanted to hear. I pushed that tiny twinge of dissatisfaction about the speaker of the words very far away into a place I'd never visit again. Once I'd read a magazine article that suggested the first flush of love, the butterflies, the compulsion to be together, that obsession always disappeared and soon gave way to something deeper and less fraught.

"Don't let the thing that makes us all, shame us," Ron whispered.

I looked at Ron, heard his words, and told myself I was just skipping the first part and leaping to the second. It felt like the most responsible adult decision I'd ever made for myself and now for the tiny person growing inside of me.

"That's what I want too, a life with you." I stood and got prepared to face my parents in a half hour or so. "You ready?"

"Casey," Ron said, taking the hand wearing his ring. "I always want to be the best part of your worst day."

That's exactly what he was, had been. Justin had shattered a small part of me and Ron Pinheiro, my soon-to-be husband, had glued the pieces back together with his thoughtful words and solution to my paternity problem. I stepped into the hallway, ready to face the future with someone by my side—finally.

36

Nicole
January 2, 2008

The flurries had never turned into a white Christmas. Instead we'd had a New Year's Day storm that was continuing over into today. Yesterday Cleveland had gotten five inches. Three were predicted for today, Wednesday.

Weather that would have shut down New Orleans was business as usual in northeast Ohio. I'd put on my boots and parka and trudged to work for my meeting with Lori Pope. She'd spared me a lecture and dressing down on the last day of the Juliana Clarke trial. Instead, today was the day the other shoe was going to drop.

I tried not to project doom as I drove at a snail's pace to the Justice Center. The scene I'd set in my head, of me sitting in Lori Pope's office as she complimented me on my diligence with the Clarke case, having the true offender in custody, and having the moniker Head of Major Crimes affixed to my door was a fantasy that quickly went up in smoke the minute I got to my office door.

The head prosecutor had taken up a spot in my office. She was in my chair, feet up on my desk, Walker murder case files in hand. Immediately I regretted not getting fortified before I'd left home. I'd planned on enjoying a sip or two of liquid courage before trooping to my boss's office. That plan was foiled.

"Plead her out," Pope said in way of greeting.

I unzipped my parka, the melted snow dripping from the shell. I didn't bother with the boot–pump switch. My airplane-sized bottles of Maker's Mark were in the same drawer as my office shoes.

"Who?" I asked while trying to tuck my boots artfully under the chair.

"Don't play dumb. Plead out Monica Ellis."

"You didn't offer a plea to Juliana Clarke."

"That self-defense story was shaky. Obviously because it was only half true. It's now public record that the deceased was an asshole of the highest order. His abuse of his wife and daughter are on the record. I watched the last day of trial. I have no doubt that Ellis would garner the sympathy of any jury. Plus her defense is solid."

"So no trial?"

"She'd get off. If I were on a jury, I'd vote to acquit. Now whoever she hires won't know all of that. We call up a public defender, Ellis takes a plea, the office has one in the win column, and you save face."

"Reckless homicide?" I proposed. "It's a third-degree felony. Jail time is optional. She could get nine to thirty-six months or probation."

"Negligent homicide," Pope countered.

"That's a first-degree misdemeanor," I protested. "Ninety-nine percent likelihood of probation, and if she gets jail time, it's only six months max."

"Negligent homicide is likely to get this pled out and done with before it can spiral into an office embarrassment. The holiday season moratorium on hard news won't last much beyond the end of this week unless we have the snowstorm of the century or something crazy happens on Capitol Hill. I'm not betting anything on either of those."

"I don't think—" I stood to try to get my point across.

"Don't." Pope's voice was firm. "This is not up to your discretion."

"Then what is?"

"Nothing yet. I have no idea why I have a soft spot in my heart for you, but I do. I watched you in court during this trial and the other big problem with your presentation..."

"Was what?" I asked. I thought back and couldn't find fault, other than having the wrong defendant. Besides that, I'd been in good form. If I hadn't called Monica Mae Ellis as a rebuttal witness, I'd have put my chances of conviction right at fifty percent.

"Was that you were drinking. No one loves coffee that much."

My protest came out in a sputter.

"You can't fool me, Ms. Long. I didn't administer a breathalyzer because everyone was off for the holidays, but I sure as shit know that you were lit. So here's how this is going to go."

I sat down again, crossed my boots at the ankles and listened. I knew I wasn't going to like what she was going to say, but from where I was sitting, I didn't have much choice.

In the last years, I'd put out some feelers to other prosecutor's offices in Ohio, but Pope had already poisoned that well. My reputation for not maintaining sobriety preceded me. The alternative was to get licensed in another jurisdiction, then look for a job. That was not the most desirable outcome either.

"What do I have to do this time?"

"Go to rehab."

"What?" I knew I had to have misheard her. "You can't be serious. I can't think of a time that's been demanded of anyone in this office."

"As cancer," was Pope's reply. She continued as if I hadn't objected at all. "You've been booked at Journies in Hocking Hills for thirty days. Insurance covers everything. The few cases you have left will be assigned out."

"What if I don't go?" My voice was mutinous and I didn't give a damn.

"Your employment will be terminated effective today."

"Jesus, you're not giving me much choice."

Sobriety scared the living hell out of me. I had no idea how to live with the thoughts alcohol numbed.

"That's the point. You'll pack your bags and drive down—sober. You get a DUI, you're fired. The director there is expecting you by Friday. That should be enough time to get your affairs in order, prepay your bills or situate your pets or whatever. Any questions?"

"What happens when I come back?"

"If I get a report that your treatment was successful, then you'll be promoted from acting to permanent head of

Major Crimes. You'll be groomed to replace me should I run for higher office."

"Why are you doing this? Why have you never fired me?" I had to ask because if not today, then last year before should have been my last.

"Years ago, I had a sister like you. Everyone pointed fingers. She was a thief. She was an addict. She was a mess. Every family occasion revolved around the question of what's wrong with Sarah?"

I couldn't think of a thing to say, so I just listened. Pope continued.

"One day she came home from a meeting. She'd been sober for a week or so. I asked her how she was doing. Sarah said she'd hooked up with a sponsor. That woman said the 'What's wrong with Sarah' question was the wrong one. The better question was 'What had happened to Sarah?'

"The woman had asked the right questions, but it was at the wrong time. My sister wasn't ready to face the what question, and she overdosed a week later."

"I'm so sorry," I said. And I was. I didn't want to think of the times I'd hoped alcohol poisoning would take me in my sleep. How many times I'd mixed drinking with sleeping pills hoping to never wake up. Pope didn't wait for a response from me.

"You're a brilliant woman and I think you can be a great attorney. So while you're away detoxing and cleaning out your system, you might want to think about what happened to you and how you're going to address that at the same time you work with the physical addiction."

"Thank you," I said moved by her compassion. For the years I'd known her, my boss had been Teflon. This was the first time I'd seen a chink in the armor.

"Nicole, I want you to know I'm not kidding. This will be your last chance."

She stood and stalked out without saying goodbye.

I stood to leave myself. I slipped my coat back on, and for the first time in a long time, I wanted more than to survive to the next day.

I was done being stuck in the past with Seth Collins tormenting me in my dreams. This was my last chance at a future and I was ready to grab it with both hands.

ABOUT THE AUTHOR

Aime Austin is the author of the Casey Cort Legal Thriller Series. Casey is almost always in trouble. Aime's full time job? Rescuing her. Good thing Aime's got experience. She practiced family and criminal law in Cleveland, Ohio for several years—so she has the skills for the job.

When Aime isn't rescuing Casey from herself, she's hosting her podcast, *A Time to Thrill*, raising her son or traveling between Budapest and Los Angeles.

www.ingramcontent.com/pod-product-compliance
Lightning Source LLC
Chambersburg PA
CBHW021456110726
47899CB00001BA/182